Praise

"In her first novel, Mary Lou G important events in the life of h_ _ _ _ _ _, _ _gg_ _ _ Eve 1964 tragedy that changed Maggie's life forever as a teenager, and a 2007 journey she takes from Virginia to New Hampshire designed by a mysterious spiritual guide to explain her past and reveal her future. Gediman skillfully unravels it all in an unforgettable adventure. You will enjoy this well-paced and insightful tale."
—Randy Fitzgerald, English Dept., Virginia Union University; columnist for *Boomer Life* and *Fifty Plus,* Richmond, Virginia; former columnist, *Richmond Times-Dispatch*

"*Journeywoman* was hard to put down. . .and I didn't want it to end. Mary Lou Gediman's writing is easy to visualize, and it's funny too!
—Julie Shoen, artist, Newport Art Museum

"Maggie is a down-to-earth, realistic character that readers can sympathize and empathize with. Author Mary Lou Gediman does a remarkable job of shifting from past to present while keeping the reader engaged and eager to know exactly what happened on that night in the church basement so long ago. She leaves us with an atypical "happy" ending that we can all appreciate. Finally, the local color of blue collar, small town New England is ever-present in the descriptions of the characters and the setting. I can't wait to read Mary Lou's next book!"
—Marylu Dalton, English teacher, South Carolina

"Christmas day 1964, two local cops were found murdered in the basement of St. John's Episcopal Church. Cops in a church, murdered? Why? And who killed them? Author Mary Lou Gediman leads us to the answer with intricate detail and seemingly insignificant conversation, but every morsel of information counts. This isn't your typical "who-done-it" mystery that takes readers through the investigation of a murder. Gediman transports us through decades from Virginia through New England and back, unraveling the mystery layer by layer. We travel with the protagonist Maggie through each moment of her journey. Maggie is your mother, your sister, your best friend. She is lively and quick, *and* courageous. The other characters are familiar; you could swear they live next door. Their conversations are speckled with familiar truisms and their mannerisms, quirks and expressions are presented in plain language that makes us feel at home. Maggie's journey reveals surprising answers to questions—some not even asked."
—Judy Peterson, lecturer, University of Richmond

Journeywoman

Journeywoman

By Mary Lou Gediman

Brandylane Publishers, Inc.

Copyright 2010 by Mary Lou Gediman. No portion of this book may be reproduced in any form whatsoever without the written permission of the publisher.

The characters, places, and events in this book are fictitious. Any similarity to real persons, living or dead, is coincidental and not intended by the author.

ISBN 978-1-883911-95-9

LCCN 2009942953

Brandylane Publishers, Inc.
Richmond, Virginia
brandylanepublishers.com

The illustration opposite the title page is a watercolor by artist Julie Shoen of Newport, RI. The original design was done in color and can be viewed on her website. For more of Julie's original watercolor designs, please visit www.julieshoen.com or contact her via e-mail at Julie@julieshoen.com.

Author's photo on back cover by Ann Bradshaw (www.saycheeez.com)

For Mark, Jen and Amy

My World

"The most important trip you may take in life is meeting people halfway."

–Henry Boye

Acknowledgements

A big debt of gratitude goes out to the following:

- My dearest husband Mark for his unending patience, love, and listening capabilities
- My children, Amy and Jen who are the light of my life
- Lloyd Webster for his infinite knowledge of cars and trucks
- Dr. Rachel M. Jones for setting me straight with medical lingo
- My dear friend Phyllis Dudding for her unwavering encouragement and support through this new adventure of book writing for me
- My good friend Nancy McGrath who is the funniest person I know
- My sister-in-law Beth Falcon for her help in marketing my book, and her husband David for his skilled knowledge of martial arts.
- My good friend Mary Peterson for her love and encouragement
- And a special thank you to Cameron Walker for bringing me up to speed in the IT world. Thanks for making my website, www.marygediman.com and blog look professional and interesting
- My friends and neighbors Jeff and Kristy Geiger, for both their support and for Jeff's legal expertise
- Thank you to my publisher, Robert Pruett of Brandylane Publishers and my editor, Sarah McCollum – you two are the best!!
- Thank you to my sisters Dorothy, Barbara and Elizabeth for teaching me that whatever life throws at you, facing each obstacle with humor is like laying your head on a soft, comfortable pillow at the end of a long, hard day
- Thank you to my sister-in-law Diane and my brother-in-law Ben and their family; my brother-in-law Bob and his family; my sister-in-law Julie and her family; my mother-in-law and father-in-law Phyllis and Al Gediman – all of who gave me so much love and support
- Thank you to all who are not mentioned here, my friends, family, neighbors, and ex-coworkers. If you are reading this, you know who you are. Without each and every one of you, this book would not have morphed from an idea into a reality.

Prologue

Looking down into my father's dead face
for the last time
my mother said without tears, without smiles
without regrets
but with civility,
"Goodnight, Willie Lee, I'll see you
in the morning."
And it was then I knew that the healing
of all our wounds
is forgiveness
that permits a promise of our return
at the end.

–Alice Walker

Part One

December 25, 1964

Chapter One

Norman Vincent Peale, the champion of positive thinking, was once quoted as saying, "Christmas waves a magic wand over this world, and behold everything is softer and more beautiful." Not so in Durham, Connecticut, a small town located just twenty miles southeast of Hartford, the state's capital. In Durham, a malevolent cloud hung low, shadowing the good citizens of the town. Murder was in the air this Christmas, murder that would inevitably change the lives of many who dwelled in this pocket-sized town. Not all lives would change, mind you. But for some, the change would be enough to turn their whole world upside down and knock it sideways. Especially after the truth got out about who was lying face down on a table in a church basement, deader than a doornail. For the friends and relatives of those poor slobs, and for the murderer too for that matter, life would never be the same again and that was for darned sure.

Today, at the top of newspapers in Durham, Connecticut as well as countrywide, big bold letters were sprawled across the top of the front page. The print read, **Merry Christmas – December 25, 1964** and headlines boasted of the grand opening of a new movie premiering in theaters everywhere, *Goldfinger,* starring Sean Connery. As soon as word got out about the motion picture coming to the big screen, almost every kid in America would want to go see it. Another story that would appear in the press would be a gloomy article alerting die-hard Cheerio Meredith fans of her sudden death at the age of 74. Many dedicated TV viewers followed Cheerio's career on the *Andy Griffith Show* ever since she made her début in 1960. During her two-year stint on the show, she only appeared in six episodes but somehow, to the American people, she made a lasting impression.

Indeed, news was a plenty on this dreary New England Christmas day in the mid 1960's. Spread out on almost every front-page of newspapers nationwide were startling reports of an attack made on George Harrison's girlfriend, Patti Boyd, by a crazed female Beatles fan.

In Durham, CT however, news of a new movie opening, the obituary of a seventy-four-year-old supporting actress, even attacks surrounding the legendary Beatles would be nothing. Yes, all of these current events would pale in comparison to what would be displayed on the front page of tomorrow's newspapers. In fact, tomorrow, headlines would read differently, much differently. Taking center stage in tomorrow's newspapers would be the story of two murdered policemen found locked in a storage room in the basement of St. John's Episcopal Church.

St. John's Episcopal Church was perched smack dab on the top of Federal Hill overlooking Durham. From the grand tower, which was now almost completely covered in ivy, one could see virtually the whole city including the new Dunkin' Donuts on the corner of Main and Trinity. Man, oh man, how that scenery had changed from its noble beginnings in the year of our Lord 1754. Peering out over the balusters from the main tower, the rows and rows of two-family homes became visible on Federal Hill. All looking near identical to one another, knit closely together in true New England fashion, the two-family homes hung there on the side of the hill like pearls strung on a never-ending wire. Each row of homes wound round and round, increasing in width with each strand that drew nearer to the bottom of the mount. The large graduated rows of pearl homes were uninterrupted, save for the single clasp of road running vertically right up the middle and horizontal railroad tracks which were laid at the very bottom of the hill. The railroad tracks stretched as far as the eye could see, separating the hill from the surrounding maze of suburbia.

The horizon, the land that reached beyond the tracks, provided a different view altogether. The invasion of newcomers, which—in New England terms—meant living in a community for less than twenty years, changed that vista from vast open pasture to one of chopped up plots of land separated by tall, thick wooden fences. On these parcels of land stood bigger, newer single-family homes with large driveways to accommodate new Buicks or Chevys or an occasional El Camino. These fancy cars were a far cry from the type of cars parked in pearl house driveways. Those cars usually came in two-tone, and not by choice. A rusted door that had fallen off often times necessitated a trip to the junkyard in search of a new one close to the make and model, matching the color was always an added bonus but not really required.

There was an occasional two-family house scattered here and there in the valley of greed, but most homes were all on one floor with sprawling yards, encompassing at least a half acre of land. Each parcel of land was rimmed with a tall fence demarcating land borders, a necessity when separating each home from their respective neighbors. All lawns at the bottom of the hill and beyond were lusciously green and well-manicured, unlike the pearl home lawns, which were usually full of dandelions and crabgrass. The newcomers in their fancy homes didn't know a lick about community though. Most of them hardly knew their neighbors first names. With such a wide patch of land between each home, how could they? Supply and demand—the price of urban sprawl; probably the same reason why a new Dunkin' Donuts emerged right in the middle of town.

No two-family house dweller would ever dream of going into a Dunkin'

Donuts. They'd make their own coffee each and every day, every morning, just as the generations before them had done. When they wanted some company, they'd just yell out of their windows to the adjacent house. What with the houses being so close to each other, they could practically pass the cups back and forth through the windows. So, when they peeked out of a side window and saw their neighbors cleaning their carpets or making their beds, or, better yet, bending over a stove concocting some homemade treat which could easily be shared among friends, they'd either rap on the windows and hold up an empty coffee cup or simply lean down a bit and yell through the screen. Once they got their neighbor's attention, it didn't take too much convincing to have them come and sit down for a good cup of joe and a lively conversation.

Coffee was usually percolated, made in a Corning Ware Cornflower stovetop coffee pot, the same one they got as a wedding gift umpteen years ago. It was brewed on top of a gas burner stove and served in slightly chipped or cracked cups with stained saucers to match. And the fragile cups and saucers were ever so gently placed on Formica-topped rectangular tables with grooved aluminum rims and chrome-plated legs. The coffee was slurped, not sipped, while sitting on vinyl-covered chairs that stuck to bare legs underneath tattered housedresses. Conversation was friendly and light, though heavy on benign neighborhood gossip.

St. John's Episcopal Church was far and away the most magnificent structural design still standing in Durham. Nothing could compare to its beauty. On the outside each round stone was strategically placed in near perfect succession. They were polished smooth over time from the harsh winters of Connecticut. And the unforgiving New England weather had successfully worn away their original auburn color until eventually each stone became a nondescript lackluster shade of tan. The grand and glorious stained glass windows, fashioned in the middle ages, told a tale to all those who observed them. The glass art was used to spread the gospel and educate the faithful. Twelve small stained glass windowpanes depicted the life and ministry of Jesus. A large rose window portrayed the arrival of the Holy Spirit on Pentecost, and three windows above the altar confirmed the risen Christ, flanked on either side by St. Peter and St. Paul.

The inside of the church was even more spectacular than the outside, if that was possible. Both the nave and sanctuary touted the same stonework as the outside of the church. The ceilings were made of thick mahogany beams placed at near perfect forty-five-degree angles. These beams pointed toward the heavens. And, just in case any parishioner had a question about where they were supposed to go after this life was over, the thick beams would indeed aim them in the right direction.

Red carpeting adorned the floors. Long crimson padded cushions provided added comfort to the broad pews, and the end of each pew was festooned with hand carved crosses and freestanding antique candelabras. Long tapered white candles made of half paraffin and half beeswax emerged from each candelabra. The divine smell of alfalfa and clover from the beeswax wafted through the air. But, on this Christmas morning neither fifty nor a hundred and fifty fine scented candles would be enough to either camouflage or suck the stench of sin out of the air.

At this 10:00 a.m. service, like all other Christmas's past, St. John's Episcopal Church had added three simple white roses to each candelabra, each rose symbolizing purity, joy and hope. The Reverend Dudley S. Session stood at the altar. Behind him hung a large ruby red velvet curtain draped on a rod as big around as Popeye's forearm. The traditional Crucifixion Cross was suspended directly in back of Rev. Session so that it appeared, when the Reverend held his hands out to signify the beginning of the service, that there were two men hanging on that cross, Jesus being on the top and The Rev. Session on the bottom.

Rev. Session examined the contents of each pew, his neighbors, family and friends—his flock. He didn't care so much about the number of people that attended church this Christmas morning as he did about who attended. He was really only in search of two families. To be more specific, he hunted the crowd in pursuit of Doris and Agnes, both with their children in tow. The teased-haired, tobacco-smelling women sat together every Sunday that is unless they arrived late and another parishioner took their usual space. Then they had to split up, which, just by looking at their faces, was an obvious annoyance to them both. Doris was a gum chewer, clicking and popping away at the big wad of Juicy Fruit stuffed in her mouth. This drove Dudley nuts, especially when he was delivering his sermon. He wanted nothing more than to come down into the isle, stand right in front her, hand her a Kleenex and tell her to spit it out.

Doris and Agnes didn't look like your typical mothers and housewives. They looked more like they should be standing on the street corner wearing a pair of stilettos and skin-tight clothes, clothes that advertised every part of their bodies, the good parts as well as the not so good parts. Reverend Session supposed these two wives dressed whatever way their husbands wanted them to. Perhaps it was a small price to pay for what they each got in return, a nice house, fancy cars and the ability to shop wherever they wanted. He knew their husbands made a lot more cash than your traditional street cop did, mostly because of all the extracurricular activities they were into. He suspected these two gals were more intrigued with the money their husbands brought home than they were with their husbands. He could be wrong though. Maybe he had been wrong about these things before, although he doubted it.

Doris and Agnes were not two-family house dwellers like the Reverend, but they had been at one time. He saw them sitting side by side in the same pew, their children sprawled across the rest of the bench. The kids looked bored and fidgety, like they couldn't wait for the service to end so they could return to their newly opened toys. The moms kept looking around for their husbands who usually met them at church service after their night shift was over. They were worried today. And the Reverend knew their worries were for good reason.

The moms knew something was wrong because their husbands should have been home earlier that morning, Christmas. It was like them to be late, to be irresponsible, to put themselves before their families, but never on this day. No, never on Christmas. They'd want to be home to watch the kids open their gifts. They wouldn't have gone out to breakfast today. They wouldn't have lollygagged with their cop buddies shooting the bull somewhere. Rev. Session felt a pang of deep sorrow, knowing that these men would never show up and that their wives would now be called widowers and their children would grow up without a father.

The Rev. Session quickly dismissed his compassionate thoughts, but left in their place was an unmistakable wave of guilt that swept over his entire body. Dudley quickly dismissed this too. The two men these women looked for were scoundrels. They were nightshift policemen who walked their beat. And in the many hours of darkness while patrolling the good streets and sidewalks of Durham, they were on the take, with deep-seated ties to the Mafia and other illegal activities. Everyone in town knew. It was also a known fact that when these two cops were around, everyone in town closely monitored where their teenage girls were at every minute. The townsfolk knew what these cops were after. You couldn't help but notice the way they looked at the young girls, mentally undressing them and most assuredly thinking vulgar thoughts about them. The people of Durham were not stupid. Yes indeed, these cops were rotten to the core, and they were also on the take big time. How else could two average families living on modest cops' salaries have been able to move to the other side of the tracks? People looked the other way when it came to dirty cops. Not only people in Durham either. People everywhere looked the other way. Maybe they were scared of what would happen to them if they became whistle blowers. So they held a blind eye and a deaf ear to the rumblings of talk pertaining to the goings on of dishonest cops. The Rev. Session thought back to his friend in the Army, Private Buster Lee, a southern boy who enlisted in the Army just to get his first pair of honest to goodness man-made shoes. Buster's favorite saying was, "Some folks just need killin." In the case of these two wayward policemen, that saying couldn't have been truer.

Now Dudley's attention turned from Doris and Agnes to another woman in the congregation, another woman with her children. Dudley felt just as bad for this mom but the Reverend needed answers from her more than he needed to empathize. Well, not so much answers from the wife and kids as from their Dad, Eddy, who was the church Sexton. He knew he would never see Eddy in church. And Eddy's wife and kids were C & E guests of the sanctuary. Christmas and Easter always, no exception. Dudley begged Eddy to attend even the C & E services but no deal. After working five and a half days at the church every week, Eddy's response was, "I've given my week doing the Lord's work. You know Dudley, even on the seventh day God rested."

And so it was, no Eddy at any of the church services, even the C & E ones. Eddy's wife Emily was there though, albeit her presence at church appeared as if it took quite a bit of effort on her part. She typically came in late and looked frazzled, her three daughters in tow. Each one of them was just as lovely as Emily. Maggie was a head turner for sure. She had a beautiful face and a body much more advanced than any of the other girls in her tenth grade class at Dover High School. While most other young girls in her class were wearing small sized brassieres, Maggie was already into a woman's size 36D, her bosoms more than filling the two large cloth cups. Maggie tried to hide her chest, but there was only so much she could do. Folding her hands across her upper body only made her elbows poke straight out. And wearing a tighter bra in an attempt to mimic the appearance of her other female classmates resulted in giving her more cleavage, which in turn, drew even more attention to her, attention she did not want or appreciate. The Reverend watched as some of the dirty old men in the congregation stared at her voluptuous chest when she walked by them. He felt bad because he knew this would be a burden Maggie would have to carry all her days. She would probably have to ward off a lifetime of dirty old men and even young ones for that matter, all with profoundly misguided sexual intentions.

Eddy would never admit it, but Maggie was far and away his favorite. He always tried to disguise this fact from his other children, Jill and Linda. Of course he couldn't hide it from his wife. And she didn't let him forget it either: "I swear Eddy Payne, the other girls will grow up with a complex if you keep focusing on Maggie like you do."

Maggie bore the markings of the Payne heritage all the way from the top of her head straight down to the soles of her feet. She was a spitting image of Eddy's mother who'd come straight from the Emerald Isle with a mischievous twinkle in her eye and more than pep in her step. All full of piss and vinegar Eddy's mother was when she came to this country. It was true that Eddy's oldest Maggie could've passed for his Mom's twin sister, comparing the two of them side by side in a picture. Plus, Maggie and Eddy shared a strong common bond–the undeniable love of cars.

Eddy's wife Emily was beautiful. She had red wavy hair and her skin was covered in freckles. She was short and pudgy–a sturdy woman, but it looked like it fit her, like the good Lord himself had meant for her to have some girth and fill out that smooth ivory white skin dotted with just a hint of light brown flecks. They made a stunning couple, Eddy with his jet-black hair, piercing green eyes and olive skin, and Emily with her unruly red mane and crystal blue eyes. Eddy was drawn to her red hair instantly and right from the very first moment they met he had nicknamed her carrot top.

Eddy was Irish and the story he always told the Reverend was that his parents came right off the boat. When they got to Ellis Island and went through the immigration screening station, their brogues were so thick, they didn't hear the first part of the name, the Mc. And so it went—from then on the McPayne family and their descendents became simply the Payne family. There was no mistaking Eddy's heritage. His face looked like a map of Ireland.

 The Reverend didn't know what was to become of the Payne family after this Christmas. He didn't want to know yet. The ramifications were much too much for the Reverend to take in at this time. He preferred to keep an open mind and an open heart for his faithful servant Eddy and his family, reserving all judgment until he heard the truth. This was a trait he set aside only for the very few. It was also a trait he would be willing to give up should his own self-preservation become threatened in the balance. As for all the other people he encountered on a day-to-day basis, well, they were dealt with as the good Reverend saw fit, based on what he required from them or what they would be willing to give him. For the time being though, he would stick by his loyal servant Eddy. But one little bit of information stuck in Dudley's craw. There was no guesswork when it came to where Eddy was last night.

 He knew Eddy was right there at the church. Dudley knew this because he had called Eddy himself asking him to fix the broken boiler after his Christmas Eve service. Dudley had felt a definite chill in the air at that service, and he could hear the boiler banging and sputtering away as he gave his sermon. He wanted the parishioners to be warm at the services on Christmas morning, so he called Eddy, the church's very own mechanical wizard. It was true—Eddy could fix almost anything he set his mind to fixin'. And Dudley knew, Christmas Eve or not, Eddy would come, being the diligent worker he was.

 Dudley knew from experience that people didn't like to be uncomfortable at Church services, and when they froze, so did their wallets. If he was going to accumulate any money in the collection plate at all this Christmas, the temperature in his church had to be at least warm enough for his parishioners to reach deep into their pockets and give generously to the good Lord.

 But the Reverend would not jump to conclusions, no indeed. He needed to get Eddy's side of the story first. On the other hand he had a bad feeling about this one. The Rev. knew nothing good could come from murder. He also knew that nothing would be the same again both in his church as well as in the modest town of Durham, Connecticut.

August 24, 2007

Chapter Two

"Mique Wush Tagooven"

(Hello My Friend)

She exhaled and watched as the smoke from her cigarette slowly mixed with the steam in her coffee; it rose and formed a murky wet gray cloud that hung above her head. Looking up she thought, "an omen."

Who was she kidding? What a drama queen. "That's no omen," Maggie thought, just a piss poor reminder of one of her many bad habits lurking above her. She didn't necessarily care about her many bad habits, because she didn't necessarily care about herself.

Life was hard for Margaret Lerner. Maggie the Maggot—that's what kids taunted her with every day from first grade until she graduated high school. And they did so for no particular reason. But kids could be cruel. Anything out of the ordinary could spur a plethora of malicious comments. If someone was too short, too tall, too skinny, too fat, wore glasses, had an unusual name or even one that rhymed with something bad, well it was all over for that poor little bastard. Once the malicious name was set in motion and caught on, well there was no hope of ever shedding it, unless you moved to a different town.

You would think she'd have gotten used to those nasty cutting remarks, but they always hurt her feelings. She just tried not to show it. By the time Maggie the Maggot hit sixth grade, all those words had done their damage, irreversible damage. That whole sticks and stones thing—well that was a lot of crap if you asked her. Even after all these years, she still heard those little voices in her head sometimes. Those voices, along with all the other little subliminal messages of worthlessness and abandonment she had acquired throughout her lifetime.

The air was muggy and it felt even stickier because of the slight mist falling from the hot August sky. She watched another puff of smoke rise and linger under the overhang of the old brick building she had come to know so intimately. Oh, how that puff of smoke reminded her of her own life. Watching her dreams go up in a dirty, foul smelling cloud of gray—loitering just long enough for her to ponder them, release them and watch them disappear, always drifting off to a land that was foreign to her. Somewhere she had never been, and she knew she would never visit. Somewhere just outside of her reach. She had her two (sometimes even four) cigarettes under that awning everyday for the past twelve years. The old-fashioned brick building, with what her ex referred to as "having a lot of character," was the place she called "work," whatever that meant.

Her desk was exactly fifty-four Mississippi's from where she smoked her morning cigarettes. That is if you counted every step and every stair, which was completely necessary to do, given the fact that one could possibly miss a stride and end up with an odd number of steps. But that was another bad habit she had, counting. Maggie counted almost everything. How many times she moved the toothbrush up and down on each side of her mouth as she brushed her teeth in the morning. The number of chews it took for each bite of her rye toast. And it always had to be an even number, never an odd number of chews, brushes, steps, etc. Odd numbers were bad and invited unwanted anxiety of some lurking doom that could possibly invade her world. And, really, who would want to risk that?

Truth be told, Maggie was fourth generation wacko. Her mother was crazy, her grandmother was a lunatic, and her great grandmother nuttier than a fruitcake. Yeah, they had issues. Not necessarily counting issues (at least not that Maggie was aware of), but other issues, like fear. But not just plain ordinary fear. No that was too easy for her family. It was the kind of fear that gets a grip on you and doesn't let go. The kind of fear that holds onto you, stops you dead in your tracks, immobilizes you, and keeps you from living any sort of normal life. Fear of making decisions, fear of meeting people, fear of leaving your own house—you name it, the whole lot of them were scared to death of everything. But the biggest fear of all—the fear of never having enough. Of anything! Not enough money. Not enough food. Not enough attention. Not enough, not enough, not enough . . .

Odd that Maggie would be teamed up in a working environment with her boss, Dr. Scottie Leonard. Two first names, that's what Maggie thought when she first met him. Scottie was very tall, but who wouldn't be, compared to Maggie's five feet, one inch? He was 6'5 and lanky with a neck like a giraffe, and Maggie imagined him in a zoo sometimes but mostly he reminded her of Ichabod Crane. He had odd habits, and he would freak if she tried to rearrange any of his medical and psychology journals on his desk. Or if she even made one remark about any of his patients—that would just set him off into a series of rants and raves that Maggie made sure to avoid at all costs. Scottie had quirks many, many quirks. Yeah, the two of them made quite a pair, OCD times two.

She watched Scottie walk past her desk. He was soaking wet because by now that light August mist had turned into a full-fledged rain. His skin was almost transparent it was so thin and pale. She could see the blue vein lines running just under his skin, jagged and pulsing beneath his high cheekbones. He reminded her of someone at the end of his stint in Auschwitz. His hair was stringy and a little too long to be called neat anymore. He took his coat off, shook off the excess water, and hung it on the little hook behind his door.

Maggie leaned over, resting her large breasts on her desktop and peered around the corner to take a good look at him. He sat down at his desk piled high with stacks of shiny magazines. Scottie was brilliant and had been for most of his life. "He's a child prodigy," exclaimed Scottie's third grade teacher to Scottie's mom. The truth was he was addicted to learning and had an unquenchable thirst for knowledge. But Maggie couldn't help but wonder how much ribbing he took as a child. With that long neck of his and those nerdy mannerisms, he must have been taunted mercilessly in school just like she had been.

Scottie pushed the button to turn on his computer; he turned around, stuck his head up above the stacks of paper and squawked Maggie's name. A wet bird, that's all Maggie could think of, a wet bird in its nest, squawking for his mother.

"Maggie, there's a piece of paper in my outbox, can you please take care of it for me?"

"A whole crap load of paper on his desk and he wants me to take one little piece out of his outbox," Maggie thought as she pondered the situation. Scottie's M.O.: he can't see the forest for the trees, and he can't see more than one tree at a time. And he sure as shit had to deal with that one tree immediately or else the world would without a doubt, come to an end. Well, stupid Scottie. Didn't he know that Maggie could absolutely not retrieve that piece of paper from his outbox? Didn't he know that one piece of paper equals an odd number? Didn't he know that she had to wait until there were two pieces of paper in his outbox? What a smart, yet undeniably stupid man he was.

Maggie turned on her computer, pretending to be busy until Scottie dropped another item into his outbox. She heard the paper land and jumped up to grab both pieces. Then, returning to her desk, once again turned her attention to her computer. "How the heck do I get so many freaking e-mails?" Maggie mumbled to herself. Staring off into space, she envisioned all kinds of wacky e-mails from all kinds of places floating down a canal, bottlenecking until the floodgates open and off they go magically propelling into everyone's e-mail accounts.

She began the deleting process by checking the little square box next to the message. Then she moved her curser to the blue and white delete button at the top of her shortcut bar and voila, all those meaningless messages were gone.

When she was almost done deleting, one of those crazy e-mails hit home for her.

In bold letters the subject line read:

Subject: A blast from the past– "Mique Wush Tagooven" (Hello My Friend)

Your MISSION: Take the Journey

I'll be in contact with you soon to further instruct you on your mission. Pay attention to the signs.

Signed: Your friend, Chickahominy Grits.

P.S. By the way, your mom and dad enjoyed the stories you wrote about them! You know they both loved you!!

Maggie froze. "What a weird, weird e-mail," she thought. Chickahominy Grits–sounds like something you eat for breakfast. Floodgates, floodgates–opening up the floodgates. This must be some kind of joke. But from whom? No one has ever read her stories about her mother and father because Maggie didn't share much of her past with anyone. And take the journey??? What kind of crap was that? She could barely get out of bed in the morning!

"Should she answer the e-mail? What would she say?" Nothing–she would say nothing because there was nothing to say. She would ignore the e-mail; delete it along with all the others, as if it was never sent to her. That's it–done, gone for good.

The rest of Maggie's day was pretty normal, or as normal as it could be working in a psychiatrist's office. Patients came and went, and each and every one was greeted with a smile from Maggie. No matter how rough and crass she was around the edges, Maggie had a great big heart that was full of compassion for the less fortunate, the weak, infirm, or mentally ill. So all in all, she was in her element in that old medical facility. Sometimes she would look out from her little desk at the people in the waiting room and think, "I'm home."

Most people who came to see Dr. Leonard had mental problems, but not the ordinary kind. They were problems born of pain and problems that came from circumstances beyond their control. Some of his patients were people who had been handed life's most gruesome and challenging of tests. His patients were people who had been pushed to the edge of the cliff and were almost ready to jump. The people who came to see Dr. Leonard either had nowhere else to turn and were ready to be admitted to the looney bin or were just being released from it.

Maggie looked around the room. There was old Mr. Patterson who was just full of nervous tics. You couldn't even watch him for a minute without him making your eyeballs hurt. He was like watching a Mexican jumping bean. Maggie usually offered all the other patients either water, coffee, or soda, but not Mr. Patterson. She learned her lesson early on–at the beginning of his visits—because the floor was a disaster zone after he got done with whatever drink he picked. "Chronic motor tic disorder" was Dr. Leonard's diagnosis. This was exacerbated by the death of Mr. Patterson's wife. He helped her end her life because she begged and pleaded with him to do so. She didn't want to go on living anymore. She knew the end would come soon enough but she just couldn't go through any more pain and suffering. Finally with tears in his eyes and a heavy heart, he crushed the last of her pain pills up, fifteen Oxycontin to be exact, and mixed them with a little water, sucked them up in an eyedropper and squirted them down his wife's gullet. Consequently, he carried the guilt of his wife's death with him for the last five years, and shortly after she died those small little bothersome tics got bigger—much bigger and much more annoying.

The courts had shown pity on the old man, judged him not guilty in the murder of his ailing wife by reason of temporary insanity. But he was remanded to the care of Dr. Scottie Leonard for outpatient visits for the remainder of his natural life or until he was deemed sane, whichever one came first. Just one look at old Mr. Patterson and you knew he wasn't right though. Any court in the country could tell that just by observing him for a little while. He was nervous, easily agitated and very, very sad looking, like he had lost his best friend. But he was calm every time he got through with his session though, and then by the time his next session came, there he was in the waiting room again—jumpy, jumpy, jumpy.

Without a doubt one of Maggie's favorite patients was a young woman who came to see Scottie once a week, sometimes twice if she felt really bad. Her name was Rebecca Wood. Rebecca had just had a baby girl about three months prior to making her first appointment. She named the little girl Mary after her grandmother on her mother's side. Her name had been Mary Louise, and Rebecca absolutely adored her.

Well, Rebecca's marriage had gone south long before she learned she was pregnant. She knew it in her heart of hearts and wasn't surprised that Mike, her husband of six years, had jumped ship shortly after Mary was born. Mike was controlling and overprotective. Whenever she left the house, Mike had always questioned where Rebecca was going, whom she would be with, and how long she planned on being away. If she didn't return home when she was supposed to, Mike had one of his buddies on the force go and look for her.

Mike resented little Mary from day one because he had never ever even wanted children in the first place. He wanted Rebecca all to himself, and he had no interest in sharing her with anyone—another issue in their long list of marital woes. After Rebecca had delivered her precious little bundle of joy, her husband bent over Rebecca's hospital bed and whispered in her ear, "I hope she dies," in the most eerie and demonic voice she had ever heard. After that freaky episode, she knew that her marriage was over for good and got a restraining order to keep him at bay.

She didn't really need to get the restraining order because Mike was gone right after he uttered those words to her. Then Rebecca was alone, but to her surprise, quite happy about it, thank you very much. She had not seen hide or hair of Mike in almost a month. She thought he had moved out of state because whenever she met any of his co-workers in the supermarket or drug store or around town she would ask if they'd seen him and each and everyone said "no." In reality, Rebecca's husband had not gone far away at all. Ever since he left his wife's bedside, he had been residing in a local hotel room plotting his next move.

Then came the day that destroyed Rebecca's life as she knew it. The only problem was that she didn't know it. An ordinary day in late March, the weather was brisk and perfect for walking with a newborn. She had seen the car slow down, recognized the make, model and driver. Mike had tried to disguise himself, but how can you hide pure evil? Rebecca had reached into her pocket for her cell phone, dialed 911, and was poised to push the send button, but in an instant it was all over. It all happened so quickly—no time to think about any kind of a reaction. Mike jumping out of his car, pushing Rebecca to the ground, the cell phone flying in the air, him grabbing little Mary and then just a blur. Mike had taken Mary out of her little navy blue stroller and thrown her on the sidewalk and she was dead as soon as she hit the pavement. Rebecca hadn't remembered any of that though. The farthest she could go back was seeing Mike driving up in his car. The rest she had blocked out. "Distorted Grief Response due to Post-Traumatic Stress" was the diagnosis on her chart. Rebecca had blocked out the worst part of the incident and had made up a story that was easier for her to handle.

Her trauma was much too much for her to cope with at this point in her life. So, as part of her body's natural response to ease her intense emotional pain, Rebecca's conscious mind had fabricated a tale that she believed with all her heart and soul to be true. She honestly assumed that some lunatic had abducted her newborn. She also believed with confidence that this madcap mental case would take good care of her little girl until the police got to the bottom of all this mess and put things right, returning Mary once again to the loving arms of her mother.

As for Mike—well, apparently he had some conscience after all. Shortly after murdering his little girl, the scumbag went back to his hotel room and proceeded to eat the barrel of his 45-caliber pistol. He took the easy way out.

At the urging of Dr. Leonard, Rebecca was to be sheltered from the truth about Mary. Scottie advised those who came in contact with Rebecca to go along with her story at least for the time being. This informed inner circle included family members, friends and a select number of policemen who had been working on the case. Even Maggie was instructed on how to deal with Rebecca. And Maggie listened to Scottie's orders obediently. The last thing she wanted was to upset the natural order of things. If the truth was revealed too soon the ramifications could be disastrous for Rebecca, perhaps sending her into a mental stupor the likes of which she would never return from. Scottie said the truth would need to come to Rebecca gradually, preferably in increments that she could handle. Hopefully, one day, all would become clear and she would come to grips with both the reality of the situation and the grief that accompanied her daughter's death.

So, consequently, each and every time Rebecca came in to see Dr. Leonard Maggie asked her if the police had found Mary yet. And each time Rebecca's response was a long anguished "no." In some ways Maggie envied Rebecca and wished that she could block out some things in her life. But this was not so. Maggie let everything come into her world. Every memory and every feeling attached to it flooded her brain with thoughts and her heart with emotions. This was sometimes a blessing, but mostly it was a curse.

Dr. Scottie Leonard understood people and especially those who had experienced grief. He understood mental illness and what it took to push people over the edge. "How had he gotten this gift?" Maggie pondered this question over and over to herself many times during her employment with him. The only conclusion she could come up with was that he was born with the wonderful talent of understanding people, enabling him to possess a unique ability to console those poor lost souls that came to see him week after week.

After Maggie met Mrs. Anne Leonard, Scottie's mom, she decided that Scottie may have been born with the wonderful attribute of intense empathy for the human race, and Anne made it her mission as a good Christian mother to make sure he used his special gift to better the world. She signed Scottie up to be a tutor at school, helping his fellow students who were struggling with their schoolwork. She signed him up for every kind of humanitarian service there was at the church including feeding the homeless, collecting clothes and necessities for hurricane victims, and helping teach Sunday School classes at church every week. Wherever there was a community need or service to be done, there was Scottie helping with the cause. So truth be told, Anne Leonard was surprised, especially after all the religious teachings she bestowed upon her only son, that her Scottie chose Psychiatry above Religion as his vocational choice. This was a career Anne Leonard knew nothing about. She would have much preferred that her son use his God given natural talents to please the Lord and enter into a more pious lifestyle such as pastor of the local Baptist Church.

Scottie Leonard was born into a simple rural family in Breaux Bridge, Louisiana (a.k.a. the bayou). He was raised in a town where folks just trusted one another. They left their doors open at night and never once had second thoughts of anyone breaking into their homes. His mom was a stay-at-home mother and just adored Scottie, little nerd that he was. She didn't mind though because that's what God blessed her with. You see, Scottie's mother was a Bible-thumping, down-home country girl with a disposition as sweet as molasses. Whatever God brought her, well that's what was supposed to happen, and she accepted it without question. If it was bad news, it was a lesson from above, a test of faith. "God willin' and the creek don't rise," was Anne Leonard's favorite saying. And, as luck would have it, God's will always prevailed, and the creek never rose high enough to flood anyone out, which was just perfect as far as Anne was concerned.

Anne Leonard believed wholeheartedly in giving little Scottie the best upbringing she could. She cooked good meals for him, was always there if he needed anything, made sure he had good churching, and tried as much as she could to help him with his homework after school. But since Scottie was so intellectually advanced, Anne couldn't really help with his homework after the third grade. Anne ran a tight ship too. She didn't allow any drugs or alcohol in her home. The only drug Anne used in her home was shooting up with Jesus, mainlining to the big guy upstairs. Consequently, her little precious son learned a lot about loving and accepting everyone, no matter who they were or where they were from. He learned from his mother Anne how to be compassionate and forgiving. In this environment, Scottie Leonard flourished wonderfully.

So many times Maggie wished she had had the same kind of upbringing as Scottie did. She couldn't help but wonder, even if her family had moved right next door to the Leonard's in that hot, muggy climate—no matter what the weather was like—her family would still be the ones just a screen door away from Hell, just like they were up north. That's just the way it was, plain and simple. Life handed Maggie lemons from the very beginning, but she could never find the recipe for lemonade.

Finally, after what seemed like days, Friday was over. Five o'clock: yabba-dabba-do time. Maggie straightened up her desk a bit, turned off her computer, grabbed her purse, and she was out the door. She was spent. She had felt for the world today. There was old Mr. Patterson and Rebecca and then there was that wacky e-mail. Maggie could hardly wait to get home. Mentally she envisioned the ice clinking against the sides of the glass as she poured her nightly cocktail of Jack Daniels. The soothing comfort of the bottle was one of Maggie's closest friends at the end of the day. Just two drinks though—that was her limit, plus that was an even number so she was happy about that limitation.

Interstate-95 wasn't too crowded. Usually a bad rainstorm would send drivers in Richmond into a panic, slowing them down to a crawl on the highway. Even so, bad weather or not, there were so many wacky drivers in Richmond you never really knew what you were getting into when you hit the interstate. People were migrating south; there was no doubt about that. "Dammed carpet baggers," Maggie thought, even though she was one herself. It was certainly less expensive to live here in Richmond, Virginia. And it was most definitely cheaper than New York or Massachusetts. So consequently, there were drivers from all over—New York, New Jersey,

Pennsylvania, and even as far away as Boston. They all brought their bad driving habits too.

Maggie immediately noticed a brand new Ford Escape–the new hybrid version. He almost hit her when she was merging onto I-64 East. He cut her off but she sped up and ultimately got right in front of him. He tailgated for a minute before he floored the gas pedal, passed her on the left and cut right in front of her. As he went by her, she got a good look at him, albeit brief. His dark black hair, streaked with a touch of gray at the temples was pulled back into a long thinning ponytail. Hanging from his rear view mirror was a half-dollar sized dream catcher with beaded feathers hanging from the bottom rim of the woven circle. He wore a large, thick colorful beaded band around his neck. Maggie surmised, from all these signs, that this man was a Native American.

"An Indian," thought Maggie. "Weird," she mumbled to herself. "Who sees a real Native American Indian anymore?" Her thoughts went back to the e-mail she had received earlier, but she tried to push that out of her mind once and for all. As the SUV passed her, the driver smiled and held up his hand. He gave Maggie an odd look as well as an odd hand gesture. His forefinger and middle finger were closely knit together with his thumb and then he sort of motioned his whole hand back and forth like he was ringing a bell or something. It was just plain weird. As he passed her, she got a close look at his license plate: New Hampshire–Live Free or Die. "Damned freaks," Maggie thought.

After being on the road for about twenty minutes, Maggie was home. She pulled into her apartment complex and saw her neighbors sitting on their front porch. "Shit" she said openly in the confines of her old Toyota Corolla. Every day was the same: Maggie would arrive home and no sooner open her car door than her next-door neighbors would start talking. Both of them–husband and wife would talk at the same time, often talking over one another in an effort to gain Maggie's attention. Most of the time Maggie would stop, gab awhile, make her niceties, and then give them some excuse just so she could get away from their verbal grip. They were old–in their late seventies maybe–but both healthy so she never felt really bad for them. They were just bored from doing nothing all day.

"Hello Maggie, how was your day?" Jim and Carol said at the same time. "That's how it starts," thought Maggie. One quick answer like "Good" and they were all over her like a fly on shit. They'd go on and on about how we shouldn't be involved in the Iraq war, or Jim would tell Maggie anything and everything about what it was like to work for the government. "Back in my day, blah, blah, blah..." Jim ranted on and on. Maggie looked at them both and immediately envisioned spiders in a web–each of them poised–ready and waiting for their next victim.

"I suppose I should be more understanding, she thought. After all, these people have been home all day just waiting for someone to talk to," Maggie mentally wrestled with her fleeting moment of compassion for the older couple. She quickly rejected that thought and replaced it with the reasoning that God gave people two ears and one mouth—to listen more than they spoke.

"Not today, no absolutely not today," Maggie decided. So she did something completely out of character for her. As she headed toward the back of the building, down the hallway to her apartment, she removed her front upper partial denture from her mouth, turned to Jim and Carol who were up and leaning over their front railing by now, and gave them both a big toothless grin. Cocking their heads, they both stared at Maggie, speechless for once. Neither Jim nor Carol knew what to say and by the time they did, well, Maggie was counting the steps to her own door—fourteen to be exact. She was putting the key in her own lock and for once she did not have to listen to the mindless dribble of her neighbors—stupid jibber jabber.

Tonight Maggie would relax. She had promised herself this on her ride home. No cleaning, no cooking, no thinking, just sitting and relaxing on her back porch and maybe eating a bag of potato chips for dinner if she was so inclined. She changed into her old cotton pajamas, and then poured herself two fingers of Jack Daniels over ice with just a twist of lemon. She slid open her screen door and plopped herself on the old wicker chair on her back deck. There were no other apartment buildings behind her, just her three foot wooden railing to separate her from the great outdoors. It was the closest to nature she got. In the woods behind her apartment Maggie sometimes spotted a family of deer or a raccoon or some birds and this would please her immensely. Today was not one of those days though. Nothing was happening out in the woods today except for a couple of squirrels playing tag with each other.

Almost as soon as Maggie sat in her chair, she could feel water start to dribble on her head. Looking up through a crack in the decking there he was, the upstairs neighbor, a.k.a. the village idiot, all dressed in his tan, olive green and red Scout Master's uniform. He was bending over what Maggie assumed to be a large blue cooler. "Must have had an outing today," she deduced. At first the water dribbled out of the little white spout on the side of the cooler. But emptying it that way wasn't good enough for Boy Scout man, so the smart ass dumped it completely on its side. Water gushed down on Maggie through the cracks in the decking, soaking her completely from head to toe. The liquid was cold and took her breath away for a minute until she gasped and yelled, "What the hell are you doing?"

With a simple sarcastic reply Mr. Boy Scout shouted, "Soooorrry"!

Maggie was infuriated. The world would not piss on Margaret Lerner today, no indeed. Flying out of her chair, she almost walked through the sliding screen door, grunting and swearing with every step. Apartment 39C would hear the wrath of an angry woman tonight. She headed straight upstairs to give Mr. Boy Scout Leader and his family a piece of her mind. A come to Jesus meeting was in order for water boy.

She banged on the door and when Mr. Boy Scout answered he looked at Maggie like she had three heads. Maggie started in: "You inconsiderate son-of-a bitch. Who do you think you are? Some Boy Scout leader you are—you're nothing but a hypocrite, pretending to do good work in that dumb-ass uniform of yours, and then dumping out your old stinky cooler on your downstairs neighbor. I should report you to the Grand Puba of Boy Scout leaders or whoever the heck it is that rules you bunch of jackasses."

By this time the whole Boy Scout family had gathered in the doorway, wife and three little monster children.

"And while we're on the subject of complaining about being dumped on, why don't you tell those little rug rats of yours that, contrary to popular belief, when you live above someone it is common knowledge that playing basketball in the house at 7:00 a.m. on a weekend is also INCONSIDERATE!"

Mr. Boy Scout looked at Maggie and his face got more and more red with each verbal assault she dished out. But being a man of few words, he looked at Maggie and simply said in a voice with a deliberate lisp and a magnitude of sarcasm, "Thorry Nanthy Nipple!"

This made Maggie's blood boil because at that very moment she realized why he answered as he did. Maggie had not stopped to put her teeth back in her mouth so every syllable remotely related to the S or TH family— came out in one great big lisp. Even worse, the cheap cotton pajamas she had on were paper thin from all the times she had washed and dried them. And when the transparent cotton become drenched, the view underneath left little to the imagination, giving her neighbors a birds eye view of her ample bosoms.

Maggie looked at Mr. Boy Scout Leader with daggers in her eyes, did not say a word but instead gave him the sign that the Native American gave her that same night during her ride home from work. She placed her forefinger and middle finger together with her thumb as if holding something and started shaking her hand back and forth. This made Maggie feel tremendously better.

As for Mr. Boy Scout Leader, well he just circled his finger around his temple and said, "You're nuts," then slammed the door.

Maggie went back to her apartment, changed her clothes and tried to relax the rest of the evening, which wasn't easy. Thinking back on all the events of the day, she decided it had been one sorry-ass day from hell. But mostly she thought of the Indian in the Ford Escape with the license plate that read: New Hampshire—Live Free or Die.

December 25, 1964
12:30 PM

Chapter Three

There were more black and whites in the parking lot of St. Johns Episcopal Church than Carter had liver pills. Brand new 1964 Ford Galaxie Sedans. More than 200,000 of them were made that year. The V-8 engine was smaller than the '58 model at only 289 cubic inches, but advancements in technology increased the horsepower to a whopping 271. They were all lined up side by side in the parking lot of St. John's Church. Sitting on the roof of each cop car was a round red plastic light that took up a good part of the hood. It looked like a pimple right in the center of someone's forehead—just ready to pop.

The place was crawling with all kinds of people. Neighbors came out of their homes to see what the commotion was all about. Parishioners who had lingered from the morning service waited in their cars with the engines still running. Even though it was Christmas day and they should have been in their own homes, everyone wanted to know what was going on, even people just passing by on their way to someone else's house stopped to see what all the fuss was about. And the parking lot, the lawn, the sidewalks and the entire inside of the church were just swarming with cops. Not only cops from Durham either. They were from all over the state of Connecticut and beyond. By 1:30 p.m. the FBI, following direct orders from J. Edgar Hoover, arrived on the scene as well. It was a given that no one in the field of law enforcement was going to enjoy a hot turkey dinner with their families on this particular Christmas day.

The imposing Chief John M. Gunderson loomed above all the other policemen in the crowd. He was of Norwegian decent with blonde and gray hair that was firmly affixed in place with a large wad of Brylcreem. But Gunderson defied the popular product's coordinating slogan, "A Little Dab'll Do Ya!" and replaced it with, "You can never have enough." His goopy hair could be seen hanging out about an inch and a half from the bottom rim of his hat, visible comb marks still running through his unyielding locks. At six-feet-four-inches and close to three hundred pounds, he looked like he should've been sporting a winged Viking helm on top of his noggin instead of his traditional flat-topped hat with the small oval scooped visor and etched shield that had the word CHIEF embossed on it.

The Chief moved his lips and words came out. His voice was deep and the tone only varied when he wanted to accentuate his point. He did this by elevating his low pitch slightly and drawing the syllables of certain words out longer than they should have been. These were the words he wanted people to pay attention to. Most of the time his speech sounded more like the roaring echo of a Blacksmith's bellow than any human voice. Looking around the crowd of people that had gathered in the parking lot he hollered, "Who called this into the station?"

The Rev. Dudley S. Session answered with a little too much confidence in his voice, "I did sir."

"I assume you're the minister in this church right?" Gunderson questioned, glancing down at Dudley's white plastic clerical collar. "Were you the one who found the bodies?" he roared. Gunderson walked slowly through the crowd of people, eventually making his way to the good Reverend.

"Yes, sir. I'm Reverend Dudley S. Session and I've been the minister here for the past ten years. I had just finished my liturgical service. It was about 11:15 a.m., but by the time everyone left and I gathered up the necessary accoutrements I typically use in my Christmas services, it must've been closer to noon. I brought all my altar things down to the storage room to lock them up."

"Exactly what do you mean by 'accoutrements'?" Gunderson barked.

"I use the standard things any priest would use to conduct my services: a paten which is the small gold dish used to hold the altar bread and an ornately carved gold chalice which has a large ruby gem in the middle of it. In case you're not familiar with our religion, the chalice is used to hold the wine and actually the wine is synonymous with the precious blood of Jesus." He spoke to Gunderson as if he was a religious imbecile. "At Christmas I also use a vessel in which I put holy water in for our sacrifice of the Eucharist. This is also very ornate and has a large gem right in the middle of it too. I'm not sure what kind of stone it is though. I use other things in my service as well. Do you need to know what they are and what they're all used for?" Dudley asked Gunderson.

Gunderson looked at Dudley. His eyes had begun to glaze over as Dudley explained his religious rituals. "They're valuable then, right Dudley? That why you wanted to lock 'em up?" Gunderson asked his question then held out his large paw in an attempt to shake Dudley's hand, "Sorry, forgot to introduce myself properly. I'm Chief John Gunderson. I'll be in charge of this investigation."

"Nice to meet you, sir," Dudley replied in his phony voice. On the outside Dudley pretended to be interested in meeting Gunderson. On the inside it was hard for him to hold back his disdain for cops, any cops. He tried as hard as he could to shield his true feelings behind a mask of heartfelt caring and sincerity. This wasn't easy, because in his opinion every single person who worked on the Durham Police Force was a total and complete moron. "Yes, they're very valuable, priceless as a matter of fact."

"Just to make things a little more simple, why don't we classify all these items you use for your service as your 'mass kit,' okey dokey?" Gunderson suggested. "Now, moving on with the investigation!" Gunderson shouted. "Is that the same storage room where you found the bodies? Do you always store your mass kit in there?" Gunderson asked brashly.

"Yes that's where I found the bodies and yes, I do store my *mass kit* in there. Typically I bring it there after every service." Dudley emphasized "mass kit," letting Gunderson know he understood that these two words would now be used to represent the items he had just informed Gunderson of, the ones typically used on his altar.

"Did you have a service last night, Reverend, and if you did, did you bring your mass kit down there after your Christmas Eve service?"

"We did have our usual Christmas Eve service at 9:00 p.m. but I decided, since we were having another one early this morning, I would just leave the mass kit out."

Dudley felt as though both he and Gunderson were reading from a script, such was the nature of each of their voices. He would not have normally spoken in such a lackluster tone but he was following Gunderson's lead, using the loudest verbal flat line voice he could muster. He tried to match the deep tone and volume of Gunderson's voice but after a while his throat became hoarse so he had to abandon these vocal imitations and go back to his normal pitch. He wanted to fit in as much as possible, make Gunderson think he was really interested in these so-called heinous murders. Dudley figured if he mimicked Gunderson's demeanor, it would be to his advantage. Calling attention to himself and his church was not what he wanted.

Dudley had never been caught in any unlawful situation and he didn't want to start now. He made sure to protect his cover at all times, using whatever method he deemed necessary to guard his secrets. Dudley could hold his ground with the best of them but, just to be on the safe side, he tried to stay away from the law's limelight as much as was humanly possible. He didn't mind helping the cops out, but only if there was something in it for him.

The Chief opened up his spiral-edged notebook and took off his gloves so that he could hold his pen better. He put his black leather gloves inside the pockets of his thick wool overcoat. The girth of his hands was ridiculous. He could have probably killed someone with just one of them. He began to write something in his notepad, one of his first observations in the case. He emphasized this observation by placing question marks in front of it.

?????Rev. Dudley Session left PRICELESS Mass Kit out on altar after C. Eve srvc to use in AM Christmas srvc

Gunderson wondered why on earth anyone would leave such valuable items out on the altar overnight. An even bigger puzzle in Gunderson's mind was, if he were to leave them out on the altar, why on God's green earth hadn't they been taken already. These expensive items were just begging to be stolen.

"Let's go inside, Reverend, and get out of this cold." John opened the thick arched wooden door with his huge hand. He motioned for the Reverend to go ahead of him. As Dudley walked past the esteemed Chief, he got a good whiff of his aftershave, Old Spice. He recognized the scent immediately, having worn the same cologne himself for many years. It had a manly smell but was not overpowering. "The Chief probably got the gift set that very morning," Dudley thought. The famous advertisement for the popular cologne was posted all over billboards beckoning wives to buy the product. The ad was just heaving with guilty messages and came with the intention of warning women shoppers, quoting: "To most men, it just isn't Christmas without Old Spice." That sure rang true for the Chief.

As the Chief and the Reverend made their way into the sanctuary, they chose to sit in the back row on one of the cushioned pews. Just as they sat down, an imposing figure strolled up the aisle and stopped right in front of the two of them, turned and started to talk. "You the goombah who's takin on this case?" the short stocky figure asked Gunderson in a low husky voice.

"Yep, I'm the goombah," Gunderson replied glancing over at the burly olive skinned gentleman.

The short man wore a long black wool coat and a soft wool snap fedora hat that was cocked a tad to one side just like the one Humphrey Bogart wore in *Casablanca*. He stared at Gunderson with a deliberate look. In one hand he held a cigar that Gunderson swore was the size of the rolling pin in his wife's kitchen. He hadn't lit the cigar yet. At least he had the common courtesy not to smoke in the house of the Lord. Taking his other hand out of his coat pocket, he scrunched up all his fingers together so they all met on the backside of his thumb, a classic Italian gesture. This was not an easy chore for him to do because of his short pudgy fingers. Holding his hand like that for a while made his hand appear as if he'd stuck the whole thing into a cup of Elmer's glue and it was now just beginning to harden. He pulsed his hand up and down directly in front of Gunderson's face. The short stocky man spoke in Italian, "*Giuro per portare la vendetta sul mio assassinio del fratello. Sue assassin desidererà che loro non era mai stato nato.*" And, as soon as he said this, bam, like a bolt of lightning, he was gone.

Dudley stared at the man in the fedora hat as he spoke in Italian. He watched him turn quickly and leave the same way he came into the church. "Look's familiar," he said to himself. "What did he say, Gunderson? Do you even speak Italian?"

"I don't speak Italian but I know some words. I think the dead cop was his brother. I'm pretty sure the word *fratello* is brother and, of course you know what *vendetta* is, don't you?"

"Of course I know what *vendetta* is." "What does this dim-witted cop think, I was born yesterday?" thought Dudley.

"So the cop was his brother," Dudley said, surprised. "I thought I recognized a family resemblance. That's not good, is it Gunderson?"

"Not good at all. You know who he was, right?"

"I don't have a clue."

"Mr. Anthony Salvatore Giovanni, a.k.a. 'Fat Tony.' He's one of the top New England crime bosses."

"Not good at all," Dudley grimaced, trying to contain the feeling of dread eating away at his insides. He couldn't have pictured a more perfect scenario, two brothers, one tied to the law and the other to the mob. Each brother wore separate uniforms for their designated professions but each brother was indeed cut from the same cloth. Talk about one hand washing the other.

Dudley wondered when people turned bad. Mostly he wondered when he had turned bad. At times he questioned his own integrity, not that he even knew what the definition of integrity was anymore. There were times when he felt he had gone from good to bad overnight, from the number one to the number ten in an instant, and then he just got stuck on the number ten. "Sooner or later if you put one bad apple into a bushel, they eventually all turn rotten," Dudley thought.

"We'll deal with him later; now let's get started again if we can hear above all this commotion." "Quiet down everyone," John hollered. "We all want the same thing here, folks, and that's justice. I can't even hear myself think, let alone gather evidence with all this racket going on in here."

There must have been at least seventy-five law enforcement officers in the sanctuary all gathering things, dusting for fingerprints, examining every nook and cranny. And there were even more in the basement where the bodies were discovered. They were hungry to pin these two murders on someone. Once they did, it would be a miracle if that person ever saw the inside of a courtroom. They'd string him up alive. Dirty or not, a cop is a cop and whoever messed with a cop didn't stand a chance no matter which way you sliced it. And then of course there was the added complication of mob involvement, which was a different story entirely. The things a cop would do to the murderer of one of their own would pale in comparison to what the mob would do. Even further obscuring the whole mess was the fact that the dead cop was connected to the mob by blood.

Chief Gunderson tried to regain his focus on the investigation, "Was the storage room door locked when you went into the basement this morning?"

"Yes, it was locked so I took out my key to unlock it." Talking to the Chief was like being on an old episode of *Dragnet*. "Just the facts, Dudley, just the facts," the Rev. thought to himself as he answered Thor's questions.

"Do you always keep it locked or is it left open sometimes?"

"Well, we are a church here, Chief. We trust people not to steal things so we keep it open sometimes. But we usually lock it when we put the mass kit inside the room."

"So it should have been open, since you left your mass kit out on the altar last night right? You didn't go downstairs last night at all, is that correct, Reverend?" A red light had gone off in Gunderson's big head. Dudley was talking out of both sides of his mouth. He was willing to leave his expensive mass kit out on the altar all night for the entire world to steal, stating that he was more than trusting of any Tom, Dick or Harry that came along. But, on the other hand, he said that he usually locked the door when he put the kit inside. It didn't make sense to Gunderson. Why didn't he just bring the mass kit downstairs after the Christmas Eve service? This mass kit was supposedly priceless, irreplaceable even. Things just didn't add up. Why in God's name would Dudley ever leave these objects out? Gunderson jotted down these acute observations in his notebook. He knew this information would probably be of significant consequence later on in the investigation. He just didn't know exactly where or when yet.

"Right. I had gotten the mass kit out of the storage room earlier in the day and set it up for the Christmas Eve service. I didn't lock the door behind me because there isn't usually much worth taking in there. We keep the linens for our altar down there as well as linens for our folding tables. We also keep all the cleaning supplies in there. You know, like mops and brooms and such. There's a small table in that room with four chairs that Eddy and I eat lunch at sometimes when we want to get away from the nursery school children. It's quiet downstairs. Not too many people know about this little room so I can easily escape there to get some solitude when I need to write my Sunday sermons or just to think."

Gunderson's ears perked up. Cocking his head to the side and looking at Dudley through squinted eyes, he questioned, "Eddy? Who's Eddy?" The name didn't ring a bell with Gunderson, but that wasn't unusual since Gunderson didn't attend this church. He was Methodist, but hadn't been to a church service in a good long while.

"He's our sexton. You know, our janitor. Eddy Payne. He's been at St. John's almost as long as I've been here. He's a hard worker. I don't know what we'd do without him. He lives close to the church, which is good because he doesn't own a car."

"Tell me Reverend, this Eddy, does he have a key to the storage room?"

"He does. In fact Eddy and I are the only two people that do have a key to the storage room." The Reverend's face flushed red. "But I lost my key for a long time until Eddy went to have a new one made for me. I need it when I'm here alone like yesterday when I needed to get in there to get my kit."

The Chief watched the Reverend. He noted the reddening of his face and the nervous shifting movements of his body. He was trained to notice everything, and something just didn't smell right here. Any number of people could have killed these two cops. The medical examiner would have to first establish an approximate time of death. Then the Chief could toss the net out wide and, depending upon the time of death, he would then be obliged to question nearly all the people who attended church on both the Christmas Eve and the Christmas morning services. Then he would use his internal sieve to cast the wheat from the chaff. It would not be easy. Plus, he wasn't stupid. He now knew at least one of these cops had mob connections. That investigation would be hardest of all, since he didn't want to tarnish his image or the image of the police force. For that matter, neither did he want to soil the persona of the church. Hopefully his investigation wouldn't escalate to that. But, from what his gut told him so far, the Reverend and Eddy would certainly be first contenders in the suspect category.

"We should get a time of death on the bodies soon. After we obtain that lovely piece of information we'll be able to narrow down the suspect list. We can't be sure of the key situation, since yours was stolen and anyone could have used it to lock that door after the murders. We'll need to question this Eddy though, so I'll definitely need his phone number."

"Let me go into my office and get it. I can't remember it off the top of my head." The Reverend started to make his way down the hallway.

Gunderson knew this was a bold-faced lie. If you work with someone for over ten years, you sure as shit know his phone number by now. But he decided not to push Dudley on this point. Gunderson knew that sooner or later, no matter how savvy people appeared on the outside, if they're guilty or covering for someone guilty, they'll eventually cave. From Gunderson's viewpoint, he decided the best way to handle this Dudley character was to let him dig his own grave. Maybe Gunderson would get lucky. Maybe the Reverend might even hit himself over the head with his own shovel and fall into his own manmade hole.

Gunderson interrupted Dudley as he started toward his office. "Give it to me later, Reverend. Why don't you go home for a while, spend a little time with your family. There are plenty of people here to handle what needs to be done."

"Good idea, Chief. I'll just go and get my coat." Dudley started toward his office again, this time to retrieve his coat from the hook on the back of his door. Or at least that's what he wanted Gunderson to think he was doing. Dudley's office was dark and scantily clad with a simple desk, two chairs and a small lamp.

The Reverend made sure to shut the door completely after he entered the room, just in case Gunderson circled back around to check up on him. He picked up the telephone earpiece from its cradle, dialed the phone and waited a minute for the recipient to answer. After three rings he whispered into the receiver, "Meet me in the little patch of woods behind Maplewood Elementary School at 8:00 p.m. tonight. Oh, and Eddy, come alone!

August 25, 2007

Chapter Four

Mother

Early Saturday morning, after she had her coffee and two cigarettes, Maggie hunted in her closet to find the maroon colored leather binder that contained all the stories she had composed for her creative writing class. She placed the binder on the coffee table for the time being. Before reading anything, a nice hot shower was in order first. She figured there was something in Mr. Boy Scout's cooler water last night, some kind of sugary drink that had leaked, because when she woke up this morning parts of her hair were stiff and stuck together.

Maggie figured Abbie must have come in when she was in the shower because she didn't even hear the door open. But, there she was, sitting on the couch when Maggie went back into her living room. And she had the maroon binder on her lap. It was open to Maggie's story, the one she had written about her mother.

When Abbie was in second grade and Maggie was totally bored at home by herself, Maggie decided to take some fun classes just to keep herself busy and possibly sane. Her husband had suggested the creative writing class, since he noticed that Maggie had a proclivity for jotting things down in her journal from time to time. Maggie would have much preferred taking a woodworking class at the local high school around the corner. Or, better yet, an instructional course in the art of auto repair. Oh, how she loved cars! And it didn't matter what make or model they were, each one was unique and fascinating to her. Sometimes she imagined herself working with the pit crew of the Indy 500, an occupation so exciting it sent shivers down her spine. She would never tell Frank this, but on more than one occasion, she even dreamt about cars.

The stories Maggie shared with her class portrayed both an Ozzie-and-Harriett past and a marriage to her husband that was nothing short of a modern-day utopia. They were hand-written yarns spun in thick, gooey Pollyanna ink. The other narratives, the ones she kept entirely to herself, these were the true accounts of her past and present. These were her real stories and they were for her eyes only and, in writing them, she labeled them as such and placed them in her special maroon binder.

She ended up performing this same double writing ritual for almost all the assignments her professor gave to her. Since the class ended up being "a journey of self discovery," as her professor aptly named it, there was a lot more personal writing than she would have liked. Although the class wasn't touted as this in the course curriculum, it really didn't matter to Maggie, since she found a way around her dilemma early on, remedying it with the double writing thing. The class might just as well have been an acting class for Maggie. She read each fake story aloud with a great big enthusiastic smile plastered across her face. The other stories, the real stories, the ones labeled "For My Eyes Only," were read in the dark of her room, turning the pages with one hand and holding a tissue with the other.

"Hi ML," Abbie greeted her mother with a great big smile. "What's up? What's in the binder?" she asked inquisitively, looking down at the title on the page, the one that said "MY MOTHER." "You okay, ML? You look like you just saw a ghost."

This is what Maggie loved about her dear daughter. She was observant about people's feelings, thoughts. She was also a great communicator, asking questions and trying her best to understand what the other person thought or how they felt about things. Looking at her lean frame sitting there on the couch, Maggie wondered where she came from. She certainly didn't look a thing like Maggie. She was a lot taller and thinner and had dark wavy hair that cascaded down to the middle of her back. Her eyes were chestnut brown. They were wide and sparkly and invited everyone who looked into them to come inside her soul and get to know her a little better. Maggie was glad for all these qualities Abbie had acquired, although she knew full well where they came from, her father. The only difference was that Abbie's personality characteristics were real. Her father's were just a whole lot of bullshit.

He was a charmer. On the outside he was friendly, open, and giving with almost everyone, even his own daughter. Needless to say, Maggie never got to see any of these wonderful qualities on the home front. There was one little thing that bothered Maggie lately. It was Abbie's penchant for greeting people or even referring to them using their initials instead of saying their first and/or last names. This worried her. Abbie had just recently turned twenty-four and about a week after her birthday this newly acquired habit had reared its ugly head. Maggie worried that this little tic on Abbie's genetic profile was her fault, even the fault of her screwed up ancestors. It was perhaps the beginning of an OCD, just like Maggie's counting.

"Good morning, dear. Why the abbreviations for my name? Why don't you call me 'mom' like most daughters greet their mothers?" Maggie asked, feeling a little annoyed or maybe even a little guilty at hearing her initials.

Abbie thought about trying to be funny and answering her mother with some funny comment but, after seeing the concern in her face, she decided against it. "I just like to call you ML, that's all. Don't you want me to?"

"I suppose it's okay, but I'd prefer mom."

"Okay I'll try to remember to call you mom. But I'm just warning you – I might slip up sometimes so don't get upset if I do. Okay?"

"Okay, thanks Abbie."

"So what's this *mom*?"

"That's the story I wrote about your grandmother," Maggie answered defensively.

"Can I read it?"

"How come you're not in school?" Maggie tried to change the subject.

"It's Saturday, ML. Remember?"

"Don't you work on Saturdays?" Maggie asked, concerned.

"I do get time off for good behavior, you know." Abbie's attention went back to the binder that was sitting on her lap. "So mom, why do you have this out?" Abbie pointed down. "I've never even seen this story before. Did you just write it?"

Then she noticed the date in the upper left hand corner, September 22, 1991. She looked up at Maggie, lifted her eyebrows and cocked her head to one side in a gesture as if to say, "Well?"

Maggie didn't want to, but she told Abbie all about the e-mail she had received yesterday, the one from Chickahominy Grits. She told her not to worry, that it was probably just some kind of spam or joke or something. Maggie did not tell her daughter about the man in the Ford Escape. Some things were better left unsaid.

Abbie stood up and the binder fell to the floor. "WHAT! she yelled. That's ridiculous. Did you tell someone about it? Did you report it? How did this character CG know about the stories you wrote about your mother and father? Did you show them to him? Who is he anyways? You need to find out who this asshole is. You need to tell him to go pound sand!"

"Relax, Abbie. Relax. I'm sure it's all a big mistake." Maggie tried to reassure her daughter that everything would be okay. She wished she had never told her about the e-mail. But, more than that, on a grander scale, she wished she had never even written the damned stories about her mother and father. She wished she had listened to her inner voice a long time ago and taken the auto mechanic or woodworking classes like she had wanted to. But no, her status-driven husband would not allow her to take either one of these courses. Having an aspiring author for a wife was a much more acceptable explanation to tell ones friends and colleagues, certainly more socially acceptable than having to admit your wife was thinking of becoming a female carpenter or, even worse yet, a grease monkey.

The never ending quest to climb both corporate and social ladders, aiming ever higher towards the status of VP or CEO, these were the aspirations of Maggie's ex. To say he was manipulative would be severely underestimating his need for control. He also had a liking for alcohol, big time. This was one vice Maggie consistently and vehemently opposed. One or two drinks were perfectly acceptable to Maggie, but time and again Frank pushed the envelope with alcohol. She suspected and ultimately discovered his addiction when she was cleaning one day and found a slew of empty vodka bottles stashed in one of the alcoves upstairs in the spare bedroom. She was wiping the cobwebs that had collected along the baseboards, and when she opened the miniature door that lead to the eaves of their cape cod house, there they were, at least fifty empty pint-sized vodka bottles. Foolish Frank, what did he think she was stupid? She should have realized there was something wrong even before she found the empty liquor bottles, what with his drastic mood changes recently. Looking back on her discovery, she wished she had kicked him out of the house right then and there. But she didn't.

Maggie tried as best she could to ignore his alcohol consumption, even when he got a little too frisky with his hands, or rather his fists. And, instead of signing up for the classes she wanted, come January, when the new catalog came out, much to her chagrin, she went along with her husband's suggestion and signed up for a class in creative writing at the local community college.

One of the first things her professor taught her was that writing was cathartic. "No shit, Sherlock," Maggie thought to herself. Learning about poetry and how it's supposed to hit you like a wave, wash over you and leave you infused with the moisture of prose, entering every pore with inspiration and awareness was just fascinating to her. The explanation of a poem alone was like a poem. This was a new vocabulary for Maggie. She felt enlightened.

Armed with all her newly acquired writing knowledge, she began the painful journey of writing about her Mother and eventually about her Father: catharsis! She wrote the story about her mother first while she was taking her creative writing class. Her father's story came many years after. It had taken Maggie a long time to find the right words to put on paper, words strong enough to decipher the feelings that surrounded her wounded heart with regard to her father.

Maggie gestured for her daughter to sit back down on the couch. She reached over to pick up the maroon binder and sat down next to Abbie. "Calm down dear, calm down." "How about we read the story together, okay?"

"Fine, ML, but you have to tell this idiot to leave you alone . . ."

"Shhhh Abbie. Let's just read the story and forget about the e-mail for right now, shall we?" Maggie sat close to her daughter and began to read the story aloud.

September 22, 1991
Margaret Lerner
Creative Writing Class

(For MY EYES ONLY)

MY MOTHER

Emily Ann Payne lived in the middle. Oh, not the middle of the street or the middle of the town, or even the middle of the country. Emily Ann Payne lived in the middle, somewhere between life and death but never choosing either one. This condition Emily suffered from was called the Scarlet Letter disease in the healthcare community, Alzheimer's. But, unlike Hester Prynne, my mother wore her Scarlet Letter "A" on the inside. A series of misguided brain cells had ostracized her from humanity. It was a kind of purgatory she could not escape from, nor could anyone enter in.

By looking at her, other than a vacant stare, you could barely tell she had the disease. She started out just forgetting things, like we all do from time to time. Then, when the disease progressed further, she would travel back and forth from no man's land to the here and now until eventually she took up residence in that vast unreachable wasteland called Alzheimer's. The last time I saw my mother the only words she could say were "I love you" over and over again. "Too little, too late," I thought.

Emily was a thick of a woman. Short and stocky just like her German ancestors. She stood only about five feet tall and weighed well over two hundred pounds. Her bulk was partly due to her insatiable appetite for sweets and partly due to heredity. Her whole family looked like that, men and women alike. Whenever we had a family reunion it was like a convention of human five by fives.

I especially remember my mother's large cumbersome hands. They were cracked and bled sometimes in the winter from being chapped. But winters in Connecticut could be cruel. Every day she hung the laundry out onto the clothesline that swung from our back porch. She never wore gloves because it was too hard for her to maneuver the clothespins with anything on her hands. This ruined her ability to keep her hands soft in the winter, no matter how much cream she slathered on them.

When I became older, I began to think about her history. I pieced the stories of her youth together from the many things I had heard at our unusual family gatherings. And I came up with a conclusion. If ever a body part could tell the story of a person's life, my mother's hands were that part. Her hands were short and stubby almost as if Mother Nature had not quite finished the job of growing them. They were stunted right in the middle of the growth process, and expanded from the many burdens she had carried and would carry throughout her lifetime. The little wounds that cracked and bled and never really healed were a constant reminder of her past and a preview of what was to come.

After I moved away I missed the family gatherings, even if they were a bit bizarre. Especially at Christmas time. Before mother got sick, most Christmas Eves were spent over her house. Aunt Clara, my mother's sister and the one we affectionately called the "Queen of Clichés," and her family, and Peter, my mother's brother, and his family all came over to celebrate the festive holiday season, so to speak. Aunt Clara had three daughters, all of whom were quite homely. They took after Clara's husband's side of the family. When my dad was alive he used to say, "If you put the whole Goodfellow clan together they'd be uglier than a bag full of assholes."

Quirky as she was, Aunt Clara was my favorite aunt and she sure could tell a story. I sat in awe of her almost every time she opened her mouth, wondering how one woman could remember so many clichés.

There was one story Aunt Clara told every Christmas. It was when Aunt Clara and Emily were children back when Grandmother Gretchen was still alive.

"Get your sister and your buckets and go down to pick me some blueberries Clara," her mother Gretchen ordered in her thick German accent. So Clara mindfully found the two silver buckets hanging on the rusted hook in the back hall and went in search of Emily. Clara found Emily quietly reading near the barn.

"Come on, Emily. Mother wants us to pick some blueberries so she can make a pie." Clara shouted loudly.

"Can't you see I was reading?" Emily answered obviously annoyed at the interruption.

"But Ma wants us to go blueberry picking," Clara repeated in her matter of fact tone of voice. "You know the early bird catches the worm."

"That would be fine, Clara, if Ma was making a worm pie, but she isn't!" she answered sarcastically. "Besides, who says you can boss me around anyways?" "You are younger than me, you know."

Clara ignored the comment and went right on talking. "We're tight as ticks, aren't we, Emily?"

Emily dropped the book and grabbed the bucket from Clara's hand. She slung it over her shoulder like a handbag, bent over and picked up the old blanket she had been laying on. She carefully folded it into a nice little bundle, put her book on it and laid it on the top flat part of the post at the end of the railing near the barn door. Then both Emily and Clara marched down the old dirt road behind the barn that led to the blueberry patch, their silver buckets swinging in their hands.

"Yes," Emily said with her teeth tightly pressed together, "We're tight as ticks."

The blueberry patch was nestled on an incline just before the train tracks about a half a mile down the road. The fresh sweet aroma of blueberries filled the air as they got closer and closer to the train tracks. "I'm so hungry I could eat a horse," declared Clara as she began plucking the blueberries and popping them into her mouth. "If you eat them all, Clara, we won't have any to bring home and Ma will be very mad at us."

"OK, OK, shut up Emily," Clara's voice echoed among the sound of blueberries hitting the bottom of the tin bucket.

Surprisingly Clara kept quiet for a long time while they both worked hard at bending and picking. Their buckets were nearly full and Clara announced that she was tired and wanted to go home. Emily was almost to the train tracks by now and wanted to fill her bucket up all the way to the top. Noticing a large patch of blueberries growing in between the wooden railroad timbers, Emily pulled herself up the hill and stood on the thick, large beam. Trying to anchor her footing while bending over to pick the blueberries, she moved one foot out and tried to reach the other timber. As she did, her foot got stuck in a triangular wedge in one of the railroad ties. She tried desperately to free herself but each time she pushed or pulled, her shoe wedged deeper and deeper into the crevice.

"Help me get my foot out of here, Clara," Emily yelled to her sister.

"How the heck did you get your foot stuck, Emily? I swear you are as dumb as a doorknob."

The sound of steam from the train engine bellowed in the distance. Clara put her ear to the track and felt a faint vibration. "There's a train coming, Emily!" Clara screamed frantically.

By now the two of them were hysterical. Emily tried desperately to loosen her foot but her fat little fingers wouldn't reach into the tiny spaces between her shoe and her ankle. Clara was crying so hard by now that it was hard for her to see her hand in front of her face, let alone Emily's wedged foot.

Emily pumped her arms wildly above her head as she looked up and saw the train coming. Clara untied Emily's shoelace and grabbed her around the waist, pulling her as hard as she could, trying to free her sister, but to no avail. Then Clara got an idea. She reached into her bucket and picked up a handful of blueberries. She squished them between her fingers and rubbed them all over Emily's ankle and as far down into her shoe as she could. She grabbed Emily by the waist again and pulled hard. The slimy fruit did the trick—Emily became free. Holding tightly to one another they both toppled down the small incline and into the blueberry bushes. They lay there for a minute or two, sobbing uncontrollably. A strong gust of wind rustled their hair as the train whizzed by at breakneck speed. After they saw the little red caboose rattle by, they ran up the hill to try and find Emily's little brown oxford shoe. It was mangled beyond recognition.

They were both so upset neither one spoke on the trip home. Clara held onto Emily's arm as she hopped on one foot. There remained only one bucket of blueberries because Emily got so upset when she saw the train coming that she flung her bucket up in the air. She later found it cut completely in half laying on one of the tracks.

They reached the front porch of the house and stood in front of the door as their mother watched from the shadow of the living room on the other side of the screen door. "What happened to you two?" their mother asked in a harsh voice. "And where is my other bucket? And your shoe, Emily, what happened to your other shoe?"

By this time Emily was in shock from the trauma of the day. She stood next to Clara with one shoe on and the other foot covered in blueberry mush and bits of gravel from the road. Her long red hair had streaks of bluish slime in it from where Clara had tried to pat her head consoling her sister after the near fatal accident.

"Emily's shoe got stuck in the railroad ties and she almost got killed by the train Ma," Clara blurted out. Her voice was still trembling from the shock. "I saved her life, Ma, I saved her life."

But it was obvious their mother didn't want to hear the details. "You two are just a mess." She shook her head in disgust as she turned to walk away with the bucket of freshly picked blueberries in her hand.

Clara peered into the thin layer of metal screen, the cage that separated their mother from her and her sister. She looked up at the shadow of the large figure of her mother in the doorway–her long reddish blonde hair neatly pulled back into a bun at the nape of her neck. On the front side of that bun was a beautiful full face with a perfect rosy complexion–eyes as green as a cat. As Clara looked at her mother and squinted as if to put a curse on her, another cliché came to mind, and she blurted it out. "Beauty is only skin deep; ugly's to the bone. Beauty fades with time, but ugly holds its own." As soon as she said it she grabbed Emily's arm and pulled her down the steps and out into the yard. They stood by the hose trying to clean the blueberry stains off their skin and clothes with a small bit of lye soap their grandmother had made. Clara figured they were both safe from a beating when she didn't hear a slam from the screen door. Emily stood staring vacantly into space while Clara scrubbed her with the burning soap and the coarse bristles of the well-worn scrub brush.

As Aunt Clara told this story over and over every Christmas, everyone laughed at the end of it. Even Clara chuckled. Her three daughters laughed hysterically as they stuffed themselves with chips and dip and bits of holiday fudge. Uncle Peter giggled too, but only after looking at Aunt Ellen to see if it was all right. My mother did not laugh though. Instead I noticed that vacant look she took on whenever she was troubled by something.

So, perhaps my mother's illness was just an exacerbation of a lifetime of vacancies. Perhaps my mother's halfway house was built long before her diagnosis of Alzheimer's. Maybe it was built when my father died, or during the great train incident. But I suspect my mother was born into it just as the many generations before her had been. Aunt Clara had her clichés, which shielded her from the world. Uncle Peter, who had been a nomad from the age of eighteen until he met Aunt Ellen, gave new meaning to his wedding vows, "and the two shall be as one." The two of them never once left each other's side. Aunt Clara used to say that if Ellen ate beans, an hour later Peter would fart.

But aside from all of their idiosyncrasies, I loved them all. And, looking at my family structure now, I know why my mother lived in the middle. She never really had a choice. Or at least if she did, no one let her in on the secret.

"That's a great story, ML. I don't remember EP too much. I just met her a couple of times and then we moved. And, then she got sick. I know she sounds a little quirky, but I sure wish I had gotten to know her a little better." Abbie looked at her mother. There were tears trickling down the sides of Maggie's face.

"So do I, Abbie. So do I."

"I'm sorry, mom." Abbie turned to face her mother. She reached out to her and gave her a big hug. Then she whispered into her ear, "I love you, ML."

"I love you too, AL." Maggie responded, holding onto Abbie for dear life.

December 25, 1964
7:00 PM

Chapter Five

The Reverend came back to the church at about 6:30 p.m., shortly after he finished eating or, rather, attempting to eat Christmas dinner with his family. He didn't see the Chief right away but then, coming around the corner in the narthex, he almost ran into him.

"Hi Chief," Dudley exclaimed, startled. "Were you able to get away? Get some dinner?" Dudley asked, all the while wondering when Gunderson would be leaving the church for good. "How long does it take to investigate a couple of murders anyway?" Dudley wondered.

"No, Reverend. One of the guys brought me a turkey sandwich but I wasn't really hungry. It's hard to eat when you know there are dead bodies in the basement."

"I know. I tried to eat dinner but I kept thinking back to earlier in the day when I opened that locked storage door and saw those cops sitting in their chairs with their heads on the table. If it weren't for all the blood everywhere I would have thought they were just snoozing. Did you establish the time of death yet?" Dudley asked tentatively.

"Yes, we did. We can definitely rule out the Christmas morning church crowd as suspects. These two men were murdered in the wee hours of the night. Their internal temperature was about the same for each of them, 74 degrees at 12:45 p.m. today. They were also both in near full rigor mortis. Are you aware of the timeline for rigor mortis Reverend?"

"Vaguely, but it's been a while since I've been in a science classroom."

"It begins with the eyelids and then progresses to muscles of the face, the arms, torso and finally the legs and feet. Within twelve hours rigor mortis has been fully established when the body is stiff and as unbending as a block of wood. Their feet were still a little pliable so we figure that meant they'd been dead about eleven hours. Also, since the body temperature falls from its normal 98.6 at a rate of generally two degrees per hour for the first twelve hours, that puts the time of death roughly between 1 and 3 a.m."

"Wouldn't that eliminate the Christmas Eve parishioners too, Chief?"

"Not necessarily. There's no rhyme or reason when it comes to murder, Reverend. After the service the murderer could have hidden for a while someplace in the church. This place is big. I'm sure it wouldn't be hard to find a hiding spot somewhere. Are you sure you saw everyone leave after the service last night? Did you notice anyone lagging behind or looking suspicious?"

"Near as I could tell, everyone was out the door shortly after the service ended about 10:00 p.m., but I wasn't really paying too much attention. I usually stand in the vestibule and shake hands with everyone as they leave. Last night was a little different. At the end of the service we sang all three verses of 'Silent Night.' Then people left when they wanted, some staying behind to pray. I would say that everyone filtered out by 10:30 p.m. at the latest. I know because I was home at 10:40 p.m., and I live right next door. So by the time I took my robe off, hung it up on the hook in my office, put my overcoat and gloves on, it was probably 10:35 p.m., and I can usually make it home in five minutes."

"But you didn't lock the doors, right Reverend?"

"That's correct. I usually leave them open for people to come and pray as they are led to the Lord. They can't do that if the doors are locked, can they, Chief?"

Gunderson detected a hint of sarcasm in Dudley's voice, or could it have been a hint of defensiveness? He thought back to when Dudley told him about how he left his priceless artifacts out on the altar overnight. It didn't make sense to Gunderson. Dudley may just as well have nailed a hand-written invitation to the church's big wooden doors, "Come on in. Grab what you like. This here Chalice has some priceless gems in it, so you might want to steal that first." He was still puzzled by that one. "You're right Dudley. People can't come in to pray (or steal for that matter, he thought) if the doors are locked." Gunderson rolled his eyes in disbelief at Dudley's remarks.

"But this makes our case that much harder because anyone and their brother could have come in here last night, the doors being unlocked and all." Gunderson went on. "The murderer could have stayed behind after the church service, knowing the cops worked the night shift, just waiting until they showed up. Maybe the killer knew these cops came into the church from time to time to get out of the cold or have something to eat or just to gab. But that's unlikely, since they would have waited a good three hours for them. If they were intent on killing, they would have most likely come back, that is if indeed they attended the Christmas Eve Service at all. Any number of scenarios could have taken place. The possibility of it being a serial killing still exists too, God forbid."

"Indeed, God forbid. So you'll still need to interview the people who attended church last night, right Chief?" Dudley casually lifted the cuff of his shirt so he could see his watch, trying to be as inconspicuous as possible. It was now 7:30 p.m., almost time to meet Eddy.

"Yes, I'll need the list of everyone who attended church last night. Do you have a sign-in sheet Reverend?"

"We do. I'll get it for you." Dudley dutifully went into the vestibule to retrieve the padded book that lay open to December 25, 1964. The book rested on an antique carved wooden stand. The stand was ornate just like every other artifact in the church.

"Thank you Reverend," Gunderson said, taking the book from Dudley. "I'll be going soon. The coroner just took the bodies down to the morgue not less than two minutes ago. All the evidence we could gather is at the crime lab waiting to be analyzed. We've got a big job ahead of us now."

"I imagine you do, Chief. Let me know if I can help you at all. I'll be happy to assist in anyway I can. Oh, Chief, do you have any idea why these two policemen were murdered? I can't imagine why anyone would want to kill an officer of the law." Dudley almost gagged as he said this. He knew why someone would kill them. He knew exactly why.

"We don't have a motive yet. But we do know how they were killed, and it wasn't just a random killing, I can assure you of that. These murders were done at the hands of a trained killer. How he was trained—well I don't know that piece of information yet."

"Why do you say that, Chief?"

"Just by the way they were killed. Plus these cops were experienced law enforcement agents. They knew how to defend themselves. So it must have been an experienced killer who attacked them."

"How were they killed, Chief?"

"Apparently it was a sneak attack from behind. From what we can tell so far, the two policemen were sitting at the table side by side, much the same way you found them earlier, Dudley. The killer stealthily came into the room armed and ready to kill. Judging from the ligature marks around the neck of the cop closest to the door, the cop on the right, the killer came up from behind, wrapped his arm around the officer's neck and squeezed, hard. With this type of maneuver, the killer would have had to lock his own arm in place by bending over a bit, getting very close to the victim, and placing the palm of his right hand on the left side of his own neck or clavicle. This would have caused an unbreakable bond and rendered the first victim immobile and unconscious within seconds. The officer probably tried to defend himself by grabbing for the killer's forearm but there was not much room to do that, since the killer was so close to the victim. Plus, it appears the victim had his hands on his lap when he was attacked. He may have even had them under the top portion of the table. He was sitting very close to the table so, by the time he was able to free his arms, he was probably already only semi-conscious."

"You figured all that out just this afternoon, Chief?"

"We figured that out right off the bat. That murder was easy to figure out. The second cop wasn't so easy. But, judging from the angle and force of the stab wound, the killer came in with the intention of killing both cops simultaneously. It's a technique as old as the hills. A martial artist would know how to do this, as well as someone who had gone through basic training, let's say as in the armed services."

"As the killer grabbed the first victim around the neck, he reached with his left hand, which already had the knife in it, and plunged it into the second cop's heart. And when I say simultaneous, that's what I mean. At the same minute he grabbed the first cop, he also instantly killed the second one. We know this because there was virtually no sign of struggle from Cop #2. There was just a lot of blood all over the place. When the killer extracted the knife from Cop #2, he then turned back to Cop #1 and did the same thing, plunging the same knife into his heart as well. But Cop #1 was probably near death by that time because the force of his neck hold collapsed his windpipe and he was in the process of choking to death even before the fatal knife wound killed him."

Dudley listened intently as the Chief explained the murders. "I hope you catch the killer soon Chief. I wouldn't want someone like that running around Durham." Dudley played right into the Chief's hands, opening his almost clear light blue eyes wide at just the appropriate times, pretending to be shocked at the gruesome details of the case. He would furrow his bushy gray eyebrows and cock his head just a little or shake it back and forth and ever so slightly pucker his lips when it became necessary to be sympathetic and compassionate. He was a good actor.

"That's not all, Dudley. Although we know the killer must have been a man just by the shear power of his neck grip and the force of the stab wounds, the M.O. appears to be more like that of a female killer. A male would most likely have done it with a gun. It would have been easier for sure. This place is just loaded with soundproofing what with these thick stonewalls and all. No one would have heard the shot that's for sure. But, this crime was personal. A lot of emotion and anger is associated with a knife to the heart. With this much emotion, it's more reminiscent of the type of crime a woman would commit. It's baffling that's for sure," Gunderson admitted.

"It sounds like you have a lot figured out already, right Chief?" Dudley shook his head up and down vigorously, opening his eyes so wide there was mostly white showing. This expression consequently pushed his eyebrows so far up it looked as if one of them was intentionally placed there with the sole purpose of holding up the thick shelf of gray hair that swooped over the top half of his forehead.

"Congratulations Chief–good job." Dudley peered at his watch again, this time in a gesture meant for the Chief to see, " I'll need to be heading out in a couple of minutes. You know, it's still Christmas and I haven't spent much time with my family today. We need to gather together tonight and say a long prayer for both victims and their families. We also need to pray for the killer in the hopes that he'll be caught soon and brought to justice. We'll pray for you too, Chief. Shouldn't you be getting home soon too? You've put in a long hard day haven't you?" Dudley put on his thick wool coat and started walking toward the door.

"You're right, Dudley. I'll walk out with you. Promise me you'll lock up tonight, okay?"

"I promise." The last thing in the world Dudley wanted to do was walk out with the Police Chief. But he had no choice, so he made his niceties, locked the door and headed toward his house. When he was sure the Chief couldn't see him any longer, Dudley ran around the back of his house, behind the church and out on the sidewalk that headed straight to Maplewood Elementary School.

The Chief got into his patrol car, revved up the engine and then pretended to be preoccupied with his notes. He could see the Reverend through the corner of his eye as Dudley pretended to go home but instead slithered around behind his house to God knows where.

All through the day the Chief had watched Dudley intently, taking in as many clues as he could for future use if need be. He was meticulously groomed, this Dudley character. His clothes looked like they just came off a laundry press. He wore brand new penny loafers with a shiny new 1964 copper penny placed face up in each one of the thin slots on the front flap of each shoe. Each penny was going in exactly the same direction. "This guy's meticulous," Gunderson thought while observing Dudley's shoes.

The Chief had noticed Dudley's shiny shoes when Dudley and Gunderson were sitting in the church pew. He had, believe it or not, been a bit distracted when a patch of light swept across the floor and wafted across Dudley's shiny new shoes. The glare was so bright that it cast a blinding ray right into Gunderson's left eye. Right then and there Gunderson had to commend his eye doctor. Had it not been for the new pair of bifocals he was wearing, he probably wouldn't have been able to even see the penny in the shoe, let alone make out the year on the bottom of the round coin. Not that the year would matter so much. But he was grateful for his new superman vision. God knows he needed all the help he could get in his line of work.

"With his swanky outfit, this guy should be on the cover of *Gentleman's Quarterly Magazine* rather than in the religious life," thought Gunderson. "What's he up to?" Gunderson wondered, sitting in his patrol car. He took off his cap and scratched his enormous head. The case was hard enough to solve without this clown mysteriously creeping around.

Gunderson was glad he left out three important clues when he explained the crime scene investigation to Dudley. He would keep all three of the clues sealed close to his vest until such time as he needed to reveal one or all of them to Dudley. It depended on which ones would possibly pull out a confession from the Reverend or even the good janitor, Eddy. One clue was big, monumental in the outcome of the investigation, Gunderson was certain of that. The fact that the entire table was filled with blood spatters except for a single blank eight-by-ten area on the corner was an obvious red flag. This finding intrigued Gunderson. The other clues he wasn't certain of yet. He needed to do some hunting first and then he'd make his assessment.

The eight-by-ten outline in the corner of the table was obvious to

Gunderson. The lack of blood splatters in that blank space indicated an object had been there at the time of the murders. "Eight-by-ten – huh. Maybe a picture? Yeah, probably a picture," thought Gunderson. "Find the picture, find the killer," the Chief said out loud in the silence of his patrol car. "Easier said than done!"

August 25, 2007

Chapter Six

My Father

Maggie sat on her couch huddled together with her daughter for a long time. Finally she got up, went into her tiny kitchen and started making a fresh pot of coffee. "Want some?" she gestured to Abbie, holding up the near empty glass carafe.

"I'd love some, ML. I mean mom." Abbie was still seated on the couch. She was still leafing through Maggie's story, stopping to read some parts again and again as she thumbed through the pages.

After the coffee had finished brewing, Maggie brought the steaming hot mug over to her daughter. She placed it on the coaster right in front of her. Abbie looked down at the cup, glanced over at the other two coasters on the table and, looking up at her mother she asked, "No more counting mom? You only have three coasters here. What's up with that? That's an uneven number, you know." Abbie was well aware of her mother's OCD. She was one of only a handful of people that knew of her malady.

"I'm getting better, I'll have you know, Abbie," Maggie replied matter of fact. Although she didn't tell her dear daughter that the other coaster was underneath the large wooden box and doily in the center of the table. After all, she didn't need to tell her everything, right? Although not telling her made her feel just a little bit guilty. Just knowing that a fourth coaster was positioned somewhere on that coffee table made Maggie feel better. Knowing that the amount of coasters on the table was an even number brought her great peace of mind. Maggie set her cup on the coaster next to Abbie's.

"I like your centerpiece, mom," Abbie said chuckling.

"Funny, Abbie, funny. Remember that?" Maggie asked, pointing to the large box positioned in the center of the doily. The box was hefty, taking up a good part of the table. Two industrial sized hinges were screwed onto the back of the lid. The whole thing was obviously hand painted with some high gloss light brown paint. There was a picture frame glued to the top of the box.

"Duh... how could I forget? What grade was I in when we made that monstrosity?"

"You were in middle school I think, either seventh or eighth grade, right?" Maggie questioned.

"I think it was seventh. Remember that stupid contest?"

"It wasn't so stupid was it, Abbie? After all, you won."

"WE won, ML, WE won! It was your idea remember?" Abbie was laughing out loud now. Maggie was laughing too.

"What was that contest all about, Abbie? Do you remember?"

"I don't remember! I didn't even want to enter the stupid contest. It was your idea. I didn't want to hand that dumb thing in. You made me!" Abbie gave out a hearty laugh.

Maggie looked down at the top of the box. Inside the picture frame was a map of the world, a flat map of the world. Inside each country was a single green split pea that had been glued to the paper map. On the outside of the picture frame, on the wooden part, were the words "WORLD PEAS". And "WORLD PEAS" was spelled out with the same kind of little green half peas that were on the inside of the frame, each half pea glued neatly to the wood. Maggie and Abbie laughed and laughed as they looked at those damned peas. Abbie opened the box and inside were little pieces of folded papers. Each paper had the name of a country on it, corresponding to the world map. And when you opened up the papers, each one had a different solution to achieve WORLD PEAS. One paper said "Israel" on the outside and then when you unfolded it the inside said, "Get over it (and get along!!!)." Ireland's paper said, "Everyone's different–deal with it (and get along!!!)." Each folded paper had a different saying attached to it, but each saying ended with "and get along!!!"

"That was fun," Abbie admitted.

"It sure was."

"Hey, ML. Where's the story about your father? I don't see it in this folder."

Maggie sighed. She hoped Abbie had forgotten about the other story. She should have known better. Abbie didn't forget about much. "I'll be right back, Abbie. I don't keep my father's story in that folder," she said pointing to the binder. Maggie went into her bedroom. She lifted her mattress slightly and there was the story, lying neatly pressed on top of the box spring. Returning to the living room she handed Abbie the papers, "Here, you read it. I don't think I can do it."

Abbie took the story and began to read it aloud.

MY FATHER

My father died somewhere between a blink and a lifetime. At least that's how it felt and still feels. It seemed as if he was here one day and the next day he just vanished into that unknown world called death. Such a mysterious place this was for me. It was a place of no return where people went at the end of their lives but couldn't come back and tell anyone about.

Until my father's death, I hadn't really known anyone close to me who had died before. But somehow I felt closer to this place where dead people went, Heaven, especially now that my father resided there.

He was fifty-two, much too young to leave behind a wife and three young children. He passed away on March 5, two days before his fifty-third birthday. He was sick for about a month and most likely longer, I suspect. But he didn't go to the doctor until it was too late, so we never found out. I don't think it much mattered though. Thirty years ago you needed something short of a miracle to survive an illness as bizarre as my fathers.

As for me, at sixteen I didn't really pay too much attention to my dad's current state of health because I just thought he would always, always be around. Or maybe I just refused to entertain any thoughts that he could possibly be sick. He used to tell me he was going to live to be a hundred, but that was usually while he was puffing away on one of his non-filter Lucky Strike cigarettes. I didn't really want to notice him getting thinner. You see I had other things, more important things going on in my life at that time, for instance hanging around with my friends. But, as oblivious as I was back then, I do remember a couple of incidents when I had that "aha" moment and realized that my father was ill.

One time he fell asleep while he was eating his dinner. There was still food in his mouth. I thought he fell asleep because he was just tired from working. Our family usually ate in the living room while we watched TV. When I brought my plate into the living room and set it on the TV tray, there was my dad slumped sideways onto the arm of the couch with the fork from his dinner plate still in his hand and his mouth was gaping wide open. He was snoring. I took one look at him and went running into the kitchen screaming—"Dad fell asleep and there's food in his mouth—he'll choke." My mom told me not to worry, and she didn't even go in to check on him. Maybe she knew something was wrong then too.

Even before I witnessed that incident with my dad, I had been paranoid about choking. The fact is my dad saved my life once because I choked on a candy cigarette. In the 1960's that was the rage in candy eating. The pack of candy came in a small hard box, which looked a lot like a real cigarette box. Inside the candy cigarette box were twenty white sticks of hard, sweet, chalky deliciousness. The ends were painted red and they appeared as if they were lit when you took them out of the box. The latest gimmick was a small gold hollow cigarette holder that you could fit the candy sticks in. My friends and I would saunter around with those things hanging out of our mouths like we were some famous movie star or something. A piece of my candy got stuck in that holder once and I tried to get it out by inhaling it through the holder. It dislodged from the gold wrapper, and I ended up sucking it right down my windpipe. I'll never forget that worried look on my dad's face when I went over to him, holding my neck and gasping for breath. He picked me up, stuck his finger down my throat, and I puked right there in the living room, right in front of everyone. I could see the little white piece of candy sticking up in the middle of my vomit on the floor. It was kind of gross, but I didn't care, at least I could breathe.

Another time I remember my dad being sick was when I got up in the middle of the night and saw him sitting at the kitchen table with all of our school books spread out in front of him. He had his head down on them and he was crying. His face was pale and drawn. When I saw him there at that moment I noticed how thin he'd become. He didn't see me watching him and I made sure I kept really quiet. Then about two days later that's when my mother tried to open up the bathroom door and couldn't because he had passed out on the floor. He was lying there in the fetal position with his legs wrapped around the commode. My mother called an ambulance and they brought him to the Veteran's hospital where he died three weeks later.

My mom brought us to see him in the hospital a week before he passed away. He was in a wheelchair and he was very, very thin. My sisters and I took turns sitting on his lap for a while, but we didn't stay very long because he had to get back to bed. He was too weak. He made the nurse wheel him backwards on his way back to the elevator so he could see us up until the last second before the elevator doors closed. I remember he looked so sad. I didn't know why then, but I do now.

He had a military funeral. During the wake, at my mother's request, there was a closed casket. I was crying so hard I couldn't breathe and my uncle had to give me smelling salts. He broke the tablet right under my nose and I jumped up and ran across the funeral parlor floor right in front of everyone. At the cemetery they had a twenty-one-gun salute. Each time the guns went off, chills ran down my spine. I watched those soldiers and they stood so straight, no emotion, guns cocked and raised in the air ready to fire. What a paradox that was. What a rigid ceremony for a man with such a kind, gentle, loving spirit. After the guns went off, they folded the flag and handed it to my mother. We got a lot of sympathy cards, especially from the people he worked with. He was a janitor at a church, and the kids in the preschool there loved him. They all made him cards and sent them to him when he was in the hospital.

Even though dad went quickly, sometimes I felt and still feel as if he died slowly, very slowly. I think Mother Nature does that to you though. She only lets bits and pieces of the loss come through at sporadic intervals. And it's a good thing, too, because if I had thought about him not being able to see me graduate high school or college, get married, or see his grand-daughter, I think it would have been too devastating for me to take in at the tender age of sixteen. The memory of my dad does come back to me at times and I feel both the joy of his presence and the heartache of his loss all over again.

I was in Starbucks the other day and there were some people right next to me in line waiting to get a coffee. It was a double line because there were two people at the register. They could have used more judging by the backup of customers. Anyways, I always get coffee to go, even if I sit there to drink it. I vowed a long time ago never to drink out of a restaurant coffee cup ever again because I found lipstick on the rim of my cup once and it totally grossed me out. Plus, I like to read all the different little prophetic sayings written on the sides of the paper cups. Words to live by they are. The people standing next to me in line obviously did not have the same issues as I did. They both asked for the standard restaurant issue white ceramic mugs.

We both ended up bringing our coffee over to the cream and sugar bar at about the same time. I put half and half cream in my cup and then offered the dairy thermos to Mr. Ceramic Mug man. He graciously took it, thanked me and put about two tablespoons of the cream into his cup. Then he took his metal spoon from the saucer and stirred the hot liquid. But he didn't stir it like most people. He slid his spoon back and forth, tapping the sides of the cup. The spoon made a clicking sound each time it hit the rim of the mug. I looked down into his cup and saw the black liquid marble, the reflection of the spoon slowly dance from side to side, and then the coffee turn a light tan. That's just how my dad stirred his coffee. I used to stare at him in the mornings, mesmerized by the way he moved the spoon back and forth in his cup. I looked forward to watching him perform this coffee ritual every morning. There was just something magical about this coffee idiosyncrasy he had.

To this day I cannot take a spoon to my coffee to stir it–I leave that job to the law that governs the motion that moves my hand and cup to my mouth. Usually by the third gulp it gets mixed up enough to resemble coffee the way I like it. It's funny how kids get notions into their heads just by observing one of their parents' little habits. Whenever I watched my father stir his coffee the way he did, a feeling of peace came over me. After I watched him stir his coffee in the morning, I just knew it would be a good day. I knew nothing bad would happen to me and I would be safe. I haven't felt that same feeling for a long time now.

I've decided that one of the worst parts about someone dying is the phone call you get. You think you are prepared for the words, the finality, but you are never prepared. And you always, always remember where you were when the phone call comes through. My family didn't have a phone upstairs at the time. But my grandmother lived downstairs from us, and she had one. When her phone rang, my grandmother called upstairs and my mother went down to answer it. We heard her scream. Then my sisters and I huddled on one bed and waited for Mom to come upstairs to deliver the news. But we already knew, even though not one of us said a word. And you know something funny, she never really told us outright–she was much too upset for that. She paced around the room wailing and screaming while all three of us just sat there like a big blob of taffy all stuck together watching her, our eyes as big as saucers.

Once that message of death comes through the phone line or wherever it comes from, that's it. Your life changes forever. No more memories are made with that person, no more moments shared, no more watching anyone stir their coffee in the morning.

About two days after my dad died I had a dream. It was so real. I was sitting in front of my dresser mirror combing my hair. I looked down for a moment and as I did, I felt something pinch my scalp. Looking up into the mirror again, I saw my dad. He was standing behind me pulling at a single strand of hair on the top of my head and laughing. My dad was always teasing me like that.

Anyways when I saw my dad standing over me in my dream he was just as handsome as ever, just like I remembered him before he got sick. His thick black hair was almost sparkling because of a small bit of light that had filtered through my bedroom window and hit his head at just the right angle. I could see his small-framed silhouette as he stood behind me. His hands were folded in front of him, but he wasn't leaning on any doorframe. He wasn't holding up the house anymore. I could see his eyes, those green eyes that could always look right through mine, right down into my soul.

One thing I knew after I had that dream was that my dad would always be there for me, standing over me with that big shit-eating grin on his face. I knew he would always be watching out for me. I also knew that nothing, not even death could separate the bonds of love a father has for his children. That kind of love is timeless, without boundaries and the purest thing I have ever known in this universe and probably beyond.

Abbie and Maggie sat on the couch after Abbie finished reading the story. They both stared at their coffee cups, mesmerized by the liquid inside. They sat quietly for a long time until Abbie piped up and exclaimed, "I sure would have liked to know him better too, ML!"

"So would I, Abbie. So would I. Hey, Abbie?"

"Yeah?"

Maggie hung her head in a gesture of embarrassment, "There's a fourth coaster on this coffee table. I put it under the box. I just felt like I needed to tell you that," she confessed.

Abbie laughed. "I figured it was here somewhere. You didn't need to tell me, you know. You could have kept that on the DL."

"I know I didn't need to but it's hard for me to keep things from you. Hey, who's DL?"

"DL—you know—on the down low, quiet, secret." Abbie was laughing out loud now.

"Oh yeah, the DL," Maggie laughed too.

"Hey, ML."

"Yes, dear daughter."

"I love you. Please don't do what that stupid e-mail told you to do. Please don't take the journey!"

Maggie was silent for a moment. She considered what her daughter said about the journey then she replied, "I love you too, my darling daughter. I love you too."

December 25, 1964

8:05 PM

Chapter Seven

Eddy had been waiting for Dudley behind the school for about fifteen minutes. They kept the lights on behind the elementary school, but Eddy didn't know why they did. "Waste of electricity," he thought out loud. It wasn't as if anyone needed the lights for anything. Who on earth would want to walk around an elementary school at night?

Eddy was cold and bone tired from staying up all night worrying. What he didn't know was, in the weeks and months to come, that one sleepless night would be the easiest night he'd see in a good long while. He really wanted to just leave, go hide away somewhere and never come out. He assumed Dudley was the one who found the bodies. He knew Dudley would be hunting for answers. The Reverend was a smart man. He would put two and two together and come up with the most logical sum—Eddy. And, if he could make this assumption, so could everyone else involved in the case.

In reality, Eddy had hoped and prayed the bodies would disappear overnight, just go away. He wanted Dudley to find them and expose of them and also get rid of the evidence. But he knew that wasn't possible. Eddy's head hurt. The high stress from the night before had taken its toll on his body. He felt as if he had been on an all night bender with the boys.

Trying to get himself warm, Dudley broke out into a slow jog. He had forgotten his hat. "It would have looked really suspicious to Gunderson if I bundled up just to walk next door," he thought to himself. The night air was blustery. The wind made snow tornados from the freshly fallen powdery snow. The wind tunnels looked like empty, crystallized ice cream cones. Dudley picked up his pace. The steam from his short puffs of exhaled breath became more and more visible as his body heated up.

Thinking back to just a few minutes ago, he questioned himself, "I wonder if Gunderson suspected anything?" The Rev. would have to wait and see. Police were a sly breed. Dudley could never figure them out. Either they were way too cool to let on they knew something or they were just plain stupid. For Dudley it was hard to tell because most of the cops he knew spoke with the same monotone voice as Gunderson did. He figured it must have been a trick of the trade.

As Dudley reached the school, he noticed a set of footprints in the snow. He couldn't imagine anyone traipsing around the school on Christmas night, so he figured the footprints must have belonged to Eddy. Dudley slowed his pace down, trying to walk in the same footprints Eddy had made in the newly fallen wintry concoction. Although his foot fit perfectly into the impressions made by Eddy's size ten boots, Eddy's stride was longer, more widely spaced than Dudley's short, tight gait. Dudley had to adjust his walking style accordingly, but once in a while he would lose his balance and miss a footprint. When this happened he could hear a loud crunch, the thin layer of ice giving way to the old snow beneath. Remnants of mosaic ice pieces were left in the new footprint's wake. Dudley looked down at the path of footsteps that lay ahead. The fragments of ice nestled inside the footprint crevices reminded him of clear, uneven chunks of peanut brittle with just a hint of white powdered sugar sprinkled on top.

Eddy stood at the mouth of the little alley where all the kids played dodge ball. The causeway was inadvertently constructed when an addition had been added to the school. For a longtime the little alley was used to store all the snow removal equipment. Then, some of the parents got together and decided to build a great big tool shed to store all the snowplows, shovels, sand and rock salt. This left the little causeway empty, so the big wooden gate at the end was removed and, *voila*, a dodge ball field! Red brick walls on either side of the alley helped a great deal with keeping the ball in the appropriately confined space. Some kids, especially the athletic ones, could throw the ball from here to kingdom come. In an open field, this would make the game go on forever, with kids chasing after wayward balls through most of the game. Not so in dodge ball alley.

After much anticipation, Dudley and Eddy finally met up. Well, actually they fell into one another's arms, Eddy balling his eyes out. In all the years Dudley had worked with Eddy, he had never seen him cry. Even when Eddy's own sister and her husband died in a car crash two years ago, he had pretty much kept his emotions in check. So Dudley figured things must be really bad.

"I didn't mean to do it," Eddy blurted out. "You would have done the same thing I know you would have, Dudley."

"Slow down, slow down," answered Dudley totally surprised and thinking to himself, "Wow, he did kill the two cops."

"Tell me the whole story, Eddy. Here, lets go back in the alley a little more where the wind isn't blowing so much." Dudley chuckled just a little as they made their way into dodge ball alley, "It's colder than a witch's you know what." In a lame attempt he tried to lighten the mood just a little, but his meager gesture was completely ignored. Eddy was much too upset to even think of anything else besides the murders.

"Well you know the first part, Reverend," Eddy started, his lips quivering as he spoke.

Dudley didn't know if this was due to the cold or to his nerves. He figured it was a little of both.

Eddy went on, "You called me after the Christmas Eve service was over, remember Dudley? I was just finishing putting together a bike for my youngest, Linda. Not that she could ride it in this messy snow anyways. But that's what dads and moms do on Christmas Eve, right? They wait until the kids go to bed and then they put together bikes or whatever else needs assembling. You know, so all that new stuff will be bright and shiny under the tree on Christmas morning." He began to cry again.

Dudley didn't say anything yet. Instead he reached into his coat pocket and handed his friend a handkerchief with the initial "D" embroidered on it. Dudley's wife had given him the white cotton hankie last Christmas, and he had kept it in his coat pocket ever since, unused. It was a little too dainty for Dudley's taste, but he would never tell his wife that, being that she worked on it so hard throughout the year. She wanted the handkerchief to be a surprise, so she tried to hide it among all her other knitting projects. But Dudley spotted it one morning after she'd inadvertently left it out on the coffee table. On the nights Dudley had church things to do, his wife, Eunice busied herself with various craft projects. He figured the hankie was for him, what with that big letter "D" embroidered all over the front of the damned thing. Little pink tulips surrounded the humongous "D," as if the "D" had miraculously sprung up from a brightly blooming garden. He was grateful to have seen the handkerchief though. That way he could try to be enthused about the gift when he opened it up, instead of scrunching up his face in a most distasteful scowl. Dudley preferred to follow the tried and true Boy Scout motto; "Always be prepared."

"Go on, Eddy," Dudley responded sympathetically.

"After I got the call from you I came upstairs to tell Emily I needed to go fix the boiler at the church. She was really mad. Said I shouldn't go. Said I should just let the people in church keep their coats on during the service. 'It won't kill 'em,' were her exact words. You know Emily–she says what she feels. She doesn't think too much about how it's gonna come out. Anyways–my oldest, Maggie, was still awake. She's quite a bit older than Linda or Jill, and Emily and I both knew we sent her to bed too early, but we just figured she'd fall asleep eventually. We figured she would keep herself busy by reading or writing in her diary or something. She said she didn't mind going to bed early because she didn't want to be awake when Santa came to the house. Even at sixteen, she still wanted to believe in Santa Claus. Maggie heard our whole conversation. She begged Emily and I to let her come up to the church to help me fix the boiler. She said it would be an adventure, plus she might learn something about how to fix the boiler too. 'Please dad, please dad,' she pleaded."

I kept telling her, 'No, Maggie. You have to stay home. It's too cold to come outside. I don't even know how long I'll be up there.' I tried real hard to talk her out of it, but she kept begging me. Emily didn't want her to go either. But since it was Christmas, I told her she could come but only if she was quiet and laid on the cot next to the boiler. I told her she could go with me if she tried to get some sleep while I worked on the furnace. She said,

'Yes, dad I will. I'll try to sleep while you fix the furnace.' Then she winked at me, the little shit. So we both bundled up and headed out the front door and down the steps, turning toward the direction of the church. Maggie was happy as a clam."

"What time did you finally get to the church, Eddy?"

"It must have been about 11:00 p.m. I vaguely remember looking at the clock but everything seems to be a blur right now. Didn't get any sleep last night, so I'm not working on all eight cylinders, you know?"

"I understand, believe me. Before you go any further, I just wanted to ask you a question." Dudley felt a little like Chief Gunderson when he was questioning Eddy. He didn't mean to speak in such a bland tone, but he didn't want to put any emotional or judgmental spin to his words. "Maybe that's why cops talk they way they do," Dudley thought.

"Go right ahead, ask," Eddy replied, wiping his eyes with the dainty hankie.

"Did anyone see you? What I mean to say is, did anyone drive past you and Maggie when you were walking up to the church?"

"Not that I can remember. We did see a lot of cars parked on the street. You know how it is on Christmas with a lot of people's relatives visiting and staying over and what not. It was starting to drizzle a little bit. You know that cold bitter rain that stings when it hits your face? I remember Maggie started to sing, 'The rain in Spain falls mainly on the Payne's.' Then she'd giggle. And then, as we walked a little further along, Maggie and I started to play our usual car game. I'd point to a vehicle and she'd give me the year, make, and model. It's our thing between the two of us. I've never seen a young lady so interested in cars, Dudley. I swear she's going to grow up to be an auto mechanic. She's a pistol too. When she came to a Volkswagen car she said the driver must be a communist. I think she's studying that in her social studies class in high school. So everyone she comes in contact with that's unfamiliar to her automatically becomes a communist." Eddy began to cry again. He buried his head in his hands and, shaking his head back and forth whispered, "That's why I had to do it Dudley, for Maggie."

Dudley took in a deep cleansing breath. The bitter cold air tore at his lungs as they filled with oxygen. "Go on Eddy, tell me the rest of the story."

"I knew something was wrong with the furnace as soon as I got downstairs. I could smell the oil. Plus there was a little bit of smoke coming from the boiler, so I knew something was off kilter. I just figured a pipe or valve was leaking. And I was right. It took me a long time to find the leak and fix it though. But Maggie was good. She did just what she promised. After about five or ten minutes, she laid down on the cot next to the boiler and fell right to sleep. She stayed asleep too, even when I heard the commotion in the storage room. There was a lot of laughing and talking, so I went to see what was going on in there. It surprised me, you know Dudley? I thought someone had broken into the church. It just didn't make sense to me why someone would break into a church and have a party in the storage room. Someone was really whopping it up in there. So I went over to see what all of the hubbub was about. It kind of scared me. I didn't know what to expect, you know?"

Dudley felt a tiny bit guilty for being the one responsible for placing Eddy in jeopardy. But, more than that, on a much deeper level he was angry that his employee, the one that would do anything he asked, put his nose in where it didn't belong. Dudley's ears perked up as Eddy continued to tell his story. He could vaguely feel them move but they were so red and cold he thought for sure they would just fall right off his head and land next to his feet without him even knowing it. He figured they would look something like those new-fangled bright red colored wax lips the kids were all playing with these days. His ears would turn into brilliantly crimson waxy blobs plastered to the sides of his head. And when they fell off, he could just pick them up off the ground and stick them back to the sides of his skull and he'd be none the worse for wear.

"Go on, Eddy," he commented flatly.

"I was done fixing the boiler by the time I heard all that commotion. I should have just left but I had to see what was going on in there, you know Dudley?"

"I understand. I would have done the same thing, Eddy." It was hard for Dudley to pull off agreeing with his friend, especially since he knew this whole mess they were in right now was due to the fact that Eddy just couldn't ignore what was going on in the other room. Dudley wanted to scream, "No! I don't understand. I would have just walked away. I would have known it was none of my business!"

"I was very quiet, you know, like how the Army teaches you to sneak up on your enemy?"

"I know, Eddy. I remember that from boot camp."

"Well, as I got closer, I saw the two cops in their uniforms sitting side by side, their chairs pushed into that little table we sit and eat lunch at sometimes. You remember, don't you, Dudley?"

Dudley shook his head. "Poor guy," he thought. As if Dudley would forget any part of the church after working in it for so many years. "He just wants me to understand."

"They were looking at some pictures, big pictures, 8x10 pictures. Big enough for me to see them from the crack in the door I was peeking through. They were holding them up and making comments about the figures in them. Nasty comments, worse than you'd make at a stag party, you know Dudley? They were talking about what they'd like to do with the people in the pictures and then one of them said to the other one, "You want some of this? I can make it happen you know. She's ripe for the picking. And her father works right here at the church, and he's a nothing. I can make it so the girl won't say anything. You know we can threaten her with anything. Girls this young are easily threatened. Even if she does talk, who would believe her anyway? They're low-life, the whole family. She's got nice tits, doesn't she?"

"Oh Eddy, they were talking about Maggie weren't they?" Dudley was mad now. He knew these cops were into anything and everything that had to do with pulling in some extra cash. But, when it came to this sort of thing, Dudley drew the line. These kinds of things were not acceptable to Dudley, even with his low moral standards.

"Yes. Yes, Dudley, they were talking about my little girl, my sweet Maggie." He hung his head for a moment. He half wanted to continue his crying jaunt but something inside him snapped, something primitive and animal like. He punched one of the bricks on the wall. He punched it again and again until finally Dudley grabbed his hand to make him stop. "I saw the picture they were holding up. It was from the summer. Maggie was wearing her bathing suit. She was with a couple of other kids at the church picnic. I didn't see who the others were but I knew they were talking about my Maggie because they were pointing directly at her while they were talking. Plus, you know how Maggie's bosoms are? She can't help it though. She takes after Emily," Eddy blushed. Eddy punched the wall again. "Those son-of-a bitches," he screamed.

"I'm so sorry, Eddy. I know how you must have felt when you heard them talking about your daughter." For a moment Dudley thought about what he would do to some pervert if they were looking at his daughter and making those comments. One thing he knew for sure, he definitely wouldn't have killed those cops. He might have had them killed by someone who owed him a favor, but he definitely wouldn't have done it himself. "Perverts," thought Dudley. Inside he was steaming just like Eddy was.

"I just went crazy, Dudley. If you asked me what I did that night I can hardly remember but I do know I grabbed the hunting knife I keep down there. You know the one I use to cut the fishing line when I bring the girls fishing down the pond at the end of our street? I used to keep the knife at home until I caught Jill playing with it one day and it scared the bejesus out of me. It was a good thing I kept it in that thick leather pouch or she would have really gotten hurt. After that happened I brought it to work with me and now I keep it down there in the basement. I'll take it out from time to time to use on different projects here at the church but mostly I use it for the fishing thing with the girls, you know?"

"I know which knife you're talking about. You use it here sometimes to cut wire or string, don't you? I think I've even used it a couple of times myself. It's that one with the big thick blade, right? The one with the serrated edge?" Dudley knew exactly which knife Eddy was referring to. Dudley hardly ever used it. He was scared of it actually. Eddy kept the knife sharp, too sharp for Dudley to be handling or walking around with. Dudley imagined what those cops' chests looked like after Eddy got through with them, big gaping holes spewing out pints and pints of blood. The thought made his stomach turn.

"Yeah, like I said, I use the knife here sometimes. Well, I know I killed them with the knife, but I can't remember much of it because I think it was mostly by instinct, like what I was trained to do in my Army days. I just heard them talking and laughing, and then I saw the picture of my little girl and I knew I had to protect her, you know Dudley?"

"Oh I know, Eddy. I completely understand. I don't know what I would have done in that situation either." Meanwhile, Dudley felt uncomfortable. After thinking about it again and again Dudley was quite sure he would never get his hands dirty by killing someone himself. He most assuredly would have had someone else do his dirty work for him. Instead, he definitely knew what he would have done. He would have run away just as fast as his legs would carry him. Eddy might be a simpler man than him, and more stupid–at least for getting himself into this mess–but he was certainly braver.

"Then I heard Maggie get up and start calling my name. I yelled to her that I was taking a shower and not to come over to where I was, just for her to wait for me to get done. I told her I got all dirty from working on the furnace. And I did actually take a shower in the little bathroom down here. I remember looking at my arms and the sleeves of my uniform and they were covered with blood, so I stood in the shower with all my clothes on and then I stripped down in the stall. After I washed up I put on another uniform exactly like the one I had on, one of the extra ones I keep down here. I put the blood soaked uniform along with the towel I used to dry off with and the knife into a plastic bag and left it in the shower. I had to hurry up because Maggie was waiting for me. I didn't know what to do with the plastic bag. I thought I could come back today and do something with it, but then everything turned to shit and the cops came and now I figure I'm pretty much fucked. Excuse my language, Dudley."

"It's okay, I know, Eddy. When I went downstairs this morning before the service I saw the plastic bag, so I took it and hid it in the shed behind my house along with the picture of Maggie and the other girls at the picnic. I saw the picture sitting on the corner of the table. It was blood splattered, but I could make out Maggie's image. I actually figured out pretty much what had happened already. Remember Eddy, I know these cops. I know what they are capable of doing, and I wouldn't put anything past them, quite frankly. I never thought they'd be into this kind of nonsense. We can't do much about the dead cops, now can we? But you and I have some work to do now Eddy, don't we?" Dudley felt like he had to keep Eddy in his pocket, following his plan. He didn't want any of this to lead back to himself. Why had he given those cops that key? He knew too well. His own damned greed.

"What kind of work? I have to turn myself in, Dudley. I can't think of another way to get out of this mess. But I can't even remember my own name right now, you know what I mean?"

"Yes, I know exactly what you mean. You're not thinking clearly. So you just let me do the thinking now. And just one more thing, Eddy. Did you hear them talking about anything else before they started talking about Maggie? Anything at all?"

"Not really I guess. Oh yes, I did hear something. They were laughing and I heard them say something about drugs. I couldn't really make out too much of the conversation. After that they started talking about the pictures and Maggie."

"I see," Dudley replied, hanging his head just a bit.

"So I have to turn myself in, Dudley. It's the only way. What else am I going to tell the cops except for the truth?"

"You leave that part to me, Eddy. I've been thinking a lot about what to do and now I just want you to listen to me, okay?"

"Okay," Eddy replied dutifully.

August 27, 2007

Chapter Eight

Old Mr. Patterson

On her way into work Monday morning Maggie came to one conclusion: her weekend sucked. It had started off on a bad note with the damned Indian in the Ford Escape on Friday night. Then things turned from bad to worse with the Boy Scout episode. And, like a horse's ass, on Saturday morning she decided to break out the old stories she had written about her mother and father. For God's sake, what was she thinking? The only good part of the weekend was the unexpected visit from her daughter on Saturday morning, but even that was far more emotional than she would have liked.

The ridicule of Friday night's Boy Scout encounter reminded her of her ex, son of a bitch that he was. He was always making fun of her or putting her down in front of others. She wondered if Mr. Boy Scout did the same thing to his own wife. Maggie could surely relate to her if that were the case. Maybe she needed to call the wife up sometime to invite her downstairs, tell her to get the hell out of her sorry-ass marriage while she was still even remotely sane. "Nah," Maggie thought–she'll learn on her own.

Early Saturday morning when Maggie read the stories about her mother and father, the essays had evoked an entirely different feeling than from her Friday night encounters. Her Saturday morning emotion wasn't anger as it had been on Friday night. In fact, reading her stories had stirred up more than one emotion in her. When the reading was done, she was left with a cacophony of long forgotten thoughts and feelings. These thoughts and emotions flooded her mind, body, and soul and left her in a state of melancholy, which lingered through the rest of the weekend and on into Monday morning. These were the thoughts and feelings Maggie had tried so hard to keep buried inside for all these years. They'd pop up from time to time but she'd just try to push them back down as quickly as she could. She could only describe them as her emotional cancer, the major symptom being an enormous internal wound, one that could not be easily healed. She was relieved for one thing though. All things considered, Maggie was actually glad she finally shared her stories with Abbie. It made her load just a little lighter to carry.

Adding insult to injury was the fact that Scottie wasn't in a good mood either. His rank disposition was obvious the minute he schlepped by her desk at 9:00 a.m. this morning. He came in grumbling about something or other with just a quick "hi" as he walked past Maggie's desk. The short greeting even seemed forced to her. He appeared to be in an even bigger funk than she was. She could already tell this morning would not be a good one. About mid-morning Maggie, feeling a desperate need to get away, decided to leave the office for awhile at lunch. She would go down to the little man-made lake right around the corner from her building, hoping the scenery would turn her foul mood around.

Promptly at noon she grabbed her lunch and headed down to the lake, plopping herself down on a small cement bench that sat next to a shriveled up willow tree. The words "Dedicated to the Preservation of this Park by the Robinson Family, June 10, 2005" were carved deeply into the cement on the top of the bench. During the summer when Maggie wore a shorter skirt and no pantyhose, rare that that event was, she was always afraid to sit on that bench. She envisioned herself getting up from the hard, unforgiving cement bench and having some of the lettering embossed onto the backside of her leg. Surely people would point and laugh at her if she walked past them with "June 10, 2005" engraved deep into the fat on the rear of her thigh as if she were a cow that had just been branded.

Sitting quietly on the bench, Maggie proceeded to eat her bologna sandwich. It bothered her that she had only one sandwich and one can of coke, because one was an uneven number. But, two sandwiches were too filling at lunch, so she'd have to live with eating just the one. Then she came up with a solution to her dilemma. She remedied her uneven problem by adding the sandwich and the coke together and, *voila* that equaled two. Now she felt happy. After eating, she smoked her two cigarettes. She was careful to flick her ashes along with the used butts into her empty Coke can. The dry pine straw mulch under most of the park's trees, plants and bushes would ignite in a minute if she threw her ashes or butts on the ground.

The weeping willow tree was nestled right next to the cement bench. Most of its branches hung over the edge of the lake, but only one limb dipped into the pond. That one branch reminded Maggie of an old man hunched over a water fountain taking a long cool drink. The landscaping people at Maggie's work had planted the willow close to the man-made pond because willows typically suck up all the water they can and, being perched on the side of a small lake was the ideal location for the tree to take root and flourish. That is until this year. It seemed as if Mother Nature had played a cruel joke on the tree this summer.

A longstanding drought gripping the south had consequently dropped the water line of the pond about four feet below normal. This unkindly natural phenomenon resulted in the slow withering away of that willow tree. The thing gradually began to wilt and die, that is save for that one single branch that dipped in the water, apparently in a last ditch effort to save itself from drying out completely. Maybe it was the willow branch's way of saying, "Screw you, Mother Nature–I'll get my own drink of water." Even recent sporadic rainstorms weren't enough to bring life back into all the dried up flora and fauna that surrounded the tiny lake.

After the smoking was done and her lunch hour nearly up, Maggie gathered her trash and started to lumber back up the small incline next to the bench, grabbing hold of the dried twisted trunk of the willow to gain more stability and steady her footing. After she had turned around to grab hold of the willow, she looked up and there he was standing right in back of the bench. That made her skin crawl, creepy it was. How long had he been there? What was he some kind of pervert? He looked different in the light of day. He didn't appear as old as he was in the office and he wasn't nearly as shaky either. He stared at Maggie with big, wide eyes. Maggie thought he might have a thyroid problem when she saw his eyes. She hadn't remembered them being so big when he came in to see Dr. Leonard in the office.

Maggie knew a girl in school who had similar eyes and that girl had some weird thyroid disease that made her eyes pop out of her head. They popped so much Maggie thought they must have been hanging on by just a couple of thin muscles and veins. But she sensed that old Mr. Patterson had done the eye thing on purpose, just to instill fear into her. If that was the case, he needn't worry. His mission had already been accomplished.

Patterson's eyes also reminded her of one of the kids in her math class in junior high. All her classmates teased him too. He had eyes as big as saucers and his name was Frederick Genovese. But everyone called him Freddie Spaghetti with the meatball eyes, probably because of his huge bulging eyes and because he was Italian. After thinking about it for a minute or two Maggie decided she must have gone to school with a lot of bug-eyed people.

"Hello, Mr. Patterson," she said hesitantly.

"Hello, Maggie. How are you today?" Patterson replied in a friendly voice. By this time he had put his eyes back to normal, so he didn't look like a deer in headlights.

She thought he almost looked and sounded normal, except for the slight tremor in his hands when he reached out to help her climb the little rocky slope next to the bench.

"I'm okay, and you?"

"Fine I guess, except I miss my wife, especially on these kinds of days. When the weather was warm and muggy we used to take a walk because she loved that–loved to sweat. My wife Pavoti said looking at the water cleaned her spirit of the evil ones. Pavoti means, "clear water" in the Hopi tribe. Did you know that Maggie? Paul didn't wait for a response. Instead he went right on talking, "Pavoti and I used to walk every day along a makeshift path worn away from years of footprints from wild animals. The path traveled right along the river, the one that ran close to our reservation.

The animals used to come down to the river to drink."

Maggie thought his reaction was kind of weird. He went straight from "I'm okay" to the subject of his wife. "Quite the instant transition. He sounds a little ADD if you ask me," Maggie thought. But when he came to the part about Pavoti being an Indian, Maggie's ears perked up and her heart began to race. "Your wife was an Indian? You lived on a reservation?" she asked, thinking back to both the e-mail and the Ford Escape. This damned Indian fixation was haunting her, pulling at her and making her pay attention when all she wanted to do was ignore the whole dim-witted thing.

"Native American is the proper term, and yes, Pavoti was one hundred percent Native American. We lived on a reservation about thirty miles from here—in a small town called Cobb's Creek. It wasn't much of a life though. Cheap government—always trying to sell us short. Never giving us what we really needed or deserved. We showed them though. Pavoti and I were happy living there, no matter what they tried to do to us. We didn't care about all the political nonsense the government threw our way."

"You don't see too many authentic Native Americans these days."

"No you don't—only a handful of them are left really," Mr. Patterson replied, looking right into Maggie's eyes—almost straight through her.

Now she was really creeped out. Maggie tried to gaze around at her surroundings, attempting to be as inconspicuous as possible. She could see nothing but a small, well-camouflaged brick path and thick woods. Not another living soul was in sight, just her and the not-really-so-old Mr. Patterson. She thought of running, but knew with her short stubby legs and her smoker's lungs, she wouldn't get very far.

Now he was coming closer to her, and she realized he wasn't shaking at all. "Have you ever lost someone close to you Maggie? Someone you loved dearly, more than life itself? Never mind, I know you have."

"How do you know that, Mr. Patterson? I really should be getting back to work," she blurted out nervously. Now Maggie was the one fidgeting. As she looked down she realized he was still holding onto her hand. She pulled it away.

"Please, Maggie, call me Paul."

"Gotta go," Maggie quickly exclaimed in an oddly loud voice. She abruptly turned and, as quick as her thick legs would carry her, started briskly waddling down the brick path towards her office.

"Wait!" Paul cried out, "I have something to tell you, something important. You need to hear this, Maggie. It's about your father."

Maggie stopped dead in her tracks, turned to look at Paul and said, "Sweet Jesus of Jerusalem. What are you talking about, you idiot? My father's dead, has been for most of my life."

Paul's ears perked up and he looked around. The sound of faint footsteps could be heard in the distance and he heard them there was no doubt. "I can't talk now, Maggie, but things will be revealed to you soon. I must be careful though. Do as the e-mail told you to do, Maggie—pay attention to the signs, zoom-zoom." Then Paul made the same familiar shaking hand signal that the Native American in the Ford Escape had made last Friday night. "Things aren't always what they seem," Paul said as he turned quickly and walked away.

"My father's dead!" Maggie screamed as she stood in the middle of the path. She noticed her eyes had become extra wide and buggy and were filled with both shock and fear. Because they were so bulged out, the little gust of wind that drifted by had dried some of the fluid in them, and she found it necessary to blink several times to lubricate them once again. She imagined this was how Freddie Spaghetti's eyes had felt or even the girl with the goofy goiter for that matter. Maggie's whole body went limp. She couldn't feel her arms or legs anymore. She had the odd sensation that all four of her appendages had virtually become detached from her core, useless they were to her—like tits on a bull.

December 27, 1964

Chapter Nine

Gunderson knew some of the cops on the force were dirty but apparently he underestimated just exactly how crooked they were. The murders of Sergeants Vincent Pinzolli and Roy Blevins were shock enough for him, let alone finding out what kind of nonsense they were both involved in. You could have knocked him over with a feather when he found out that not only was Sergeant Pinzolli kin to the infamous Fat Tony, but like his mob brother, Vincent was also deeply entrenched in all the Mob's dirty dealings. When he learned of their blood relation, he knew things would get complicated during this investigation. He also knew the motto of the mob was "blood for blood." It was no wonder Gunderson didn't put two and two together with these two brothers though. Turns out they had the same mother but two different fathers, thus their different last names. He was sure one of the dads got whacked somewhere along the way for doing something stupid.

Gunderson would have to be very careful with this case. He felt disillusioned, almost as if he'd found out one of his own family was corrupt. When he first became a cop he vowed to rid the world of wrongdoing. That didn't last long. He soon found out how utopian his way of thinking was. Not too long after getting out of police training he realized that nothing or no one in this life was a hundred percent legit, although some people turned out worse than others. He came to the conclusion that this case leaned toward the worse than others category. These days Gunderson just wished he could jump ahead to the future about ten years so he could retire.

Gunderson needed to do his homework before he spoke to Dudley again and before he had a man-to-man with this chump Eddy. He still had a gut feeling about these two jokers. So he laid low on Saturday, did his groundwork all day and figured out the questions he would ask each and every one of them. Plus, hopefully, today he'd catch up with his trusted informant. Then he'd have a better idea of what was really going on here. Being the diligent Chief he was, he wouldn't come to any conclusions until all the facts were on the table.

At about eleven on Sunday morning, while most everyone else in town was in church, Gunderson perused the streets of Durham looking for his stool pigeon, Willie the snitch. He usually found him in the vicinity of either the new Dunkin' Donuts or in front of Woolworth's. Being Sunday, neither one would be open, so he didn't know exactly where to look for him. But, low and behold, open or not, there he was loitering in front of the Dunkin' Donuts.

Willie spent his time in front of these two establishments because, plain and simple, he needed to eat. In the morning he hung around Dunkin' Donuts and begged for money to buy coffee and a glazed crueler. An extra large coffee with cream and sugar usually set Willie on the right path for the day and, more importantly, jolted him out of his previous nights drinking-induced coma. In the afternoon the Woolworth's grill counter provided his dinner, even if he didn't have enough cash to cover the meal. The waitress at Woolworth's had a soft spot in her heart for Willie and always, without fail, slipped him an extra large helping of meat and potatoes.

Everyone in Durham knew Willie the snitch, and Willie knew pretty much everything there was to know about every single person in this drowsy little town too. He could recite verbatim conversations held between two friends at the Woolworth's counter, without them even knowing he was listening. Gunderson didn't know how he did this, especially with his drinking habits being such that they were. Not many people knew Willie had this talent and Gunderson was glad for that. He obtained more information from Willie than he did from any crime scene investigation. And the information was worth much more than what Willie received in return, a meal or two. Even slipping him a twenty wouldn't be enough to pay for his priceless knowledge.

Gunderson drove up close to the sidewalk in front of D & D, reached over and rolled down the window of his police cruiser. Bending over a bit so that he could see Willie's face, he hollered to him, "Get in."

"Yes, *sir*." Willie obediently replied, snapping his feet together and raising his hand to his brow, in a gesture of a mock solute.

"No nonsense, Willie, or I'll arrest you for loitering."

"Oh, I'm scared," he answered, fake shaking.

"Just shut up and get in, will ya?"

Willie opened the car door and slipped low into the front seat. He was always cautious when it came to being seen with the police chief. If other people saw him getting into a cop car with Gunderson they might suspect he was a snitch. They might even be more cautious around him; speak softer so Willie couldn't hear them or even avoid Willie altogether. And the last thing Gunderson wanted was to be seen with Willie. He figured, as innocuous as Willie seemed to everyone, the Mob was probably onto him. For all Gunderson knew, they probably had some wise guy watching both of them right now.

No, the risk of people seeing Willie getting into Gunderson's police cruiser would not bode well for either one of them. Gunderson didn't want to risk losing his prime source of information, and Willie didn't want to risk losing his prime source of income. Gunderson covered his expenses for Willie through the petty cash fund down at the station, a source of money easily able to be concealed from the rest of the force's expenditures. They had bigger fish to fry besides noticing a few bucks missing from Gunderson's play money.

"Let's cut to the chase shall we, Willie? What do you know about the murders?"

"Murders? What murders?" he questioned slyly, raising his eyebrows and rubbing his hands together in front of him as if he were about to consume a delicious steak dinner.

"Don't bullshit me, Willie. Cough up the information."

Willie gazed over at Gunderson, giving him the stink eye. "First let's see the cash."

"Don't worry, I'm good for it."

"That's not what I asked. I said, first the cash, then you get the information, *capiche*?"

"*Capiche*." Gunderson answered back, reaching into his pocket for a twenty-dollar bill.

"Oh, this will cost you more than that, my friend."

"How much more?"

"Shall we say five times more? You know as well as I do what I got to tell you is worth much more than that. But, since you're such a good friend, I'll cut you a break and give it to you for a hundred."

"Fine. But I don't have that much on me right now. Can you wait? Otherwise I'll drive you down to the station to get the money."

"No, no. I know you're good for it," Willie protested. Going down to the station was the last thing he needed.

Gunderson wished he hadn't told Willie to get in his cruiser. The new car had a more than optimal heating system, blasting hot air through vents on the dashboard at a force great enough to rattle even Gunderson's slicked back coif. The hot new-car smell was slowly but surely mixing with the less than pleasant odor emanating from his informant. He was sure he'd need to fumigate his cruiser later in the day. Or at least douse the seat covers with Lysol or some other disinfecting agent. Gunderson looked over at Willie. The obviously homeless man wore a dirty pair of Dickie's bib coveralls covered with about a month's worth of grime. The old pair of black cloth Keds he wore were minus the laces, and the tongues of both shoes were sticking out over the top part of his toes. He didn't have socks on his feet but he almost appeared to be wearing a dirty pair, such was the buildup of crud on the upper part of his forefeet. Gunderson figured this was where part of the foul smell was coming from. Sticking out from the pocket of Willie's tattered wool jacket was the green plastic tip of a fly swatter. "Aiming to kill some snow flies are you Willie?" he asked, gesturing one of his big fingers in the direction of Willie's pocket.

Willie smiled, revealing a set of five short black twig looking things hanging from his upper gum line. They were what Gunderson assumed had once been his teeth. "Yeah, so what? Don't like my choice of accessories?"

"I could give a damned what you wear. Just tell me what you know."

"Okay, okay, don't get your knickers in a knot. I'll tell ya." Willie sat for a while thinking, remembering. Gunderson wished he'd hurry up. He was about to wretch from the smell. "You see that place across the street?" Willie waved his hand in front of Gunderson's nose, pointing to the exact location of the restaurant. Another pungent wave of stink crossed in front of the Chief, making him almost lose his breakfast.

"Yeah. I see it. That's Dingus McFee's place right?"

"Right."

"So, what about it?"

"Ever wonder why his joint's never been raided?"

"He's on the up and up. We've checked him out a bunch of times just like all the other places around town. What are you talking about, Willie? Give it to me straight, no beating around the bush."

Gunderson was very familiar with Dingus's restaurant. He brought his family there every week for the Thursday night special. Hands down, Dingus made the best fish and chips Gunderson had ever eaten. Plus, when McFee served him his pint of Guinness he'd always wink at Gunderson and say, "a bit o'cheer for ya den." This offered unparalleled authenticity to his meal, which made it taste all the better.

"Good ole Dingus. He's got a room in back, see? He uses that room for all kinds of stuff, see?" Willie smiled coyly at the Chief.

"I said straight, Willie! Give it to me straight!" Gunderson reprimanded.

"Okay, okay, straight. You're really making me earn this hundred. I shouldn't even tell you without my money in hand."

"I'm good for it. You know I am. Haven't I been good for it before?"

"Yeah, you're good for it alright, I guess." Reluctantly, Willie went on, "So, I'm not sure for certain what all Dingus does in that back room, but I know one thing he's involved in is illicit gambling. But he pays the street tax, so he's safe."

"Street tax? What street tax?"

"You know, protection."

"What kind of protection?" Gunderson asked, his face starting to redden.

"Protection from everything, so he can go on doing what he does. About fifty percent of the businesses in town pay it. They pay the Mob; the Mob makes sure they don't get caught doing what they do."

"So how does the Mob protect them?"

"That's where it gets tricky, see? It sure does help when you got a brother on the force. Word gets around the station about Dingus's back room, dirty cops get a whiff of it, they tell the Mob, and the Mob tells Dingus so he has time to 'clean up' before the raid."

Gunderson's pride interfered with his judgment. Realistically, he knew things of this nature went on around town. But he obviously didn't realize the extent of the corruption. Maybe he didn't really want to know just how shady everyone was. "What other things were these two cops into? What kinds of dirty dealings were they into, Willie? Do you know?"

"Sure, I know. I know everything," Willie grinned. "But just so's you know, Gunderson, there's more than two cops, many more than two. But these two in particular, the two you're referin' to, see? They was into a lot of under-the-table stuff—labor racketeering, political corruption, extortion, loan sharking, manufacture and distribution of drugs, money laundering, assault, homicide, bribery, mail fraud, prostitution, theft, and liquor law violations. Just to name a few," Willie announced, proud of the information he knew and kept under his hat.

"So, here's the big question, Willie. What's most puzzling to me is why they were in the church in the first place. You know why?" Gunderson stared at Willie. Without a doubt he knew Willie knew the answer. He had a tell, just like in poker. When he had a good hand so to speak, he'd blink twice. Of course, the snitch was completely unaware of his revealing facial gesture.

Willie blinked twice and admitted to Gunderson, "Sure I know, Chief. What better place to do dirty business than right there under God's nose so to speak, see?"

Gunderson let go of a big sigh. "Dudley know?"

Willie blinked twice again. "Let's just say the underside of that white collar he wears isn't as clean as the outside is, see?"

"Yeah, I see," Gunderson replied, shaking his head in disgust. "Want to tell me anything else, Willie?"

"If you want to pay me some more money, sure I'll tell you more. I'll squeal like a pig."

"No thanks, not if it's gonna cost me more. I think I can figure out some things on my own."

"So we done, Chief? You sure? I'd tell you more if you weren't so cheap, see?" Willie laughed, showing his nasty, rotten teeth.

"I'm sure. We're done for now. But stay close, Willie, in case I need more info on anyone, see?" Gunderson made a point of using the word "see," as it obviously was a word Willie was both fond of and understood quite well, having used it in nearly every sentence.

"You know where to find me," he replied, pointing back and forth to both establishments, first to the Dunkin' Donuts and then to Woolworth's.

Gunderson had never been happier to see someone get out of his car. The smell of Willie still lingered for a good while after he left. Freezing though it was outside, Gunderson didn't care, he opened up his windows fully to air out the inside, trying to get rid of the stench. The fresh air felt good on Gunderson's face. It cleared his head, made him think a little better. After processing all the information Willie gave him, he felt sufficiently armed and ready to go on to the next step, questioning both Eddy and Dudley. He already had what he thought was enough ammunition to pin it on either one of these two goons, that is after he found out exactly who the guilty party was. Heck, for all he knew, they could've been in on it together.

August 27, 2007

Chapter Ten

Maggie was visibly shaken when she returned to her desk after her bizarre lunch encounter with Paul. She sat for a while just staring into space, keeping her hands folded tightly on her lap in an effort to hide her trembling fingers. "Maybe Scottie won't notice how nervous I am," she thought. No such luck. He was trained to observe people's behavior.

The minute Maggie returned to her desk, he got up from behind his desk and stepped through the doorway, ducking a little to clear the top of the molding. As he stood right in front of her, the blank, emotionless stare she was wearing was a clear indication that something was terribly wrong. He tried to make eye contact with her. His eyes were the color of milk chocolate with little flecks of black scattered throughout the irises. They reminded Maggie of puppy dog eyes. Maggie also knew these same eyes possessed the unique ability to peer right through to her inner soul. Of course his eyes appeared much larger than they actually were behind his coke bottle prescription lenses. She looked up into his eyes for only a brief moment before anxiously turning her head away. She thought back to her lunch hour, "What is it with today? Does everyone I meet have gigantic eyes?"

Scottie watched Maggie's every movement, every expression, the body language, and, most of all her lack of eye contact. Hovering in front of her computer for just a minute, he tried to get her attention again. She didn't bite. No looking up into Scottie's eyes. That would be a death wish for her now. Scottie eventually leaned over the top of her computer and, tilting his head a bit to the left, made an effort to mimic his face after the Joker in Batman. Shutting his mouth very tight, he grinned so wide it made his cheeks hurt. His antics didn't work; he ended up just looking like a fool. Then, ever so gently, he reached over the computer and touched Maggie's arm, much like she imagined a dad would reach out for his hurt little girl, and finally asked, "What's wrong, Maggie?"

She pulled her arm away and snapped back at him, "Nothing," although she didn't mean for it to come out the way it did. The events of the past few days were beginning to wear on her psyche. Her dull but predictably constant world was beginning to crumble.

Scottie stood up straight and pushed his head back slightly. This made his giraffe neck look even longer than it was, like he was about to reach up and eat the bark off an imaginary tree or something. Obviously hurt, he mumbled as he walked back into his office, "God don't like ugly."

"Ugly? Did he say ugly? Apparently he's talking about my attitude because with those thick coke-bottle glasses, how could he even see my face?" Maggie thought. She turned to her computer and released the lock she had placed on it before leaving for her infamous lunch. As Scottie returned to his office, she said something under her breath but loud enough for him to hear, "If God don't like ugly, he sure as shit must hate you."

He was halfway to his desk and just about ready to sit in his chair when he heard her mutter some comment. He couldn't make out what it was though. But, then again, he didn't really want to know what the remark was either. He could only imagine. Although he wasn't in such a good mood himself, her mood was the one killing him because he didn't want to see her hurt or frazzled. Scottie cared about Maggie, especially when she was upset. There was obviously something wrong. What it was he couldn't quite figure out just yet.

Standing there in the middle of his office, he yelled back at her through the half open door, "Have I done something to offend you Maggie? Do you need to talk? Are you still upset about Frank leaving you? Did he do something to upset you again? You know, Maggie, that was a long time ago. We've talked about this many times, and it's been years and years now. You really need to forgive him. I know it wasn't right what he did to you, but if you don't forgive him you won't be able to move on. You're only hurting yourself, Maggie."

"What is it with the third degree?" she asked herself. How presumptuous it was for Scottie to think that every little upset in her life was due to a man walking out on her. Even so, it would be a cold day in hell when she forgave Frank for dragging her down to Virginia and then cheating on her. For all she knew, that was the reason he brought her down there in the first place. Not that she would have liked it any better up north. It was time to leave Connecticut but she never thought in a million years Frank would cheat on her with his secretary. "Leave Frank Lerner out of this, Scottie. Just because I'm upset doesn't mean it has to do with Frank, you know. And I have forgiven him. I even prayed for him the other night. God Bless Frank and that slut he married. Don't worry about me, Scottie. I'll be fine. Just fine."

Scottie chuckled, "That's good." He didn't want to but he got the biggest kick out of her sometimes. "Oh, I almost forgot—Paul Patterson stopped by and left an envelope on your desk. He said you would know what it was for," Scottie yelled as he sat down at his computer.

It was a damned good thing Scottie was back in his office because, for the second time today, she was the one sporting enormous bug-eyes. If he had seen her reaction, he would definitely know something was wrong. The expression on her face was enough to worry even an impartial passerby.

Maggie turned around, saw the envelope sitting on her desk and glared at it with bewilderment. The writing said "confidential." "How could that slug make it here so fast? I just stopped for a minute to go to the bathroom on my way back to the office," Maggie questioned. "Who is this guy, Superman?" This Paul Patterson was starting to get on her nerves.

The acid began to churn in Maggie's gut just like it always did when she got nervous. The worst part was when this happened, she knew that not long after half her lunch would end up in her throat. The first puke burp felt as if someone had poured battery acid down her esophagus. Plus it made her breath absolutely stink. Her husband used to say her breath was bad enough to knock a buzzard off a shit wagon. "That's nice of you to say, dear," was Maggie's standard sarcastic reply.

Looking back on her marriage there were more of those demeaning statements than she cared to remember. One time when she and Frank were working in the yard, one of his friends drove by. He rolled down his car window and looked at Frank, pointed to Maggie and said, "I'll give you two donkeys and a wheelbarrow for her." It took Frank a good long while to answer his friend because he looked as if he was honestly contemplating the offer. But then, after declining the offer, and after his friend drove away, he turned to Maggie and said, "You look awful. You're all sweaty and nasty. You look like you been rode hard and put up wet. Why don't you go and clean yourself up?" The sad part was she usually went and did what he said.

She didn't have what it took to stand up to Frank. This was a double whammy for her because it made her already low self-esteem go down the shitter even more. So most of the time she tried to disguise her miserable life with a good shower, some perfume and a mask of Maybelline Smooth Result medium beige pressed powder. Then she would add some fire-engine red lipstick with a coat of high shine clear lip-gloss over top of it, giving her lips that sexy wet glow that Frank loved so much. Then she felt beautiful again.

"I'm not opening it," Maggie declared, her eyes fixed on the envelope. "Confidential my ass," she mumbled. But the envelope had a pull on her. The feeling was akin to nothing she had ever experienced before. She just knew it contained something that would frighten her. Maggie stared at the envelope, frowning with intense purpose, telepathically willing it to do as she commanded, "No more surprises," she begged to the envelope. "I don't want anything else to upset my apple cart." She had her routine; get up, go to work, go home. That was it. She was happy!

"Have you seen my next patient yet, Maggie?" Scottie yelled through his open door.

"No. Pearl hasn't shown up yet," Maggie answered, glad for the temporary diversion from her current state of anxiety.

"She's late, isn't she?"

"Just a couple of minutes. Not bad. Maybe she got caught in the lunch hour traffic." She thought of the name Pearl and how, when Scottie had first gotten Pearl as a patient, he made a big deal about her name. "What's in a name anyways, Scottie?" Maggie had said to him. Well that was a big mistake. This started a tangent that lasted nearly twenty minutes. "I'll tell you what's in a name Maggie . . . blah, blah, blah."

Apparently, Scottie had a sister who was stillborn. They named her Pearl. He ended up doing quite a bit of research in college about why people name their children the way they do, even writing a very long paper on the subject. Imagine that.

"Pearl is a unique name, very southern. But also with a great deal of underlying meaning," Scottie said matter-of-factly. "I have pondered many times about why my mother named a baby who died at birth a name like Pearl and, after giving it a great deal of thought, the answer became clear to me. Just the connotation of the word has a very embryonic feel to it. How the pearl is cultivated in the womb of a shell, surrounded by nacre, which is a natural liquid substance that coats the pearl and makes it grow. Nacre is also called mother-of-pearl. When the pearl is fully matured it is a beautiful treasure, but not alive by any means. I believe that's why my mother named her stillborn Pearl."

"Here she is, Scottie."

"Sorry I'm late, Maggie," Pearl announced.

"No problem. Scottie will be with you shortly. Just have a seat. He'll come out to get you in a minute," Maggie stared at Pearl. She didn't mean to stare, but oh my God! What this young girl had done to her face was just a travesty. She could have been beautiful if it weren't for all those piercings on her head. It looked like she fell face first into a tackle box. Everything clicked when she talked, metal hoops through her lips, bars through her tongue, and a huge metal rod stuck through the little piece of cartilage separating her nostrils. God forbid she got caught in a rainstorm. Everything would rust and she'd come down with a nasty case of tetanus. When she blinked Maggie could see the tattoos she had painted on her eyelids. They were of full, open eyeballs, same as the real ones stuck in her head. So, blinking or not, it looked as though her eyes were always open.

When Pearl had gone in to see the doc and when his door was shut and she was once again alone, Maggie picked up the envelope. "No more putting off the inevitable," she thought. "Just open it, for God's sake."

It was a train ticket with a note attached to it:

Ask for two weeks off, Spider. It's time for your journey to begin. Have fun on your trip to the Nutmeg State. I'll pick you up in Durham. I'm sure you know where it is don't you? When you get off the train, look for the Ford Escape. The one you saw the other day. And don't think about backing out, telling anyone or calling the police. Tell Dr. Leonard you need to go out of town for an emergency. Say it's personal and has to do with your daughter. Oh and Maggie–do trust me please. This is what

your father wanted. He said you would know to trust me if I called you Spider. I hope that little fact will help you to have faith in me. Eddy said it was a pet name between the two of you when you were little because you used to be deathly afraid of spiders. I know this whole thing sounds so strange to you now but it will all become clear during your journey, you'll see. Don't worry about bringing any money or having a place to sleep. Your father handled all the arrangements. This was his dying wish, Maggie. Please follow his last request, won't you?
Signed,
Paul

Gritting her teeth and mumbling she said to the note, "You son-of-a-bitch. When I get my hands on you I'll kick the cowboy shit out of you!" How could one person like shaky Paul have so much influence on her? Holding her head in her hands she began to openly cry, "Why me?" she questioned. "Why me?" She might as well have been born with a sign on her forehead that read, "shit for luck." She felt as if her whole life had been a series of one piss poor event after another. Remembering each event was much the same as rearranging deck chairs on the Titanic.

There was no way she could stay in the office now. Her nervous stomach, coupled with the lingering smell of patchouli from metal-mouth Pearl, made her feel as if she would lose her lunch. She began to write Scottie a note. Taping it to his door, she quickly grabbed her handbag and scampered out the door. The note read:

Scottie– I'm going home. I don't feel well. I should be in tomorrow but if not, I'll give you a call.
Thanks, Maggie

After thinking about it for a minute and feeling a wave of guilt wash over her, she added a P.S.: *I'm sorry I was harsh with you this afternoon.*

Every one of her body's senses was on fire. Her heart was thumping wildly in her chest. Fight-or-flight mode was definitely kicking in. Her regurgitating lunch made her mouth taste foul, and she reached for some gum in her purse to settle her stomach. It helped a little but not much. Stomach acid was pumping out faster than water from an open fire hydrant.

On her way home she saw no traffic on the freeway except for a school bus filled with rowdy kids jumping all over their seats. She saw an older model white Ford E-150 XL van, the kind with a 4.6-liter V-8 engine. From the side view she knew it must have been some kind of plumbing truck because it had a huge roof rack on it with different sized pipes attached to it. As the van drove past she read the back, "Johnson's Plumbing–A Straight Flush Beats a Full House." "Clever," Maggie thought. "But was this a sign?" She supposed if she thought about it long enough, anything could be a sign, but doubted this was one of the mysterious ones she was called to pay attention to.

There was no question the next one was a sign because the same Indian that was driving the Ford Escape was also driving this car. It was a Honda Element, the color was so bright it was like looking into the sun: intense orange with a scary looking flame decal on the side. The devil himself may as well have been driving. "What was Honda thinking when they designed this vehicle?" Maggie contemplated. "If you slapped the word 'Wonder' on the side of this odd looking vehicle it would have been more fitting because the shape of the damned SUV looked just like a bread truck." A personalized license plate on the Element read: *EFEDRA.* And as Mr. Authentic Native American drove by, he gave Maggie the same weird hand signal as before.

"Oh crap," Maggie thought. What do I have to lose? I'll show him he can't toy with me like that. Who does he think he is anyways?" She grew some balls because she gave him the same hand signal back. He stared at her as he passed her by and just grinned.

"For fuck's sake, what in holy hell is *EFEDRA*?" she thought.

December 28, 1964

Chapter Eleven

Gunderson would choose his words wisely as he spoke to Eddy. He had had two full days to think about what he wanted to ask him. Plus there was the interesting interview yesterday with Willie the snitch, which had revealed more information than Gunderson wanted to know. All the information he had gleaned from yesterday's meeting with Willie would stay hidden for now. In fact, Gunderson hadn't decided yet whether to use this newfound knowledge at all, ever.

Gunderson waited until Eddy was back at work to question him. He chose not to go to Eddy's home yet. He decided to interrogate him right there in the church, right where the crimes had taken place. "No need to upset his whole family yet," he thought as he waited for Eddy in the sanctuary. Gunderson had checked with Dudley about what Eddy's work hours were and then decided to make an impromptu visit first thing Monday morning. "Better to catch him off guard a little," Gunderson thought.

As Eddy lumbered into the sanctuary he tried as hard as he knew how to be as inconspicuous as possible. He really wanted to just melt into the woodwork. He tried to remember all the things Dudley had told him to say but wondered if he could actually pull this whole thing off.

Gunderson greeted Eddy with a hearty good morning. Eddy answered back a bit subdued, "Good morning," trying as hard as he could to stick to the suggestion his good friend, Dudley, had made during their meeting behind the school night before last, "Use as few words as possible."

"As Dudley may have told you, Eddy, I'm Chief Gunderson, the one who will be in charge of the murder investigation."

"I know, Chief Gunderson. Dudley told me just a little while ago that you wanted to speak to me this morning."

"Good. Now let's get right down to business, shall we?"

"Okay. It's awful about what happened to those cops isn't it, Chief?" Eddy commented, although this sounded more like it was rehearsed than sincere. Eddy was tired from lack of sleep. Dark circles ringed his anxious eyes.

"Yes, it is, Eddy. It's just a shame about what happened to them really. I'll get right to the point, Eddy." Gunderson didn't mince his words. "Dudley already told me that you and he are the only two people in this church who have keys to the storage room. Is that correct?"

"Yes. But he lost his key for a while, and then I went to have another one made for him."

"When was that?" Gunderson was surprised. Both Dudley and Eddy's stories jived. Was this the truth or coincidentally staged? Gunderson would have to wait and see.

"Not too long ago, maybe a month or so. I can't remember the exact day."

"That's fine, just an estimate of the time frame will be good enough. One more question. Were you up at the church anytime Christmas Eve or early Christmas morning?"

"No, I wasn't. I was home putting a bike together for my daughter for Christmas."

"Is there anyone who can vouch for that?"

"Yes, my wife, Emily. All my girls were in bed early though, about 8:30 p.m. That's our tradition on Christmas Eve. They are all expected to go to bed early since Emily and I know they'll be up at the crack of dawn to open their gifts."

"Yeah–I know what you mean. I have two girls of my own, probably about the same age as yours. How old are your girls, Eddy?"

"The two youngest, Jill and Linda are actually Irish twins, born just eleven months apart. Jill is nine and Linda is eight. Maggie's the oldest. She's sixteen."

"Wow–you have your hands full don't you? I can't say as I envy you, especially when the boyfriends start coming around. I have an eight-year old too. They probably go to the same school. Is your Linda in Girl Scouts?" Gunderson asked, knowing full well what the answer would be. He had proof of it in clue number two, the one he found at the scene of the crime.

"Yes, Chief Gunderson, both Jill and Linda are in troop 314. My wife is one of the leaders," thinking to himself what a weird question that was. "Maggie is one of Emily's helpers. She was a Girl Scout too when she was younger. She likes to help out with the troop."

"You're a better dad than I am. I can't say that I even know what troop my little Betty's in. All I know is that my wife just ordered her that new book from Sears Roebuck and Company called the Junior Girl Scout Handbook. Cost me an arm and a leg. Does your daughter have one of those?"

"Probably, but my wife would know better than me. Like I said Chief, my wife is one of the leaders."

"Oh yes, right. I almost forgot," bluffed Gunderson, playing coy with Eddy. "And Maggie is one of your wife's helpers." Gunderson put more emphasis on this last part, making a point of drawing out the word "Maggie" a little longer than was normal in everyday speech. "Okay back to business now, enough family talk, although I could brag about my girls forever, couldn't you?"

"Yes, I could. They're good girls, Chief, don't give me any trouble at all."

Gunderson ignored the comment. Although it may have appeared that Gunderson was speaking with Eddy on a personal level, this couldn't have been further from the truth. Everything Gunderson did and said was strictly to gain information. He wasn't interested in families or Girl Scouts or, for that matter, Eddy's bragging rights. He had to keep an unfaltering impersonal barrier between him and his suspects otherwise this case, as well as any other case he worked on, would have been shot to hell. Indeed, Gunderson didn't let any personal feelings get in the way of his investigations. "Yes, well just another question or two and then I think we're done," Gunderson continued. "How well do you know Dudley?"

"Very well I guess. I've worked here for almost as long as he's been here. He's good to my family and me. He pays me well, much more than I could earn at any other church. I trust him. He's a good man."

"That's good since he's your boss and a Reverend to boot," Gunderson replied with a slight chuckle. "I hear he was in the Army, is that right Eddy?"

"Yeah, that's right," Eddy replied, wondering why in the world he was questioning him about Dudley when Eddy should have been on trial here, or so he thought. This questioning was not at all what he'd imagined. If he didn't know better he would have thought Dudley was the suspect here.

"Were you in the Armed Forces, Eddy?"

Eddy answered the question obediently, thinking all the while, "Another weird question. I wonder what he's up to?" But Eddy dutifully answered Chief Gunderson's question as briefly as possible, just as Dudley had instructed him to do, "Yes, I was in the Army too, Chief."

"Were you stationed together with Dudley?"

"No. He's a little younger than I am. I got out in '44, right when he was enlisting. I guess we did all the grunt work, and he got all the glory, right? He saw some combat action, I imagine, mostly with wounded soldiers and prisoners of war. But he got to celebrate the end of the war, and then I guess he managed some clean-up projects. I don't think I would have wanted to see all those prisoners from the concentration camps released at the end of the war. They must have looked pretty sad, all skinny and malnourished and all." Eddy paused for a moment, wondering if he had revealed too much information. When it came to the war, Eddy could talk all day, endlessly reminiscing about his Army days.

Gunderson shook his head, agreeing with him, all the while writing down various comments in his little notebook. Looking up he said, "Okay. I think that will be all for now. Thanks for your time. I'll probably need to question you again. Any objections to that?"

"Nope, none sir." Eddy scooted out of the pew and grabbed his mop and bucket that he had previously tucked in the corner of the narthex. He started swabbing the floor back and forth, a motion that comforted him after his awkward questioning. With each swipe of the mop and each dunk into the sudsy liquid in the bucket Eddy thought, "That wasn't so bad after all."

Gunderson sat in the pew for a long time. Eddy watched him from the corner of his eye as he mopped the floor. For a minute he thought he might be called back in for a second round of questioning, but then Gunderson got up and walked to the front of the church, took a left at the baptismal font and headed toward Dudley's office.

The Chief knocked on Dudley's door but he didn't wait for an answer. He pushed the door slightly open and poked his head in.

The Reverend was on the phone and looked up from his desk at the looming shadow of the Chief. Dudley was obviously annoyed. Cupping his hand over the receiver, he sternly asked the Chief, "Can I help you?"

The Chief waved his gigantic hand back and forth, and mouthed, "I'll wait."

Gunderson sat in one of the generic chairs in Dudley's sparsely filled office. In the meantime, Dudley went back to his phone conversation with one of his parishioners, sympathetically giving his condolences on the recent death of the man's grandmother. After the phone call ended, Dudley glared up at the Chief and somberly spoke to him in a parental way, "There is a reason my door is closed sometimes, Chief. Much of my work is of a private nature and necessitates the utmost confidentiality. If you had waited for me to answer before barging in here, I would have asked you to stay out in the hallway and wait for me until I was done with my phone call."

"Oh sorry, Dudley." Gunderson replied sarcastically. "Let's get things straight shall we? This is a murder investigation. Are we clear on that? You understand that don't you, Reverend? That means that this church and all the things inside this church are under my jurisdiction, at least for the time being, until the murders are solved. That means no closed doors, no secrets, and no backtalk. Do I make myself clear, Dudley? Deal?"

"Deal." Dudley acted annoyed, which he was. He wondered how the questioning went for Eddy. He wondered if Eddy had spilled the beans to the Chief.

"Okay, now let's get on with it, shall we?" Gunderson roared. His loud voice echoed in Dudley's office, bouncing off the wood-paneled walls.

"Get on with what, Chief?"

"The truth," Gunderson declared, looking point blank into Dudley's eyes.

"I've told you the truth," Dudley shouted back, waving his hands up in the air in a gesture of frustration.

"Well, it seems you've left out one little detail, Reverend Session."

"And what's that, Chief?" Dudley asked sarcastically. Outwardly he appeared cocky and aggravated, but inside he could feel his nerves fraying, wondering all the while what this small detail was that Gunderson was referring to.

Gunderson reached in his pocket and grabbed the little square notebook with the silk cord wrapped tightly around it. On the end of the cord was a key, which fit nicely into a lock at the side of the open border of the book. On the front of the pink silk cover in dark pink embossed lettering were the words, "MY DIARY."

Dudley looked puzzled when he saw what Gunderson was holding in his hands.

Gunderson opened the notebook to the last entry, held it out so that Dudley could see it and then read the inscription:

December 24, 1964–almost midnight

It's Christmas Eve, and I went with my Dad to the church. Dad's boss called him to have him come because he had to fix the furnace. Mom was very mad but not so mad that I had to stay home. I'm glad. I love to do things with Dad alone, without my sisters. Plus I think I might get a chance to see how this furnace works. I'm pretty tired though. I might see if Dad will bring me, Jill and Linda and their Girl Scout troop back here so he could explain to all of us how it works. Because I'm helping with the troop, I'll ask Ma if she thinks there might be a badge they could earn for this. Maggie

Dudley looked shocked when he saw the entry in the Diary. "Where did you find this, Chief?"

"Well, Dudley, I found it underneath the pillow on the little cot next to the furnace in the basement. Now do you want to tell me the truth, or do I have to go and talk with Eddy again and show him this little bit of information I found downstairs?"

"Oh God," thought Dudley. "On to plan B," he whispered softly.

"What's that, Dudley? I can't hear you."

"Okay, okay. Come with me. I've got something to show you." Dudley guided the Chief down the short hallway that lead to a side door out of the church. They both stepped outside into the snow, made their way across the side yard toward the back of Dudley's house.

Eddy watched the Chief and Dudley from the small window at the end of the narthex. They were heading straight for Dudley's shed. "Oh shit," Eddy exclaimed out loud. "I thought I could trust Dudley. Shit, shit, shit," Eddy reiterated as he dropped his mop, and shook his head back and forth clutching the sides of the small window. This was the same window Eddy had tried his best to open the whole time he was at St. John's, using every tool possible, including a hammer and chisel. But the window never would budge for Eddy, no matter how hard he tried to pry the damned thing open.

August 31, 2007

Chapter Twelve

After much internal contemplation, Maggie actually decided to take Paul up on his offer. She was curious about learning more about her father. And, if Paul was correct, he'd be the one to teach her. She thought about what Abbie had said, how she told her not to take the journey. But Abbie had a full life with school, work and her live-in boyfriend. Maggie's life was not so full. In fact it was quite stagnant. She felt like she desperately needed a change, something new. Still, going on this trip was a leap of faith for Maggie. But then she decided, "What the hell."

She thought back to one of Aunt Clara's sayings about Marilyn Monroe. Apparently, from what Aunt Clara said, whenever the famous actress was in a quandary about making a decision she was quoted as saying, "Ever notice that 'what the hell' is always the right decision?" So, if it was good enough for Marilyn Monroe, it was good enough for her. Her "what the hell" decision felt like the right choice. Not to mention, she wanted to do this one last thing for her father. Was this his dying wish, to take a journey? She sure hoped it was because if it wasn't, old Mr. Patterson was playing one heck of a joke on her.

She didn't know how Paul had come to know her father so well, and that scared her a lot. But she was coming to trust Paul Patterson. She had no other choice. He obviously knew things about her and her family, things she needed to know too. It was at least a small comfort to her that, looking back at her work history with Scottie, he had trusted Paul as well. Scottie would never steer her wrong. So if he said Paul was a good man, she knew it must be true.

She remembered Mr. Patterson's first visit. When Paul was finished and left the office, Maggie asked Scottie about him. "He's originally from New England, Maggie, just like you. He really is a kind old man who just so happened to have ended his wife's life by giving her pills. She was in great pain. He thought he was doing the right thing for her, and maybe he was. Who are we to judge, right Maggie?" Scottie had asked her.

The train trip, or what old shaky Patterson so kindly referred to as the first part of "Maggie's journey" was a true mystery to her. She may live to regret this trip but, hopefully, it would be a life-altering experience. That was a chance she would have to take. She was so very young when her dad died. Maggie had so many questions she needed to ask Patterson, questions that had plagued her for almost four decades.

In some ways she was glad to go with Paul, if indeed he could give her the answers about her past she desperately sought. "How could he know so much about my father?" Maggie wondered over and over again. This one question vexed her. Searching back into the depths of her memories from her youth, she couldn't place anyone that her dad knew by the name of Paul Patterson. She certainly didn't remember him ever coming to the house for a visit. "Maybe he was someone from the Church," Maggie considered. "He's got to be legit. How else could he have known about my pet name Spider?" she reasoned. "But why's he gotta be so damned mysterious?" she wondered.

Maggie told Scottie she needed to go away for a while. She said she'd be gone for two weeks as of Friday, August 31st. Scottie balked a little bit because he usually required at least a week's notice for her vacation leaves, since it took time for the temp agency to adequately replace her during her vacation hiatuses. But this time, Maggie followed Paul's advice and told Scottie that her only daughter, Abbie, desperately needed her mom. After hearing this, Scottie made an exception to his rule. She hardly ever lied to him, so she wondered if he would catch on to her little made up story about her daughter. He bought it. So, on Thursday at 5:00 p.m. on the dot he demanded she leave so that she could get ready for her trip and then handed her an envelope with 200 dollars in it. "Use this any way you need to Maggie. I hope everything is all right with Abbie. Give her my best, will you?"

"Oh, thank you, Scottie. I will," she replied, gathering up her things and heading out the door.

Maggie woke up very early on Friday morning. She set her alarm for 5:00 a.m. "Can't miss the train," she mumbled to herself, looking at her ticket again. It was dated August 31st -Richmond, VA to Durham, CT, train #97. The ticket was for reserved coach on the Silver Meteor, and it was slated to pull into Durham at 3:00 p.m. that same day. Maggie's stomach was a little upset, so she swigged a gulp of Pepto-Bismol, drank the rest of her coffee, took one last good look around her apartment, and then shut and locked her door. She frugally packed one medium sized bag, hoping there would be a laundromat available for her use along her journey. If not, oh well, she'd rinse some things out by hand. She was low maintenance, and if need be, she'd just wear dirty clothes for a day or two. Nothing to worry about; she'd done that more than once in her lifetime.

The train station was jammed packed with every type of person known to mankind. There were short people, fat people, young people, and old people. There were ex-hippies and executives and an occasional freak dressed in all black with hair dyed jet black to match his outfit. Goth was the term Abbie called this look. Glancing around, from Maggie's viewpoint the train station was a virtual feast for visual consumption. She was in her glory. She sat on one of the curved wooden benches, ones she'd guessed had been around since the early 1940's or maybe even before. As people passed her by, she imagined what their lives were like. She could read people pretty well, but if she couldn't figure someone out, she'd just make up a yarn about their life, adding bits and pieces of flavor to her internal imaginary story as she went along. Not that she'd remember any of them! These days Maggie's short-term memory wasn't any longer than a sentence.

Maggie stood in the long lines, which were about four people wide and a hundred people deep. Waiting in line with the other train passengers, she felt a bit like a penguin, waddling back and forth in rhythm with the other penguins as they made their way to the rail cars. Once inside the train she went to the furthest car, the one with the least amount of people in it. She placed her medium sized bag on the metal shelf just above her seat. She hoped no one would sit with her during her long ride but doubted this would be a reality for her, especially when they stopped in Washington and New York.

Once she got situated, she took out her paperback book and placed her ticket in the back between the last page and the cover. Then she turned to the spot where she dog-eared the page and started to read, waiting patiently for the ticket taker to come by. After about fifteen minutes, she spotted the attendant at the front of the car. The ticket taker lady was very short and wore blue tuxedo pants with a shiny strip of darker blue running down the outside of each leg, a white shirt, and a blue matching vest. She had on the usual ticket taker's hat, the one with blue and red stripes that were shaped like a train. Maggie couldn't help but notice this hat held back the most unruly hair she had ever seen. It was long, gray and so wiry it looked as if the hat was hovering on a very large brillo pad. The ticket taker huffed and puffed her way down to Maggie, rolling her eyes and clicking her tongue on the roof of her mouth all the way down the isle, obviously annoyed at having to walk the extra distance down the car. When she got to Maggie she looked at her as if to say, "Go ahead–make my day!" Glaring down at Maggie from her wire rimmed glasses the ticket taker furrowed her brow, which looked like two great big gray furry caterpillars stuck together and glued to her forehead, and then she barked, "Ticket, please."

Maggie looked at her nametag. It read, "Twinkle." "Good God," thought Maggie–"she doesn't look like a Twinkle." Maggie handed her the ticket.

"Sign it!" Twinkle snarled, raising her eyebrows, inviting Maggie to resist her. Twinkle pushed the ticket back into Maggie's half opened hand.

Maggie pulled back a bit and sarcastically thought to herself, "Twinkle, mouth of the south." She wondered what Aunt Clara would say in this situation. It would probably go something like this, "Now Twinkle, honey, when you walk around with a hammer, you look at everything like it's a nail." She contemplated saying this but ultimately decided to keep her big mouth shut and her cynical thoughts to herself, obediently signing the ticket and handing it back to Twinkle, who promptly tore off the stub and nearly flung it back into Maggie's lap. After stuffing the ticket stub in the same spot in her book, she looked up at Twinkle and politely said, "Thank you."

Maggie tried to read her book but found much more enjoyment people watching. Every stop along the way yielded a new set of human wonders. At the stop in Fredericksburg a middle aged woman got on. She was clad in a pair of khaki shorts with a plain black tee shirt, an average outfit, nothing out of the ordinary until you looked down at her legs. Wrapped around each knee was a wide ring of duct tape. It was the kind you could get at any hardware store. Maggie stared at her in disbelief. She had heard duct tape was used as an unconventional method to clear up warts, and she could only imagine what kinds of lumps were hidden underneath that sticky tape.

At another stop, a young mother got on the train, her little son in tow. Maggie guessed he was about five or six years old. Every article of clothing he had on was backwards, except of course his shoes. She could only speculate why he was dressed as he was. "Perhaps a new fashion trend?" she pondered. "Or maybe, just maybe he was a young exhibitionist who ripped off his clothes any chance he got. Denying access to buttons and zippers was probably the only way his mother could be assured he would keep his clothes on," Maggie concluded, proud of her investigative deduction.

The train was starting to fill up. She watched as all the seats were taken by singles or some couples and then by random people asking others, "Do you mind if I sit here?"

"What was someone supposed to say, no?" thought Maggie. Her time would come she knew this. And then she spied him, a 300-pound, plus-sized man walking sideways up the isle. He stopped in front of Maggie and asked the question, "Do you mind if I sit here?"

Maggie looked up from her book. She was pretty sure she would rather have him stick needles into both her eyes. "No, go right ahead," she said, displaying her fake smile.

After the big guy shoved his bag up on the shelf right next to Maggie's, he turned around and made an attempt to sit down, wiggling back and forth to squeeze as much of himself into the seat as possible. She looked out of the window, trying not to stare at him but when all was said and done and she looked back at his very large stomach hanging over the armrests, the first thing that came to mind was a muffin top. Maggie tried to go back to her reading but her curiosity got the best of her and with her peripheral vision she looked him over–top to bottom, trying to be as inconspicuous as possible. From the side view she could tell he was sporting maybe two days worth of hair growth on his very large face and chin. Underneath his stubble were moles and an abundance of pockmarks left over from what she imagined had been either a bad complexion or chicken pox. There were other all kinds of suspicious looking cysts and what not growing underneath the beard as well. "He's got more things growing on him than a sunken ship," Maggie thought.

As her eyes moved downward she spied his feet, what little she could see of them. He was wearing red plastic shoes, the kind with little holes in them. They were held in place by thick red plastic bands that went around the back of each ankle. Underneath his bright red shoes was a pair of bright white ankle length athletic socks. Bits of fat-laden skin oozed through the holes in his shoes and it also hung over the flap in the back, held back ever so slightly by the thick white socks. These made his red shoes appear to have dough rising in them. What on God's green earth would possess a 300-pound man to buy a red pair of plastic shoes and wear them out in public, she would never know. "What are people thinking when they get dressed in the morning?" she ruminated.

Red shoes didn't stay on the train for long, thank God. He got on in DC and got off in New York. For the rest of the trip, Maggie had the whole two seats to herself once again. The nearer she got to Connecticut, the more she started to daydream out the window at the adventure she imagined awaited her at her old stomping ground in Durham. For a moment, Maggie felt a wave of guilt wash over her about staring at all these people and making judgment calls about them. "What would Scottie think?" she questioned silently. "What he doesn't know won't hurt him," she finally concluded.

Looking out the train window at the horizon, the large oak trees swayed back and forth in the cool autumn breeze, boasting just a hint of color change the further north she got. As she looked a little closer to the train tracks, she noticed a series of great big telephone poles placed about twenty feet from the tracks. She watched the never-ending stretches of tall thick wooden beams strategically placed at about fifty foot intervals. Each pole held four thickly braided wires pulled pretty tightly together, and then, as they reached each pole, they appeared to collectively merge. These wires reminded her of thick strings on a cello, vibrating only slightly with each gust of wind as if an excited musician was ever so gently plucking at them. As Maggie closed her eyes, she could only imagine how the high wires might sound.

Maggie looked at her watch when Twinkle bellowed out, "Next stop, Durham, Connecticut." It was 2:55 p.m. She felt a chill go down her spine and goose bumps covered her slightly wrinkled skin.

Standing up, she reached on the shelf above her and retrieved her bag. Then she made her way to the door and waited for the train to stop. As she exited the train, she noticed there were three stairs going down to the platform, an uneven number. She hadn't noticed this when she got on the train. Wrestling with her compulsion, Maggie decided to just grin and bear it. "So three's an uneven number, so what?" she thought. "What the hell," she mumbled and then gave out an ever so slight giggle. She quickly climbed down the three stairs and immediately recognized where she was. Memories of her youth started to flood her brain. It was as if time stood still here in Durham. Not too much had changed really. The train station was just as she remembered and, as she looked over to her right there stood the Dunkin' Donuts on the corner of Main and Trinity.

Maggie had traveled this road more times than she cared to remember. Every day for nearly six years in middle school and high school the bus stopped just before it got to these tracks as it made its way down Federal Hill. As a teen, she remembered looking out at the little train stop where all kinds of white collared men stood waiting to make their daily trip into Hartford to go to work. Her school bus stopped just before it got to the tracks and the driver would put his warning lights on, open the door to the bus, wait for a minute, close the door again, and then be on his way. These were pleasant memories for Maggie, riding on the bus with all her friends talking and giggling, mostly about boys.

She saw him waiting, just as he had promised. The Ford Escape was parked in the little lot right next to the small train station. He sported a big grin on his face. Maggie walked over to the SUV, opened the passenger door and got in. "Is it okay to put this in the back seat?" she asked as she lifted her bag and motioned it over her shoulder.

"That's fine, Maggie. It's so good to see you. I'm so glad you decided to come. If your father were here today, he would be so proud of you," Paul said, his bottom lip quivering slightly as he said the words.

She couldn't tell if he was just shaking like he usually did or if he was on the verge of tears. Either way, Maggie knew she made the right decision as soon as he uttered his greeting. "I'm glad I came too, Paul. By the way, where are we going anyways?"

"I thought we'd go past your old house and then the church where your father worked, take one last good look before we head up to New Hampshire."

"New Hampshire!" Maggie exclaimed. "Why New Hampshire?"

"Patience, patience my dear. Remember this is a journey. The destination really doesn't matter so much as the ride along the way."

"Okay, be that way Paul. Don't tell me why we're going to New Hampshire. See if I care. So, what are you waiting for, Paul Patterson? Let's get a move on, shall we?"

Chapter Thirteen

Case Study #28
Chart Number 5453397
Memorial Veterans Hospital
Newington, CT
March 8, 1965

"Hell of a day down in Alabama yesterday wasn't it, Raines?" Dr. John Sellick looked at Raines point blank as he spoke to him–scanning his young, vibrant and healthy appearance. No large black rings beneath the eyes, telltale signs that the accompanying years of medical school had not yet marked his youthful complexion. Raines always sat in the front row and always right in front of John. He was bright and eager to learn.

"You can say that again Dr. Sellick–wouldn't want to be down there in Alabama today–their ER's probably a nightmare right now," Dr. Cliff Raines replied. "I sure hope they have a good triage center in Selma. I hear they're calling it Bloody Sunday."

"Yeah, not a good time to be an ER doctor I guess. The whole country's going to hell in a hand basket. I don't know which is worse, Vietnam or the civil rights movement. Either way–it means loss of life, which is never good."

Dr. John Sellick turned to face the maze of white coats seated in the upward graduated U shaped auditorium. He couldn't help but think how much they reminded him of little white guppies–swimming in the sea of medical hard knocks. "They won't know what hit them pretty soon," thought Sellick as he perused the crowded room of first year residents. "All these young whippersnappers in first year medical school came here declaring they want to cure cancer or even just the common cold. They're giddy and fresh with enthusiasm, but mostly they're just idealistic and very, very naïve."

"Talk to me in four years," thought Sellick. "Talk to me after you've racked up thousands in debt. After you've experienced endless nights in the ER checking in every nut case and every derelict and drunk scraped off the streets of Connecticut. All those nights that just won't end. Talk to me after you've been on call for thirty-six hours, the whole time standing on your feet. That kind of tired will be unparalleled to anything you've ever experienced, and it might be enough to send you right off the edge. Make a life or death decision under those conditions. But never, ever make a mistake, because doctors are perfect. Just ask anybody in the good old USA or the world for that matter. Then come back to me and tell me what you think. I'll make a wager that all you future lifesavers will want to do is to get out of debt, do your time as physicians, hopefully saving a few lives along the way, but mostly you'll just want to live as normal and comfortable lifestyle as possible."

Thanks to the kindness of the state of Connecticut's generous taxpayers, Memorial Veterans Hospital was an okay place to be right now for Dr. John Sellick. The diagnostic equipment was more than adequate. The nursing staff was plentiful and well educated. The hours weren't bad and he got to teach, which was John's passion. Memorial afforded him ample wages and he was only on call one weekend a month, thanks to an alternating on-call schedule shared between three other very competent colleagues. So all in all, Sellick lived the comfortable lifestyle he had aspired to.

"Let's get started," Dr. Sellick yelled to the group, waving his hands in the air in an effort to quiet them down. Two young gentlemen, lost in their conversation, giggled in the back of the room. Sellick pointed to the young interns, "Care to share with us?"

"Oh, it's nothing, Dr. Sellick," Gary Links replied. "Just a patient I came across yesterday who said something funny."

"By all means, Gary, stand up. Share with the group, let us in on your little secret."

Gary stood red-faced, embarrassed at being put on display by the great Dr. Sellick. "I was doing a medical history on a forty-two year-old black male. I asked him how he was feeling. I asked him if he knew how serious his condition had been. He told me he was feeling pretty sick and he did know his diagnosis must be pretty bad because the doctors had called it the 'sick-as-hell disease.' I told the patient I thought the doctors must have meant 'sickle cell disease.'"

The whole auditorium busted up with laughter and, after a few seconds, Sellick, touting a big smile on his face, held his hand up once again, calling the group to order.

"Great story, Gary. I see why you two were laughing back there. Now lets get started with our case review or we'll never make it to rounds at 9:00 a.m. today."

Dr. Sellick turned on the overhead projector, the newest addition to Memorial Veterans Hospital. In John's opinion this little adjunct piece of equipment was just as vital as any x-ray machine ever made because it allowed him to share information with the whole assemblage of people in that room and all at the same time. No mimeographed handouts necessary. No questioning whether his students were following along. All he had to do was just turn on the light and there it was–the transparency came to life. With pointer in hand and with CASE STUDY #28 in full view, Sellick began:

52 Y.O. white male who was brought by ambulance to Memorial Hospital at approximately 7:30 p.m. on Saturday, February 13th after being found unresponsive at home.

PHYSICIAN ON CALL: Dr. John Sellick
CHIEF COMPLAINT: Overall:
- Loss of appetite
- Weight Loss
- Malaise
- Increased anxiety
- Intermittent dizziness
- Sense of impending doom
- Jitteriness
- Headaches
- Insomnia
- Weakness

HISTORY OF PRESENT ILLNESS: The patient states that over the past month or perhaps longer he has experienced the above-mentioned symptoms. These symptoms have varied in intensity but have had a cumulative effect on his well being and ultimate health. Most recently the patient recalled experiencing a severe bout of dizziness while on the commode. After apparently passing out, his wife heard the noise and came into the bathroom where she found him on the floor, unresponsive to verbal stimuli. She immediately called an ambulance and paramedics came to their home to attend to him. The ambulance arrived at this institution at approximately 7:30 p.m. on Saturday, February 13th.

PAST MEDICAL HISTORY: The patient is a 52-year-old white male who states that he does not routinely go to the doctor unless he feels something is "out of kilter with him." Other than his recent bout with the above-mentioned symptoms, the patient states he has been relatively healthy except for an occasional cold or a rare case of the flu. He denies other past medical history or prior surgeries. He was brought to this institution because of his prior status as Army captain in World War II and also his lack of other medical insurance.

In early January 1965 the minister in the church where this patient works as a janitor referred him to Dr. John Sellick, an attending physician at Memorial. The patient had accidentally slipped and fell on a piece of ice while taking out the trash at the church. The minister, The Reverend Dudley Sessions, is an old friend of Dr. Sellick's. Evaluation at that time revealed a cracked rib and slight pain in his back at T11, T12. The patient refused any workup. Consequently, the extent of his back and chest injuries was not known at this time. During that office visit palpation of the patient's chest revealed one suspected cracked rib. The patient's chest was wrapped tightly to secure the rib, thereby precipitating further healing. The patient did not return for follow-up care.

ALLERGIES: No known drug allergies.

CURRENT MEDICATIONS: Pain medications as prescribed by Dr. Sellick in early January.

PHYSICAL EXAMINATION:

VITAL SIGNS: Blood pressure 130/80 upon admission. Blood pressure spiked to 190/110 within the short period of examination and then quickly returned to baseline. Pulse 80, spiking to 150 at intermittent intervals. Oxygen saturation was 99% on room air. Respirations 18. Temperature 98.8.

GENERAL: The patient is an underweight white male in no acute distress. The patient is alert and oriented to person, place and time. He appears nervous and agitated.

HEENT: Atraumatic, normocephalic. The pupils are equal, round and reactive to light. Extraocular movements are intact.

NECK: Supple with full range of motion. No lymphadenopathy.

CHEST: Nontender.

LUNGS: Clear to auscultation bilaterally.

HEART: Regular rate and rhythm at initial examination, but escalating to tachycardia at approximately 150 bpm when checked again during examination.

ABDOMEN: Soft, nondistended, nontender with normo-active bowel sounds. No masses or organomegaly. No costovertebral angle tenderness.

EXTREMETIES: Unremarkable. Strength 5/5 throughout.

NEUROLOGIC: Anxious and hyper-reflexic throughout. Exaggerated response to both verbal and touch stimuli with an increased response time. "Parkinson like" tremor of the hands and face.

LABORATORY: Complete blood count normal. Urine grew no abnormal bacteria. All other blood and urine tests normal except for elevated serum catacholamines.

FINAL DIAGNOSIS:
1) xxxxxxxxxxxxxxxxxxxxxxxxxxxxx
2) xxxxxxxxxxxxxxxxxxxxxxxxxxxxx

The patient passed away on Friday, March 5. (Physician on call–Dr. John Sellick, covering for Dr. Bruce Gartner, who was on vacation)

After a few minutes Sellick addressed the crowd of interns, "Okay–is everyone done reading this patient's medical assessment?" He looked across the auditorium and saw a sea of nodding heads. "What do you think? Perhaps a more important question would be, why did this patient die? Any takers?"

Raines studied the overhead transparency intensely, until it appeared as though he wanted to slip right into the machine if it would give him any answers. He moved his left hand up and with his long, piano-playing forefinger of his right hand, started twirling the little ringlets of blond hair at the nape of his neck, making them dance with every diagnostic thought he entertained. He was sure of himself, speaking as though he already knew the answer,

"With the strong physical complaints of anxiety, weight loss, nervousness and sleeplessness coupled with an increased level of catecholamines in his blood, I'd put the diagnosis somewhere in the adrenal malady category?" He looked steadily at Dr. Sellick as if to ask for his approval before answering the question.

"Am I right? Is it Addison's disease or maybe a Pheochromocytoma? How about adrenocortical carcinoma? How about Waterhouse-Friderichsen syndrome?"

"Covering all your bases, are you, Raines?" Sellick answered, snickering at Raines' overwhelming enthusiasm. "You're on the right track—good thinkin' Lincoln!"

"You're almost there, Raines. Differential diagnosis is difficult at best because of the lack of laboratory confirmation needed to back up the patient's symptoms. So, with this in mind, I concentrated more on his past medical history and history of present illness."

"But there was very little history to go on wasn't there, Dr. Sellick?" Sickle-Cell Intern piped up from the back row. "The only history you know from him is that he fell on a piece of ice and broke a rib this past January. Did the rib puncture his adrenal gland, sir?"

"Bingo minus the go! You're almost right Gary! Any other takers?" Sellick looked around guppyville at all the bewildered faces. "Keep in mind that this patient was brought here because he was an ex-Army captain. Upon further investigation and explanation of his stint in the Armed Forces, the patient revealed that he was on the front lines during most of his time in the Army. He also revealed that he did in fact come in contact with an explosion in which his good friend standing next to him was 'blown to smithereens,' while the patient only received three relatively small pieces of shrapnel in his lower back. Army physicians had deemed it safe to leave the shrapnel in his lower back because there was virtually no threat of it ever moving and/or puncturing a vital organ."

Sellick paced back and forth as he informed the crowd of his findings. He had a habit of putting one hand in back of him as he walked. In the other hand he held a metal pointer, which he used to point things out on the overhead projector with. He waved the pointer around while he walked, much like a conductor would do when leading his orchestra.

"So, after I found out about his combat history, I did some investigating on my own. I researched his medical history in the Army archives. The x-rays taken at the time of this accident revealed three pieces of shrapnel at approximately T11/T12."

"Remember also that because this patient had fallen in January he most likely ruptured T11/T12–the two discs closest to the adrenal glands and also to the shrapnel. My guess is that when the discs ruptured and swelled, the adjacent shrapnel moved closer to the adrenal glands. This little fact was enough to prompt me to get an x-ray of his lower back and spine," Sellick held the set of x-rays he had obtained from the Army alongside the ones he had just taken of Eddy's chest, abdomen, lower back, and spine. "You can see from the current x-rays how the shrapnel has been moved, due to the rupture of his discs at T11/T12."

Sellick continued, "The shrapnel caused irritation of the adrenal glands at varying intervals unknown to the patient or this physician. My best guess is that the irritation occurred when the patient moved. And of course he moved a lot, especially at work. As you know, the occupation of church janitor typically necessitates a good deal of physical exertion throughout the day. This patient's day involved mopping floors, cleaning banisters, stairs, and bathrooms. He had a very strenuous job. When the patient moved, especially when he did a lot of bending and twisting, the shrapnel that was wedged in his back pressed against his adrenal glands and caused them to release various kinds of catecholamines such as epinephrine (adrenaline), norepinephrine (noradrenaline), and dopamine. All these stimulants led to his current health status and symptoms. This cause and effect process was directly linked to the patient's subsequent intermittent symptoms of nervousness, weight loss, and increased blood pressure and heart rate. So, essentially, he was in a near constant state of 'fight or flight' mode."

"That being said, Dr. Sellick, this doesn't seem like it would be enough to kill him—right? He was in good physical health with no known or suspected chronic diseases," Gary added.

"Bingo again, Gary! Although the patient was weak and emaciated, his heart was still strong and he had not yet suffered the debilitating effects of over exposure to adrenaline in the short time frame that he had ruptured T11 and T12."

"What did kill him then, sir?" Gary piped up and asked, looking around the room at all the other puzzled faces, knowing full well that everyone wanted to ask that same question.

"A back rub, Gary. A back rub killed this patient."

"What?"

"You heard me, it was a back rub," Sellick exclaimed with some excitement in his voice. He couldn't wait to deliver this bit of news. He knew these gullible students would be shocked beyond belief. He knew the news would blow their minds.

"On the evening of March 5, the nurse on duty entered the patient's room. Hearing him complain of persistent back pain, and thinking that it was the result of him lying in bed for long periods of time, the nurse offered the patient a 'back rub.' She pressed deep in the underlying tissues of his dorsal spine. This deep tissue manipulation ultimately was sufficient enough to move one of the pieces of shrapnel so that it punctured his renal vein. Because the puncture was relatively small, and because the patient was given a strong sedative at approximately the same time as his back rub, he was virtually unable to feel any pain that would have been associated with internal bleeding. So, while the patient slept, slowly but surely over the course of the night or earlier (time of death unknown), he eventually perished due to internal exanguination."

Gary's hand shot up again. "Was the nurse ever charged with anything, Dr. Sellick? Negligence? Murder?"

"No, Gary. She was devastated when she found out he was dead. And it didn't help that he's left behind a wife and three young daughters. I think his wife's name is Emily, if I'm not mistaken. Pavoti felt so bad about the whole thing that she put in her resignation today. Nurse Patterson, as of two weeks from today, will no longer be working at Memorial Veterans Hospital. Her husband Paul who works in our laboratory, quit as well. This morning Pavati told me she and Paul were moving to New Hampshire to live on a farm that's been in her family for years. It's a shame really, because she's such a good nurse and her husband is very competent at his job as well. It will be a loss for this entire institution, that's for sure."

Part Two

August 31, 2007

Chapter Fourteen

The Ford Escape climbed slowly up Federal Hill, took a right just before St. John's Episcopal Church and headed straight toward Maggie's childhood home. As they made their way up the hill, Paul asked Maggie how her train ride had been. "Good," she replied with a slight smirk on her face. She proceeded to go into great detail about all the people she had encountered on the rails. She told Paul about Mrs. Duck Tape knees, backward boy, and Rudolph shoes. He got the biggest kick out of her, chuckling with each story she laid out in front of him. Maggie watched Paul's reaction as she told him about her big train adventure. To her surprise, she was having a good time too.

"Did you see any communists?" Paul asked.

Maggie raised her eyebrows and turned to look at Paul, "Did my father ask you to say that too?" she questioned.

Maggie smiled, "Oh yeah, now I remember. I was such a dork."

Driving down the street, Maggie looked at all the old two family houses. This was where most of her childhood memories had been made. This was where she grew up, and for reasons beyond her control she had needed to grow up long before she should have. Everything looked so different now, so unimportant, and so very, very small. Almost every house on Foley Street was in disrepair. Each home looked weathered and worn, each one leaning a different way. 78 Foley Street, Maggie's old house, had had the front porch replaced. The railings on the new porch were straight and painted bright white, but the rest of the house appeared to be bending forward, sinking into the slight curvature in the hill. There was a row of maple trees across the back of the house so that, from the front of that old house, the tops of the trees gave the illusion they were resting on the roof. The house looked like an old wrinkled face with bright shiny new dentures and a receding leafy hairline. The driveway had long shoots of grass growing up between uneven cracks. And to Maggie the house appeared so much more insignificant than she remembered as a child. Growing up, and being short to boot, she would often look up at her bedroom window and think, "My house looks as big as a mansion." But now it appeared so very, very small to her.

Paul and Maggie parked right in front of her old house and stared at it for a while. Maggie pointed at a single door that sat all alone on the side of the house directly in the middle and on the first floor of course. She giggled. "Paul, see that door on the side of the house?" she asked.

"Yeah, what about it?"

"That's where the most embarrassing thing in my life happened to me," she answered chuckling out loud.

"Must not be too important now 'cause you're laughing about it."

"It was at the time. Hey, I was a teenager. Everything's embarrassing when you're a teenager. But this was especially embarrassing." Maggie admitted. "So, of course you know it's a two family house right?"

"Duh...sure I know. My eyesight's not completely gone yet."

"Oh, stupid question, right?" Maggie was surprised to hear Paul's reaction. Maybe he wasn't so serious after all. Maybe this trip would be mysterious and fun at the same time.

"Right!"

"So, my grandmother lived downstairs and my family lived upstairs. When you open up that side door," she explained, pointing again to the door in the middle of the faded old green house, "there's a couple of stairs and then there's a flat wooden landing about five feet wide by six feet deep. At the landing was the door that went into my grandmother's house. If you turned a little to your right when you're standing on that landing, you could take another set of longer stairs to the upstairs where my family lived."

"I got the picture."

"One night when I was about fifteen or so, my boyfriend came over. We hung out upstairs in my living room for a while, and when it was time for him to go home, he walked me down our stairs and we stood on the landing. I guess you could say we were making out. We were only there for a couple of minutes, and my grandmother must have heard something. She lived alone downstairs. My boyfriend and I could hear her jiggling the doorknob so we stopped kissing and looked at the door. When she opened it, there she stood in all her glory, completely naked. I swear to God, Paul, she didn't have a stitch of clothes on. Have you ever seen a seventy-two year old, heavy-set woman with size fifty-two breasts? Well there they were, the two breasts that had fed all six of her children just dangling free for the entire world to see. And, believe me, her children ate well as babies, I can assure you."

"What did you do?" Paul asked, laughing openly at her awkward story.

"I didn't do anything, Paul. I couldn't move I was so shocked."

"What did he do?"

"He did what any respectable boyfriend would do, he ran. Needless to say, we never went out again, and we never ever talked about that incident either. But I'm sure he told his friends about it because after that happened, the next day in school I could see a couple of them look at me out of the corner of my eye as I walked past, pointing their fingers and laughing."

"I guess things could have been worse right, Maggie?" Paul asked, trying to downplay the whole situation.

"How much worse could they have gotten, Paul? Tell me, how much worse?" Maggie laughed, even as she scolded him.

"Point taken, Maggie. I'm sure that must've been humiliating for you."

"Yeah, ya think?"

They both took one last good look at the old house before driving off. "Now say goodbye to 78 Foley Street. Next stop, St. John's Episcopal Church," Paul said, still chuckling.

Maggie stared at the old house with the brand new front porch. She felt such a mix of sweet and sour emotions. She held her hand to the window, pressed against the glass and whispered, "Goodbye old house."

"Can we just park in the parking lot for a while, Paul?" Maggie asked as they approached the old church. She took her cigarettes out of her purse and held them up for Paul to see. Maggie was having some serious nicotine withdrawal. She was in desperate need of her two cigarettes.

"You should quit those things, Maggie," Paul reprimanded. "They'll kill you."

"Yeah, well a lot of things could kill you. Just walking across the street could kill you."

"I know but that would be an accident, not self-induced," he said in a firm, fatherly tone.

"Okay, okay. I'll just have one." As she said this a title wave of panic hit her full force. "I mean I should have two, since we probably won't be stopping for a while," Maggie offered, knowing full well that one was an uneven number, and that fact alone would probably bother her more than any nicotine withdrawal she could feel during her travels up to New Hampshire.

"Why don't you just have one for now, Maggie? We can stop again if you want to smoke some more. We can stop again if you want another *one*, okay?"

"Okay then, I'll just try to have one cigarette and see how it goes." Maggie was a little irked. First this guy tells her that she's got some big journey to go on through her past, then he tells her not to smoke so much. Where does he get off? But he did have a point, she conceded. Those cigarettes were straight up cancer sticks, or at least that was what Aunt Clara liked to call them.

Paul and Maggie pulled into one of the empty spaces in the side parking lot near the vestibule. The archaic stone silhouette of the church rimmed their left sided view but looking out to the right, parts of Federal Hill became visible along with a great view of the newer section of town in the valley down below. "It's beautiful isn't it, Maggie?"

"Yes it is," she said as she stepped out of the car and lit up her cigarette. The smell of leaves burning permeated the air. This was a longstanding tradition in New England, the burning of leaves in the fall. The ritual took place in one's own back yard and it brought Maggie back to her youth immediately. She thought of her father and mother raking up what seemed to be mountains of leaves, putting them in one massive pile in the far corner of their backyard and then setting fire to them. "This is quite a blast from the past," she added, closing her eyes and breathing in the sweet smell of smoldering maple and oak.

"Indeed, a blast from the past." Paul got out of the car too. He stood right next to Maggie. "Do you remember when your father worked here?" he asked, pointing to the large stone church.

"Vaguely. I was young, very young," Maggie answered, drawing a big puff of cigarette smoke into her lungs.

"You remember that Christmas Eve, don't you?" Paul asked as nonchalantly as he could.

This caught her off guard, and she choked a bit as she exhaled the smoke from her lungs. "What Christmas Eve?" she asked innocently.

"Come on now, Maggie. It's quite all right. You're safe with me. Always remember one thing, I know pretty much everything about your father, his family and especially this church. Your father had my ear for quite some time."

"And when was that, Paul?" Maggie asked, staring at him sideways and cocking her head while she took another drag from her cigarette. "I've taken this whole leap of faith trip not knowing a thing about you or my father's so-called last wish. And why is it just me that needs to take this journey? Why aren't my sisters included on this excursion? What makes me so special, Paul? And why, in Christ's holy name, now? After more than forty years, why now? I'm fifty-eight years old. Why now?"

"Well, to answer your first question, let's just put it this way, although I knew almost everything there was to know about your father's life, the timing of our friendship isn't relevant. What is relevant is your age. You are just a little older than your father was when he moved on. His request was to have you take your journey at about the same age that he took his journey. I know you're not the exact age as your father was, but close enough. Don't you see, Maggie, your journey *is* his journey? And you may ask, 'why me?' The answer to that is simply; you need this trip. You need answers. Linda and Jill do not."

"You're scaring me, Paul. You even know my sisters' names, don't you? Does this mean my father wanted me to die on this journey? Tell me again, Paul, how did you know my father so well? Tell me how?" Maggie asked, terrified. This guy was really creeping her out now. Maggie wanted answers so badly that she'd convinced herself to go on this "journey," but now all she could think of was the cold can of mace in the bottom of her purse. She had never used mace before, but there was always a first time for everything.

Paul could see the fear in Maggie's eyes. "No need to be scared. I didn't mean to put a damper on your mood. I'm sorry, Maggie, really I am. I wish I could fill you in on all the details of your father and my relationship right now, but I just can't. I can assure you that the furthest thing from your father's mind was to have you die on this journey. In fact your father wanted you to live your life to the fullest and he felt this adventure you are taking right now would be an opportunity for you to do just that, live. I can't tell you everything all at once. Actually this was your father's request. "Just give her a little bit at a time—don't overwhelm her," were your father's exact words. He said you'd be stubborn. He knew what you'd be like on this trip. He knew you well." Paul reached into his pocket and took out a crumpled envelope. He opened it and pulled out the small piece of paper, a handwritten note from Eddy. He handed it to Maggie.

"Did my father really write this, Paul?"

"Yes he did, before he died."

Maggie accepted the paper hesitantly. The handwritten note said:

My Dearest Maggie,
What a brave soul you are for taking this trip even before you knew that much about it. Somehow I knew you'd be adventurous enough to accept Paul's offer though. You always were a pistol! Forgive me for not getting in touch with you earlier, but you'll understand soon enough why I couldn't. I know it's hard, but please try not to be so stubborn. All things will become clear soon enough. I know you don't understand yet but for many reasons—even for your own safety—none of this could have been revealed to you at an earlier time. Love, Dad.

"Wow, Paul. My father really wrote this, huh? I guess he really did know me, even though I was young when he died." Maggie looked longingly at the note. She touched the paper gently. She wished with all her might that her father was standing in front of her telling her this in person instead of her having to read his words from a crummy piece of paper.

Paul inched his way closer to Maggie, put his hand on her shoulder and kindly asked, "What I originally meant to ask you before is, 'Do you remember the last Christmas Eve you spent with him?'"

"Well, I don't really have a choice about you revealing things to me now do I, Paul? If you say I'll be told, I guess I'll be told. If my father said I'd be told, I guess I'll be told. But I still don't understand what all this mystery is about. And I don't really remember too much of anything from that Christmas Eve. Just that I lost my diary," she answered carefully.

"Where did you lose it, Maggie?"

Maggie thought for a minute before answering, "I don't know."

"Are you sure you don't remember?"

"Yes, Paul, quite sure."

"Do you remember your last entry?"

"I was sixteen. How am I supposed to remember my last entry into a diary from when I was sixteen?"

"Try."

"I don't know," she answered frustrated. "I don't remember! Since you know everything, why don't you tell me?"

"You don't remember, or you were told not to remember?" Paul questioned. "I do know what the last entry was, as a matter of fact."

"You do?" Maggie inquired, staring at Paul, her eyes pleading with him to tell her, although she already knew the answer. She wanted to hear it and then she didn't want to hear it, wanted to hear it and didn't. She felt a bit like the pushmi-pullyu character in *Dr. Doolittle*.

Finally, holding her hands over her ears, one hand still holding the half smoked cigarette, she screamed at Paul, "No. Don't tell me!"

"I don't have to tell you. You already know, don't you?"

"So what if I do?" she answered sarcastically.

"It's okay, Maggie. You're safe with me, remember?"

"But how do I really know that?"

"Trust me. Just trust me. Let go of all the memories that are covering up the truth and just trust me, won't you?"

"Okay. I do remember. It was something about the church, right?"

"Yes. It was something about being at the church that Christmas Eve to be exact."

"I remember." I also remember my dad saying to me on the way home from the church that same night, "Don't tell anyone you were at the church tonight. Do you understand, Maggie? Promise me, okay? I promised him Paul. I promised him with my Girl Scout promise hand."

"I know. I know," Paul answered sympathetically, nodding his head.

"That's why it's bothered me all these years about my diary. I promised not to tell anyone but I wrote it in my diary. I never told my dad. I never told him that," Maggie answered, tears in her eyes.

"He knew you wrote it down in your diary. He saw you writing it down when he was working on the furnace. You were sitting on the cot and had your back to him remember? He looked over your shoulder and read your first couple of lines."

"I've always thought that's why my dad died. It was because of that stupid diary. But I never knew why. I think it was because he got sick and died right after that, so I could never figure it all out. Not only that, I knew he didn't want anyone to know about us going to the church that night. But I wrote it in my diary anyways, and then I lost it. I was worried someone would find it and then our secret would be out. You know, Paul?"

"I know. Well, I can tell you one thing, Maggie. Your diary never killed your father, you can be assured of that."

"I think I knew that deep down inside. But I could never understand why it was such a big secret."

"Do you remember what was in the news that Christmas?"

"Sort of."

"Do you remember what happened at this church?" Paul asked, pointing his finger at the large stone structure, the one that held so many secrets.

"Sort of," Maggie answered, pretending she hadn't remembered.

"The two policemen who were killed? Do you remember that?"

"Yeah, I do."

"Do you think that's why your father didn't want you to tell anyone you were there that night?"

"I thought about that. He probably didn't want anyone to think we had something to do with it, since we were there the night before they were murdered."

"Is that what you think? You think they were murdered on Christmas day?"

"Yes, weren't they?"

"No, Maggie, they weren't."

Maggie felt confused, frustrated. She didn't want to listen to Paul anymore, be at the mercy of him doling out information. She wanted to find things out for herself.

"I want you to look on that stupid map of yours and tell me where the closest library is. I want to go look up these murders for myself. There's still got to be a lot of information out there like old newspaper articles, something, anything."

"Suit yourself Maggie." Paul fumbled with his map, trying to read the symbols on the colorful paper to see where the Durham library was located.

"Oh, forget it, Paul, I know where it is. I used to live here, remember? She pointed left and said, "Go down this street about a half a mile, turn right and go up the hill. It's not far." She was obviously annoyed.

"Okay. Will do, Maggie." Paul agreed obediently.

"I'm starting to think you brought me on this trip to torment me, tell me lies."

"That wasn't your father's intention. And I certainly don't want to make you feel bad. He just wanted you to know the truth."

"And what is the truth, Paul? Tell me, what is the truth?"

August 31, 2007

Chapter Fifteen

"Yes, well the truth isn't always so blatant and one dimensional," Paul responded, testing her level of tolerance for his avoidant behavior. All he had to do was stall her for a little while. Even though she gave him specific directions to the library, he decided to make his own way there, taking the most roundabout way possible, heading down streets he knew would take much longer than the route she explained to him. He didn't want her to start putting the pieces together quite yet, not before he got a chance to explain a little bit more about her father, Eddy Payne. He wanted her to know the real man, not the violent act Eddy committed that Christmas Eve so very long ago.

"You are just like your father. Do you know that, Maggie? Just like him."

"In what way?" she answered, still irritated.

"In a lot of ways."

"Go ahead tell me some of them. Enlighten me," Maggie said sarcastically. She put her cigarette out and desperately wanted to light up another one but resisted the intense urge. Instead she turned around, walked a couple of feet back and started to get in the car. Paul followed her lead, slipping behind the wheel of the Ford Escape once again. "What kind of boondoggle trip is this anyways?" Maggie asked.

"I like that word, boondoggle. It sounds funny." Paul tried to lift her darkening mood and also change the subject. "Your dad was like you in so many ways, really. He was a little apprehensive of strangers, often judging them sooner than he should have. But if he got to know you and liked you, well, you were his friend forever. Sound familiar?"

"Just a bit," she returned, giving an ever so slight hint of a smile when she thought back to not more than an hour before on her most recent excursion, the train ride to Connecticut. And, since she knew and loved most of Scottie's patients, the latter part of Paul's statement was true too. Maggie was and always would be dedicated to the well being of all of Scottie's patients. Plus there was Abbie. She was incredibly proud of her darling daughter and would do anything in the world for her. "The apple doesn't fall far from the tree does it?" Maggie asked, boasting a proud Payne smile.

"Nope, it doesn't."

"So I guess I have no choice but to be the passenger here, right Paul?

"Sit back and enjoy the ride, Maggie. Now let's talk about your old man again, shall we?"

"Okay. I really do want to know more about him. What else can you tell me?" Just then Maggie realized that Paul wasn't following the directions she gave him, the ones to the library. "Hey Paul, this isn't the way to the library. Where are you going?"

"Oops. Made a wrong turn. Don't worry I'll circle myself around this way," he said pointing down another street. While Maggie was busy telling him her directions, he had already looked on the map and figured out an alternate route, a much longer alternate route.

"I'll get us there don't fret. Now, where were we? Oh yeah, back to your dad. What else do you want to know about him? How about we start with his physical characteristics? Do you remember what he looked like?"

"He had jet black hair, green eyes and olive colored skin."

"Do you remember how tall he was?"

"Yes, he was very tall."

"He was five feet, six inches tall," Paul shot back, emphasizing the six inch part.

"That's not very tall at all," Maggie answered, surprised. She looked down at her short little legs and then thought about her five-foot tall mother. "I didn't have a snowball's chance in hell at being taller, did I?"

"I'm afraid you didn't," Paul offered, laughing openly. The Ford Escape roared loudly as it made its way up the hill, but neither one could hear it over their loud giggling. He looked over at the fifty-eight-year-old woman sitting next to him and wondered where all the years had gone. How fast they melted away from decade to decade.

"What else can you tell me about him?"

"He was in the Army. Did you know that?"

"Yeah, I kind of remember. He used to show my sisters and me the scars on his back from where he was wounded."

"Shrapnel wounds."

"Is that what it was? I never really knew. I thought he got shot. He didn't talk about it too much, at least not to my sisters or me. He talked about all his buddies in the Army, all the stuff they used to do. It sounded like they had fun sometimes, but basically I think the Army was hard for him. Well, not hard so much as I don't think he was the kind of man to hurt anyone else. He was gentle, Paul, very gentle."

"Yep, that was Eddy. He was such a gentle soul, not a huge talker either, but when he did say something it was exactly what he wanted to say, straight from his heart to his lips. I think I know someone who's sitting right next to me who's a bit like that, don't you?"

"Very funny. Go on, tell me more."

"Did you know he earned the Bronze Star? It's a medal that's awarded to someone who enlisted in the Army after December 6, 1941 and who served in World War II. And it's given to a distinguished member of the armed forces who was involved in a heroic act against the enemy. Did you know he was stationed in Morocco and Tunisia?"

"I think I heard him say something about Africa, but I had no idea about the Bronze Star thing," Maggie answered intrigued. "Tell me more." She fastened her seat belt as Paul proceeded to maneuver his way around Durham in search of the local library. By this time Maggie was so consumed with both the stories of her dad and finding the library, she had forgotten all about missing that second cigarette, the one that would make things even.

"He also received a Good Conduct Medal, the American Defense Service Medal, and the European-African-Middle Eastern Service Medal. But the Bronze Star was his most prized possession. I'll go into detail about how he got it in a minute. First let me fill you in on the particulars of where he was stationed. Humid as hell it was over there in Morocco, even in November. That was something your father had to get used to right away. The weather wasn't like that in Connecticut was it, Maggie?"

"Not in Connecticut, but it sure is in Virginia sometimes."

"I can vouch for that, Maggie. Sometimes it's so humid in Virginia I can sit on my little deck and almost watch the mold grow on it. Anyways, to get on with my story, Eisenhower himself was ordered to take command of the North African Campaign invasion, so in November of 1942, Army technicians modified commercial vessels to serve as landing ships and Army infantry troops were ordered to put down along the Atlantic coast of French Morocco, near Casablanca. When your father's ship landed, it was driven away from the mouth of the Sebou River by heavy shelling. The landing boat finally beached at Mehdia Plage. His battalion fought along the coast for a month or two before making their way into Tunisia. Troops had to get adjusted to operating their equipment far inland on the African continent. American soldiers found the terrain much different from what they were used to in Morocco and Algeria."

Paul went on, "Tunisia was some 400 miles east of Algiers, a much smaller area than they were accustomed to, stretching only 160 miles from east to west and 500 miles from north to south. Hills and mountains that soldiers were used to in the north had leveled to large sandy stretches in the south, the northern part of the Sahara Desert. The northern coast of Tunisia, most accessible to the Axis, was where most of the combat took place."

"I don't think I've ever been to a place like that before. It sounds like it was hard to navigate both on foot and with tanks," she interrupted.

"You're right about that, Maggie. It doesn't sound like fun does it? Plus, there were times when torrential rains turned the countryside into quagmires, making it even more difficult to navigate. Your father was a trooper though, strong and courageous and dedicated to the point of compulsion to his regiment, the 50th Infantry, 10th Infantry Division."

"I really wish I had gotten a chance to know my father better now. I bet he was quite a man, huh?"

"Yes, he was, quite a man. He was brave beyond measure."

Maggie looked over at Paul, her eyes moist with tears, "So tell me, how did he earn the Bronze Star?"

"It was April 21, 1943. He was deep in the Tunisia interior. Both German and Italian troops were poised and on the ready for incoming Americans to traipse on by. On Hill 610 Eddy's regiment encountered the enemy. As they approached the hill, Eddy watched his friend, Billy Roscoe, take the brunt of a grenade. Billy was so badly injured Eddy couldn't even make out who it was after the blast had gone off. Poor Billy's body was mutilated beyond recognition; his arms and legs had been blown clear off his body. The only blessing was that Billy didn't even know what hit him. But Eddy was marching behind Billy, and he was wounded in that blast too. He heard the blast go off and tried to turn around to get out of its way, but when he did, he took some shrapnel in his back. He didn't pay too much attention to his injuries though. He was more concerned about his friend Billy.

He was so mad when he saw what they had done to poor Billy that your father fought back, war wounds and all. He crawled on his belly around to the perimeter of where the battle was and, with complete disregard for his own safety, with his bayonette clutched in his hands, he snuck up on the German machine gunners that were entrenched in their firing dugout. They were both dead before they knew what hit 'em. He did this to three other dugouts. His courage and aggressiveness gave his regiment the offensive tactics needed to defeat the enemy."

"He was so brave. He was humble too, wasn't he? Because he never went around boasting about his medals from the war."

"He wasn't proud of killing people but he knew that if he didn't get rid of those gunners, it would jeopardize his whole regiment. So he did what he needed to do to keep everyone safe."

"He was quite a man. Thanks for telling me about his war days, Paul. That means so much to me," Maggie said, leaning over and resting her head slightly on Paul's shoulder. Maggie's angry mood had lifted a little, but it was soon replaced with sadness at the realization of what she had lost so many years ago, the chance to get to know her father better. Although she was grateful for all her newfound knowledge, there were times during this trip that she felt as though she were on an emotional roller coaster ride, happy and laughing one minute and sad and crying the next. She looked down at Paul's hands that were gripped tightly to the steering wheel. They were bony, thin-skinned, and dotted with darkly pigmented age spots. Probably the way her father's hands would look if he were alive.

"You are very welcome, Maggie, very welcome indeed. I just wish the civilian world would give medals to heroic people for their acts of courage instead of punishing them for doing the right thing."

"How do you mean?"

"Never mind, I'll tell you later, Maggie." Paul and Maggie had reached the library now.

Maggie asked him to wait in the car for her while she went in to do some research. She made her way through the huge wooden doors of the old library and into the back room, the room with the microfilm machines in it. Scrolling down on the microfilm she searched for newspapers from around the time of Christmas, 1964. Lo and behold there it was, the article about the two murdered policemen. Maggie asked the librarian if there was any way she could print it out to take with her. She felt better after she had the physical copy of it in her hands. She began to read. There it was, right there in black and white.

TWO MURDERED POLICEMEN FOUND DEAD IN THE BASEMENT OF ST. JOHNS EPISCOPAL CHURCH

Although there are several leads, no suspects have been implicated in the murders yet. Law enforcement officials confirmed the murders were committed sometime on Christmas Eve..........

"Maybe all that Paul is trying to tell me really is for a purpose," she thought. It looked like there was a lot more to her past than she had previously cared to admit.

August 31, 2007

Chapter Sixteen

Maggie read and reread the photocopy of the article but didn't say a word until she and Paul were about an hour into their trip then she piped up and said, "I'm gonna need a drink after reading this. You know that, don't you?"

"I kind of figured you'd need a little bourbon. It's a lot to take in all at once, I know."

"So these two cops were killed on Christmas Eve, right? Just about the same time as when my dad and I were up at the church, correct?"

"Yes, that's correct."

"Why haven't I seen this article before? Shouldn't I have seen it? Wouldn't it have been in our house? We got the paper every day back then. I remember because sometimes I'd have to do stuff for school that had to do with current events, and I'd have to look in the paper."

"Like I said, Maggie, your mother and father went to great lengths to hide all the newspapers that had articles about these murdered policemen. For weeks after the murders, your father would take all the morning newspapers to work and burn them in the incinerator at the church."

"So does this mean my dad knew something about the murders? Did he have something to do with them? I remember going up to the church that night and lying on the cot next to the boiler while my dad tried to fix that stupid thing. It was dirty and grimy and he was swearing the whole time at it. I must have fallen asleep because the next thing I remembered was waking up and my dad was gone. I called out to him, and it was a while before he answered. He told me to stay were I was because he was taking a shower. I was kind of used to him saying that to my sisters and me whenever he took a shower at home too. Poor guy. It must've been hard to live in a house full of women. I guess he needed a shower because he had gotten filthy working on the boiler. I never really thought anything of it that night either, so I stayed put on that cot until he came back to the furnace."

"Yes, that's correct. All of that is just as you remembered. There's just one thing missing."

"What's missing, Paul? Tell me. What's missing?" Maggie asked in a panic.

They hadn't gotten very far along the interstate when Paul announced that he needed to take a break already. "I'll tell you in just a bit, Maggie. First let's stop and get something to eat and drink." I'm famished and tired. I'm not as young as I used to be, don't have the stamina to drive very far. Plus, we have a big day of driving ahead of us tomorrow. You must be exhausted too."

"I must admit I'm pretty tired too." In some ways Maggie was glad for the change of subject. She wanted to know about that Christmas Eve way back in 1964 but, then again, she didn't want to know, all at the same time.

"I've also reserved a hotel room for us right around the corner, just outside of Mystic, courtesy of your father. After we eat and have a couple of drinks to calm your nerves, we'll talk more about that night."

"But you can't tell me now, right Paul?" Maggie pushed, still halfway wanting to know about that infamous night which had become more of a blur to her than a reality.

"Believe me, you'll need a couple of drinks in you for that story. Trust me. Let's just enjoy our dinner, and we'll talk later, okay?"

"If you say so," Maggie answered reluctantly.

They stopped at a little restaurant right off the highway, a place called Catch of the Day Seafood. It was a quaint restaurant, specializing in local seafood caught mainly in and around the Mystic area. "Your father loved seafood. Did you know that, Maggie?"

"Can't say as I did. My mother never cooked much seafood because it was kind of expensive. We never went out to eat much either, again, too expensive."

"Well, he did love it, especially trout. Was your mother a good cook?" Paul asked inquisitively.

"Not really. She just cooked the basics like meat and potatoes, nothing fancy at all. She made great chocolate chip cookies though. Except they never made it to the plate because my sisters and I would eat them straight from the cookie sheet, every last one of them. She could hardly keep up with us."

Maggie thought about her own cooking skills. She wondered what Abbie would say was her mother's most famous dish. Maggie was not a good cook at all, an unfortunate skill or lack thereof she had inherited from her own mother. In fact, if you asked Abbie, she'd probably tell you the things her mother cooked were either severely underdone or burnt. Abbie was lucky to have survived her childhood without a bout or two of salmonella or E. coli.

A smile came to Maggie's face as she thought about the time Abbie went over her friend's house for dinner. When she came home, she said to Maggie, "Allison's mom cooked dinner and the smoke alarm went off in her kitchen. I thought it was time to eat when it went off, mom. You know that's like the dinner bell for us around here." Hearing her daughter tell that story made Maggie chuckle to herself. In fact, that story became their running joke. After that episode whenever Maggie yelled, "dinner's ready," Abbie would answer, "Is it time to eat? I haven't heard the smoke alarm go off yet," then they would both laugh hysterically.

"I'll have a Jack Daniels on the rocks," Paul said to the waitress after he and Maggie were seated right next to the big plate glass window facing the river. "And one for the lady too," he added.

"Thanks, Paul. Make that a double," she said looking up at the waitress and raising her eyebrows in an expression of need rather than want.

In memory of Maggie's dad, both she and Paul ordered the trout. It was delicious just as he had predicted. "This might become my favorite dish too," she said in between mouthfuls. After they finished their meal and paid their bill, Paul suggested going straight to the hotel to talk.

"Whose room?" she asked innocently.

"I've booked us a suite, Maggie. Two bedrooms. It's like a little apartment with a kitchenette, couch, a couple of chairs, and a TV."

A look of concern emerged on her face. "You aren't planning to try anything funny are you?"

Paul smiled, "I'm flattered, Maggie. Obviously you haven't noticed that I'm just about as old as dirt. Fact is, I couldn't do anything even if I wanted to. Damned doctors got me on so many medications it'd be a medical enigma if I even thought about sex again. Plus, I would never even consider that with you. I'm here carrying out your father's wish, remember? But really, this is your journey. I'm just the messenger."

"A girl can never be too careful, you know."

"Believe me, I know," Paul answered, his tone of voice resonating a profound sadness. Trying to ease his own foreboding gloom, he joked with Maggie, "It's not that I haven't been hit on in the recent past mind you. I've seen a couple of 'mature' ladies look my way with longing in their eyes. You know what they say, the older the berry, the sweeter the fruit."

"Funny, Paul, very funny." Maggie couldn't remember the last time she was hit on. But, then again, even if a man did look her way, she'd probably say something rude or sarcastic to squash any romantic notions he had. She might even clobber him if he tried anything funny. She hadn't had too much luck with men in her life and she was pretty sure, journey or no journey, that part of her life would never change.

Paul checked into the hotel while Maggie waited in the car for him, room 310 with a balcony view overlooking the Mystic River. After they settled into their separate bedrooms, they met again in the main living area. "Will you go out to the balcony with me, Maggie? It's such a beautiful night and it would be grand to be able to look out at the water. The water always brings back good memories of my Pavoti."

"Okay," she agreed apprehensively. She was afraid of what he would say about the murders. Dark thoughts had weighed heavy on her mind all evening, but she could no longer push them away.

Paul had a bottle of Jack Daniels in one hand. Stepping into the kitchenette, he grabbed two glasses, filled them with ice and headed toward the balcony. Maggie took the two ice-filled glasses from his hand and said, "Here, let me help." She put them down on a small round table on the balcony. Pouring them each a drink, Paul sat down slowly on one of the wrought iron chairs. With a single thin cushion between the chair and Paul's bony rump, the metal chairs didn't provide much relief for his aching back and thin-skinned spindly legs.

After they sat for a while, watching the waves lap up against the rocky coast, Paul finally broke the awkward silence, "Want to hear the rest of the story now?"

"Yes, please tell me the truth," Maggie whispered, taking a big gulp of her drink, looking desperately at Paul and then pointing to the empty glass.

As he filled up her glass, Paul began to tell the story about what really happened that night in 1964.

Maggie listened carefully in disbelief as old shaky Paul told her all the details of how her father had murdered those men. He didn't leave out a thing. And, as the alcohol mixed with the truth, she listened and learned of the monstrous act her father committed that infamous night so very long ago. "Why?" she pleaded with Paul. "Why did he do it? Who was in that picture, Paul? Tell me, who was it?"

Paul excused himself, leaving only long enough to retrieve the photo, the one he had placed in his suitcase before he left Virginia. Handing the old tattered and blood stained print to her, Paul answered, "This is why he did it, Maggie."

Maggie squinted, trying to understand the image staring back at her from the old photograph. She remembered the day it was taken at the church picnic. Two policemen came and talked to the whole Sunday school class that day. The Sunday school teacher had asked Maggie to be a teacher's helper on that particular weekend because she knew the class would be large. Maggie didn't mind being an aide but it bothered her that everyone just expected her to help take care of the kids just because she had two younger sisters she was always watching out for. She remembered what those policemen said as if it were just yesterday. "You can trust the police. We're here to help you." She remembered the bathing suit she wore that day, the old yellow and white one. Her mother had to add some material in the top part of the suit to accommodate for Maggie's well-endowed bust line. She never wanted to wear it but her mother insisted. "Everyone will have a bathing suit on, Maggie," she said. "Reverend Session is putting up the new pool in the back of the church for all the kids to swim in." Maggie remembered answering her mother, "But I'm not a kid anymore, remember Ma?"

She looked across the little glass table that held both their drinks and then fixed her eyes on the old wrinkled man sitting next to her. Shaky Paul appeared sad but strong at the same time. In the midst of his withering shell, an unmistaken glow of internal power radiated from his inner core. She imagined him in his heyday. "What a fine specimen of a man he must have been," she thought. Maggie longed for her father now. She wished he were right there sitting next to her, just as Paul was. She would have loved to ask him the questions she was asking old Mr. Patterson. Instead, in between big crocodile tears, she asked shaky Paul, "It was because of me, wasn't it?"

He wished he could take her in his arms, comfort her and protect her from the shit storm he had just delivered. "This was not your fault, Maggie. Please don't ever think it was. These men, policemen who were supposed to not only enforce the law but also uphold it themselves, were bad news. God forbid they went through with their plan to take advantage of you. That would have been even worse for everyone. Your father would have killed them anyway, especially when he discovered his little Maggie had actually been hurt in that way. And he would have found out, believe you me."

"So that one night changed everyone's life, didn't it Paul?"

"Yes, it did, tremendously. More so than you can imagine."

"I remember the detective coming over our house to ask my father some questions about the murders. But he didn't come over much, just two or three times. Then my father started to get sick. Do you think that's why he got sick Paul? Was it because of all the stress from that night? And did they suspect my father?"

"We'll talk about that tomorrow, Maggie. Tomorrow's another day. How are you doing so far?"

"I think I'm still in shock." Maggie sighed. "Dumb ass Paul. How does he think anyone would be doing after being told that kind of news?" she thought. Shock couldn't even begin to describe how she felt. She would never in a million years have suspected her father of murdering those policemen.

"You're right we should talk about it tomorrow Paul. I don't think I can take any more surprises today."

"You're right, tomorrow is another day, remember?" Paul agreed. It will definitely take some time for this part to sink in."

"There's more?"

"Yes, there's more, Maggie, but not now, tomorrow."

"Yes, tomorrow," she repeated, her voice cracking.

They sat for a while, silent until she spoke, "Thank you for telling me," Maggie said between sniffles. "Thank you for telling me the truth. You know when people say, 'time heals' they don't really know, do they? A person mourns a death and time goes by and eventually the psychological trauma subsides, but that's not the whole story, is it? Not the whole story at all. Because the grief never really goes away, it just gets pushed aside in longer and longer intervals. Time never actually heals, does it? That old saying is just something people say when they don't know what else to say.

So they say it for a while until eventually so much time goes by, they don't have to say it anymore. And then, after a while, the death becomes just something that happened a long time ago. Hey, Paul?"

"Yes, Maggie?"

"What on God's green earth could possess grown men, policemen to boot, to act like that? I mean that takes a really sick person to even think about doing those kinds of things with a young girl. You know?"

"Some men are crazy. I don't know why. You're right, it's sick. Some men just figure if a child's old enough to crawl, they're in the right position."

"Do you think my father was sorry he killed those cops?"

"I really don't think so, because he knew what was at stake. Plus, you can't put the toothpaste back in the tube. Believe me I know."

"How do you mean?"

"Oh, well, you know, because of Pavoti. You know that story, don't you?" Paul answered, visibly twitching.

"Yes, Scottie told me about you and your wife. I'm sorry."

"Thank you. It was hard to give her all those pills, but I'm not sorry for what I did. After she took those pills, she looked so peaceful just lying there. It was a tough decision though."

"I imagine it was."

"Hey Paul, not to change the subject but what ever happened to my diary? Did anyone ever find it?"

Paul hesitated for a moment, trying to decide how much more he would tell her tonight or ever for that matter. "How well did you know Dudley?"

"Dudley? What's he got to do with anything? He was the minister my father worked for, wasn't he?"

"Yes."

"Well I didn't..."

"Never mind," Paul interrupted. "We'll talk about all that tomorrow. Now just try to relax a little bit. The things I told you tonight are a lot to absorb. Little bits at a time remember? Little bits at a time."

"Okay, we'll talk about it tomorrow then," Maggie reiterated. "I loved him, you know, Paul. I loved my dad more than you know. I didn't want him to die. And I don't care what he did to those cops, because they deserved it. I just wish it wasn't because of me," she said, burying her face in her hands.

"Stop saying that, Maggie!" He answered back firmly. "It wasn't because of you. Anyone in the same position as your father was in would have done the exact same thing. I'm sure of it."

"You're probably right."

"Damned right I'm right."

"I still loved him even if he did kill them."

"I know you loved him. And believe me, he loved you. He didn't want to leave you, your sisters or your mother all alone. I know he would have done anything in the world to stay with you but he didn't have a choice." He hesitated a minute before speaking, "Your father's death," Paul stopped for a brief moment and chose his words carefully. He cleared his throat and continued, "was simply the unfortunate result of divine intervention."

September 1, 2007

Chapter Seventeen

After a fitful night's sleep, Maggie woke up not nearly as refreshed as she would have liked. She changed into a new set of clothes and then put a comb through her hair. She wondered what was in store for her today. "Good God almighty who knows?" she thought. "Maybe he'll tell me my father was an alien, and we're going up to New Hampshire because that's where the Mother Ship is. Maybe they want to beam me up, back to my home planet." In the distance she could hear Paul rustling in the kitchen. The smell of fresh perked coffee made its way underneath the small crack of air at the bottom of her bedroom door.

As she stood in front of the mirror putting the final touches of makeup on her face, she could almost see the coffee aroma seep in through the bottom of her door and take the shape of a big black bean hand. With an ever so slight circular gesture, she imagined the coffee-aroma hand beckoning to her, "Come, take a taste of my bittersweet nectar." She did as the hand commanded and made her way into the small kitchenette where Paul was standing behind the stove. He was making a pan of scrambled eggs. On the counter were a plate of buttered toast, two coffee cups and two individual cartons of orange juice.

"Hope you're hungry, Maggie," Paul announced with a big grin on his face, proud as punch at the spread he had concocted. He looked at her face. Her eyes were still puffy from last night's crying episode. "Are you feeling any better today?" he asked with concern.

"A little. Boy, that coffee smells good."

"Here, have a cup," he said, raising the pot to her mug and pouring. "I got up early and took a trip to the Seven Eleven next door. Hope you like Folgers. It's all they had."

Maggie inspected the cup. There were no lipstick rings around it. She had no choice but to drink from it, seeing there were no paper cups anywhere in sight. "Oh well. You know what they say, Paul, 'The best part of waking up is Folgers in your cup.'" Maggie recited verbatim from the well-known commercials she had seen on TV, adding the accompanying melody to the jingle as well. She smiled at Paul. He smiled back. "Really, anything is fine. I'm not fussy," she answered, yawning.

"Good. Hey how about you drive today, okay?"

"Whatever you want," she answered complacently.

They finished their breakfast, cleaned up the dishes, packed up the rest of their stuff and left. When the elevator doors opened, there stood a young teenage girl holding a small baby. The baby was making cooing noises and the teenage girl was talking to it softly, lovingly. A tall blonde man stood next to her. He looked too old to be her boyfriend or even her husband, so Maggie assumed it must have been her father. He was doting on the baby too. Maggie stared at both of them. Paul just took one look and then turned away, carrying a great big smile with him as he made an effort not to stare at the mismatched couple with the infant.

When they got out into the parking lot, Maggie said to Paul, "Oh my God. Did you see how young that girl was?"

"Yeah. She was pretty young, wasn't she?"

"Too young to have a baby, that's for sure."

"That's none of our business is it, Maggie?"

"Well it's none of our business, but we sure can imagine can't we?"

"Imagine what?"

"The possibilities are endless."

"Like what?"

"Oh forget it, Paul." She knew it wasn't worth getting into with him. He just wasn't imaginative when it came to people like she was. He probably wouldn't get it anyway.

"That was a cute little baby girl, wasn't it?"

"Yeah," she agreed. "She reminds me of my Abbie when she was little. She had this hair that stood straight up. It always made her look as if someone just scared the living daylights out of her."

Paul laughed.

When they got to the car she nonchalantly threw her bag into the back seat, got into the driver's side, turned to Paul and in between yawns said, "You should get a GPS, Paul. Then you wouldn't have to always look on that stupid map. The thing is so big it covers part of the windshield. I can hardly see the side mirror," she said, annoyed. Maggie moved her head back and forth trying to find a spot that wasn't covered by the unfolded road map.

She started the engine, and headed for the interstate. They drove for a good forty minutes, until they got to the Massachusetts border, then they made a pit stop to take a much needed bathroom break. They briefly parked at the rest stop, but when Maggie got out of the car and looked around she didn't see any freaks, duck-tape-kneed people, or newborn babies this time, so she was a little disappointed. This truck stop was a dud as far as Maggie was concerned. She did see something that interested her though. It was a mailbox. She had written Abbie a letter the previous night.

Even in light of all the troublesome information that was unveiled yesterday, Maggie tried to make the letter sound carefree and upbeat. She had checked her phone yesterday and there were more than ten missed calls, all from Abbie. So she knew she needed to fill her daughter in on her recent disappearance. She hoped the letter would get to her daughter before Abbie had the FBI put an all points bulletin out looking for her long lost mother. Maggie dropped the letter into the mail slot on her way into the Ladies Room. The letter read:

Dear Abbie,

My darling daughter, why is that every time I write to you I feel as if I'm asking for advice in a newspaper column?? In any event, against your better judgment and probably mine as well, I've decided to take the journey!! Yes indeed, I've officially joined the ranks of your ancestors and have become certifiably nuts! I'm informing you of my plans through what you call snail mail because by the time you receive it, I will probably be in another location and cannot be traced. Which is to say that I know what I'm doing, and this is my decision, so don't try and stop me! I'm traveling with a very elderly and kindly gentleman named Paul who is a bit shaky (I'll fill you in later). Paul keeps me informed as to the nature of my journey as we go along. I'm letting him think he has the lead, for now at least. I should be back in two weeks and I'll call or write to you then to let you know I've arrived home safe and sound.

Last night we stayed in a small hotel with a river that runs close by (separate rooms of course). I could hear the water rushing just before I drifted off to sleep.

As a sidebar, took the train up here and there was much to see. You would have loved it, Abbie. I did see a young gentleman who looked amazingly like an old boyfriend of yours. I believe he was a Rastafarian. Is that the right term? Anyways I wish I had carried my can of ant and roach spray with me because I could swear I saw bugs crawling around in that mess on the top of his head. Oh Abbie, the man desperately needed a haircut but I'm not sure conventional shears would have worked on him. I'm not sure even a bush hog would have even done the trick. He was with a woman who wore a long colorful dress. The woman was rather large, especially on the back end (I believe you call this "junk in the trunk"), and when she got up, her dress got caught in the crack of her ass. This reminded me so much of your grandmother, Abbie. I realize you didn't know the woman that well, but trust me–this was a common sight for me in my youth. It might even have led to the invention of the "thong." HAHAHAHA..........

Ta-ta for now. I'll keep you posted as my journey progresses.
Signed your mother,
Maggie–A.K.A. The Road Warrior

Maggie returned from the bathroom and slipped back into the driver's seat.

Paul was standing in a line at a kiosk right in front of the car. He looked back at the Ford Escape and yelled to her, "Want another cup of coffee?"

She poked her head out of the window slightly and shouted back, "Yeah, I'll take cream and sugar."

Maggie watched Paul sip his hot coffee with one shaky hand and try to fasten his seatbelt with the other. "Need some help there, Paul?" she asked. She was more than a little nervous about him spilling that hot cup of coffee on his lap. She felt much better when he was all buckled in, and she saw that the lid and contents of his cup were intact.

"I think I got it."

"So I was wondering if we could talk about Dudley now. He sounds like an interesting character."

"Sure," Paul agreed.

"Great then, let's talk about Dapper Dan."

"Why'd you call him that?

"That's what my mother used to call him. After dad died, he used to come over the house at least once a month. He was always dressed as neat as a pin. He had the best-looking clothes I've ever seen a minister wear. He gave my mother a thick white envelope every month too, said it was some collection the church had started up to help us out with food and bills."

"Interesting," commented Paul with a look of skepticism on his old, wrinkled face.

"He did that for years, at least until we all graduated high school. I don't know what happened to him after that. He just stopped coming around. Then my mother had to go out and get a job working in this local factory to support herself. She got Army benefits from my dad for health insurance and stuff but not living expenses, at least none that I can remember. Of course, it was a long time ago. I could just be having a brain fart."

Paul chuckled. Maggie laughed too and added, "When he came over my mother always shook his hand and asked him how he was. His answer was always the same, 'yippy-skippy,' which really didn't sound as if he meant it in a good way, more like he was bothered by I don't know, whatever."

"He probably *was* bothered by something. A man like that almost certainly had a lot weighing on his conscience."

"What do you mean? He was always nice to us and he was great to my dad, especially when he was sick and in the hospital."

"Remember when we met in the park? Remember when I told you that things aren't always what they seem?"

"Yes, I remember that. You scared the shit out of me!"

"Sorry, didn't mean to do that. I needed to make a point, get you on board with this trip, you know? Plus, now that we're on the subject of the park, how about you giving me an apology for calling me an idiot? Whata ya say, huh?"

"I'm not quite sure you needed to scare the crap out of me to get me on board with this trip. You catch more bees with honey than with vinegar, you know. You're just lucky I agreed to go with you after that park thing.

As far as the idiot comment is concerned, I'll admit I had no right calling you that. It was a little harsh. I'm sorry. Better, Paul?"

"Much better. Thank you, Maggie. So let's talk about the Reverend, shall we? You ever wonder how the grand and glorious Reverend Session afforded all those clothes? The new car he drove? The envelope he gave your mother every month?"

"I don't know. I suppose he got it from the church, why?"

"Did you ever notice the people who went to that church? Well, if you can't remember, you might want to be reminded that they were all your neighbors on the hill. They didn't have a pot to piss in, none of 'em. That collection plate was lucky to see any paper at all on Sunday mornings. The contents of the rusted old plates usually contained nickels, dimes, and an occasional quarter or two. You can't run a church on that, no matter how conservative and frugal you are. Just heating the church for one week alone during those Connecticut winters was more than they collected in a month's time."

"So what are you saying then?"

"Dudley never lost his key like he told Gunderson. He gave it to someone. He gave it to one of those cops that got killed."

"What!" Maggie exclaimed, shocked.

"He gave it to them so they could come in the church anytime they wanted."

"So when they were mysteriously found there on Christmas Eve back in '64, they didn't just pick the place because it was open? They didn't just go there to get out of the cold? It wasn't random? It wasn't just a place to go and talk about that stupid shit they were into? Not like what the article in the paper said?"

"No, it wasn't random. Those cops met in the basement of that church almost every night. They made their drug deals there. They met mobsters there to talk about monthly collections at the local establishments and in the garbage industry. They plotted and planned and connived, all the while under the untouchable cover of that pious church. There were Mafia connections big time. In fact, one of those cops was the brother to one of the biggest New England mobsters of all time, "Fat Tony." With all their dirty deals, those two cops made some of the best under-the-table dirty money ever made in Durham."

"You are kidding, Paul? Right? Dudley the minister, Dudley, he's the one you're talking about? He gave those cops a key to his church basement so they could do their dirty work right there under God's nose? Didn't anyone see those people going in and out of the church at night?"

"Who was gonna see them? They walked their beat at night remember? They usually slipped in through the side door of the church. No one in the neighborhood was up at that time of night. The second shifters were home by then and the third shifters were long gone, most of them working away at their boring jobs at the largest factory in town, the ball-bearing plant.

Even if someone saw them, they probably wouldn't think too much about it, them being cops and all. Probably thought they were just patrolling the place, keeping an eye on it, you know?"

"So why did Dudley give them the key? What did he get out of it?"

"A kickback, big time. He was in cahoots with those men, letting them use the sacred halls of that beautiful church for evil purposes. And who was going to suspect anything illegal was going on in a church basement? Not that it mattered all that much because I guess those cops could have been meeting anywhere. But, just in case someone came sneaking around and suspected something, the cover of the church was a good one to use, you know? Especially with goody two shoes Dudley there to verify their stories. Surprise, surprise right?"

"Oh my God. That's terrible. I would never have thought that about him. I thought he was a good man."

"He wasn't all bad. He gave quite a bit of the cash to people on the hill who came to him, desperate for money. People who had lost their jobs and people who couldn't pay their bills, put food on the table, or even pay their rent or mortgage, although he usually wanted some favor in return."

"How did you find out about the lost key?"

"It wasn't me who found out. It was Chief Gunderson. There were a lot of things he discovered at that crime scene that he kept hidden, close to his vest. One of them was a key to that basement storage room. Dudley claimed there were only two keys to that room. He had one and your father had the other. Then he told Gunderson he had lost his key and Eddy went to make him another one. But obviously it wasn't lost at all because Gunderson found that key. It was right in the cop's pocket. Gunderson got to it first, before all the rookies tore the place up. He spied it when he was examining the two bodies trying to determine what the time of their death was. After all the fingerprints had been taken, Gunderson felt around for stuff in the two cops pockets, evidence, you know? He came across the key by accident. He didn't know what it was at first, but he suspected it was the key to the storage room. The cops probably didn't put it on any kind of key ring because more than likely they passed it back and forth between the two of them, maybe more cops too, who knows. Gunderson grabbed the key and slipped it in his own pocket and then waited for everyone to clear out. When all the other cops left, Gunderson tried it and wouldn't you know, a perfect match to the keyhole on the storage room door. He suspected Dudley right away because Dudley told him about losing his key."

"So Dudley didn't know about the key, did he? He didn't know the cop had a key in his pocket right? What else didn't he know? Tell me, Paul. Be honest. Did he know about the dirty pictures? Did he?"

"That's one thing I really don't think he knew about. Even though he was as dishonest as any minister gets, that's one thing he would have objected to. I'm sure of it, especially when it came to you. He loved your father.

Heck, he loved your whole family. And I think in some ways he was really torn by what he was doing. I think in some ways he wanted to stop but he loved the money too much. Plus I think, as dishonest as he was, he really wanted to help the people in his community out in hard times, whether he got something in return or not."

"So Dudley-Do-Right was really Dudley-Do-Wrong. Damned fucker. If he didn't give those cops that key, they wouldn't have been there that night and my dad wouldn't have seen what he saw and killed them."

"Lot's of 'if's' with this story, Maggie. Even if your father didn't see the cops that night, that wouldn't have stopped those policemen from going after you. Then, like we said before, your Dad would have found out, tracked them down and most likely killed them anyways."

"You're damned right there's a lot of 'if's.' Good God Almighty, I really would never have thought anything bad about Dudley. That's such a shock."

"I know," Paul answered, shaking his head in disgust. "And the sad thing about it was that your dad actually did the right thing by whacking these guys. And Dudley-Do-Wrong got all kinds of credit for helping everyone all the time. If they only knew how he came by all that money, they sure wouldn't have thought too much of him, I guarantee."

Paul continued, "Only a handful of people knew about his dirty dealings with those cops. Not that Dudley wanted to be so underhanded, mind you. It was just that he did what he thought was necessary to help himself and those around him. I really think deep down inside he was a good guy who made the wrong choices. He hated those dirty cops as much as the next guy, but he needed or thought he needed the money more than keeping his own honesty and morality intact. I don't think your dad knew about Dudley's underhanded dealings until he started to put two and two together. Even at the end he didn't want to believe it, what with them being as close to each other as they were."

"Yeah, well, close only counts in horseshoes and hand grenades," Maggie replied sarcastically, her face just about as red as a beet. She was angry, so very angry with the whole muddy mess. "Wow!!!" she screamed.

Paul held his hands over his ears. "Yeah, wow," he whispered under his breath.

Neither Paul nor Maggie spoke for a while. Maggie was obviously taken by this last bit of information, moving her head back and forth over and over again and repeating the same thing, "I can't believe it. I just can't believe it."

"I know, Maggie. It was a shock to me too."

"How did you find out about it? Did you know Gunderson?"

"No, not really. Your dad told me about most of this stuff. The other things I put together myself just by prying around a bit."

"When? When did he tell you, Paul?"

"Yikes!" Paul yelled, looking down at his pants. The lid came off his coffee and some of the now tepid liquid fell right in his lap. The timing couldn't have been more perfect. "Let's stop at this next exit, okay Maggie? I should clean myself up a bit, looks like I peed my pants. Besides, I'm hungry again."

"Again? What've you got, a hollow leg?"

Paul laughed. "That sounds like something your father would have said."

"Really?"

September 1, 2007

Chapter Eighteen

It just so happened the next exit was a hop, skip and a jump away from the tollbooth that led into New Hampshire, a mere mile and a half from where they were. And it also just so happened that this same exit had the biggest liquor store in New Hampshire, where all purchases came with the promise of no sales tax. Nada. None. It couldn't get any better than that for Maggie and Paul, both Jack Daniels junkies. Plus there was a hotdog stand right in front of the place so they could kill two birds with one stone.

They pulled into a parking spot, got out of the car and Paul instructed Maggie to stay put while he went into the bathroom to clean up a bit. He was banking on the hand drying machine to suck dry enough of the coffee liquid on his pants to make it appear to the general public that he wasn't just an old man who could no longer hold his urine.

As she waited by the car, Maggie lit a cigarette and looked up into the clear blue sky. It was an absolutely beautiful day. There wasn't a cloud in sight. She held her free hand over her brow as she looked up. Billowy trails of white crisscrossed each other, creating some form of argyle cryptic message. A small silver object she could barely see led the most current streak of white. The streaks were exhaust fumes from big jetliners. The planes probably took off from Boston because they were too high up to have taken off at any nearby airport. The jagged puffs of smoke from the plane's engines seemed to form bits and pieces of an archaic writing pattern that Maggie imagined could only be seen from way up in the atmosphere. It was as if God himself had taken hold of the knobs of a gigantic blue and white etch-a-sketch and was trying to communicate with us poor slobs down here on earth. If Maggie were up in outer space right now she sure would love to read that message. It'd probably go something like this: "People, work with me will ya? Stop using this place I made for you as your own personal toilet. Signed, The Big Kahuna, God. P.S. I love you all."

A sudden wave of guilt hit Maggie square in the kisser. She thought about every Styrofoam cup, every plastic container, and every wad of trash she dumped on this planet during her fifty-eight years here. She thought about how many times she chose plastic or paper in lieu of bringing her own bags to the grocery store. Mentally, she tried to multiply her trash habits times the number of people on earth and immediately became overwhelmed. "Don't shit where you eat," she said out loud.

"What was that, Maggie?" Paul asked, returning to the car. He had just the faintest hint of a stain on the front of his light tan khaki pants, hardly noticeable unless you looked really close.

"Nothing. Your pants look good Paul. The stain came out. Ready to go inside?" she asked.

"Yep, let's go get some Jack Daniels."

"Do you want to get a hotdog first?"

"Naw, lets get the good stuff first."

"Alright then. Hey, Paul?" Maggie asked as she threw her cigarette on the ground, stepped on it and then started walking toward the door. Briefly pondering what she had just done she stopped dead in her tracks, turned around and picked up the cigarette butt.

"Yes. What is it, Maggie?" he responded, turning his head to watch her little cigarette butt fiasco.

"Is that your car?"

"You mean the Ford Escape?"

"Yea, the one we're driving remember?"

"Duh, I know what you were talking about. Yes, it's my car. Sort of."

"Then who was driving it the other day on my way home from work? You know, the guy who almost ran me off the road?"

"Oh him. That was my brother-in-law, Pontiac. He's Pavoti's brother."

"So, his name is Pontiac, and he was driving a Ford? That sounds like some kind of line from an old Abbott and Costello movie. Don't tell me. Let me guess. Pontiac's an Indian right?"

"Native American, remember Maggie? Native American."

"Oh yes, right, he's a Native American. Happy now, Paul?"

"Quite happy thank you very much," he snapped, half joking and half serious.

"So this car actually belongs to you. What made you buy a hybrid?"

"This car was given to me temporarily, but I can use it anytime I want, at least for a while."

"I've never driven a hybrid before. It rides nice, a lot smoother than I would have imagined. What kind of engine is in here? A V-6? How does this hybrid thing work? Do you know, Paul? What kind of gas mileage does it get?"

"Whoa.....too many questions. I don't know that much about cars but I bet I know someone who does."

"Who's that?"

"Pontiac."

"I'd like to get my hands on that bastard. He scared the bejesus out of me the other day."

"Awe, Maggie. Don't be that way. Pontiac's a good guy, you'll see."

"Are we meeting him or something?"

"We'll see. Maybe. Hey, you like cars don't you, Maggie?

"Love 'em. I've always loved them."

"I know."

"How do you know so much?"

"I just know. Let's leave it at that for now okay?"

"Alright then but at some point during this journey-trip I want to know about all these things I've been asking you. I bet you own that Honda Element too don't you?"

"No. That one's not mine. It was given to Pontiac temporarily to use anytime he wants."

"What is that some kind of Native American tradition, lending cars to people?"

Paul chuckled, "I guess you could say that."

"So that license plate on the Element. The one that says that goofy word EPHEDRA. What's that supposed to mean?"

"All in good time, my pretty. All in good time."

"You sound like the wicked witch of the west in the Wizard of Oz."

"Didn't mean for it to come out like that."

"Whatever. Let's just get our stuff and ditch this joint."

"Yeah," Paul said. "Let's get our stuff and ditch this place," he reiterated. "What is that some kind of new saying? Ditch this place."

"Yes, it's a new saying," Maggie answered, exasperated. "And it's joint, not place."

"You're not sick of me yet are you, Maggie?" Paul asked laughing quietly.

Maggie stepped on the little silver foot at the bottom of the trashcan and the lid opened. She checked the cigarette butt to see if it was completely cool and then put it in the trash. Turning to Paul she answered, "No. I'm not sick of you yet. It's just that it is so frustrating sometimes to have so many questions and not be given the answers right away. I should be a little more patient, I guess."

"I'm really sorry. Your dad's orders, remember?"

Maggie ignored him, went through the revolving door of the liquor store and picked out a shopping cart. There was more liquor in this one store than she had ever seen before, isles and isles of all different kinds of booze. Paul and Maggie headed straight for the bourbon section where Paul picked up four bottles of Jack Daniels and put them in the cart. Maggie looked at the pushcart and then looked back at Paul, "Do you think we'll need this much? Tell me Paul, how much more do you need to tell me about the past, and is it so bad that I need to be put into a booze- induced coma to tolerate the information?"

Paul laughed. "You're funny. I'm picking up two bottles for home."

"That's still Virginia, right?"

"Right."

"Then how come you have New Hampshire plates on this car?" So much was unclear to her. There was still so much to figure out, and Maggie was inquisitive, there was no doubt about that.

"Long story, Maggie."

"Yeah, I'm sure it is," she replied under her breath.

Paul took out his credit card and paid for the Jack.

"You need some money?" Maggie asked. "Scottie gave me some before I left."

"No, I don't need any money. Remember, this is courtesy of your dad. And that was nice of Scottie to do that for you. He surprises you sometimes doesn't he?"

"Not as much as you do. And how did my dad know how much money we would need on this so-called journey? That was over forty years ago. There is such a thing as inflation, you know."

"You are just full of questions today aren't you?"

"I know, I know, all in good time right?" She felt frustrated. "Is there such a thing as good time? No, there was only Paul time on this trip, and that was whenever he felt like telling her things," she thought. She had no control over any of this and damned if that didn't make her mad.

"Now you're catching on."

They got back in their car and hit the highway again. "How far up into New Hampshire are we going today, Paul?" Maggie asked, hoping this question would be answered.

"We're heading up to North Conway. It's beautiful up there. You'll love it."

"How long are we staying there?"

"I figure it will be about four or five days and then we'll head back."

"But you said two weeks, Paul. That's not two weeks. We're going back to Virginia, right?"

"Right. But there's a place in Virginia I need to show you too. Trust me. This will be an informative trip. All your questions will be answered. I guarantee."

"Okay. If you say so then," she said with a sigh.

"So can we start to talk about Gunderson now?" Paul asked.

"Be my guest. You start."

September 1, 2007

Chapter Nineteen

"Ahh, Gunderson," Paul groaned as he continued to watch Maggie merge into the middle lane of traffic on the highway. "Let's see what I can tell you about Gunderson. He was tall, blonde, and he was Norwegian. And he was also very, very smart, although he didn't look it. He had that kind of modern day Columbo mentality, you know? Yes indeed, he was a real Cracker Jack gumshoe. He pretended to be out of it but he knew exactly what was going on, always."

"I remember the tall part. When he came over our house once to talk to my mother he towered over her. He looked like the Jolly Green Giant to me. Can't say as I remember him being goofy acting, but I guess I was too young to get that part."

"Well, he only acted goofy. He was smart, believe me. Like I said before, he suspected both your father and Dudley of the murders, but he didn't say anything to anyone. He was lucky he could easily conceal them as suspects because mostly all those prints they took at the crime scene were your dad's, the dirty cops', or Dudley's. No big surprise there because all of those prints were supposed to be there, what with your Dad and Dudley working at the church and all. All except for the cops' prints of course. But those could be easily explained because the church was part of their night beat and supposedly they went in to check on things from time to time. But something just didn't jive with Gunderson. He could feel it in his gut. There was the lie about the lost key, the blank 8 x 10 space on the table, and a couple of other things Gunderson found at the crime scene that he didn't tell anyone else about."

"If he was investigating the crime, why didn't he tell anyone about all those clues he found?"

"That's simple. He knew better. If word got out to the Mafia or other illegal cops, both your father and Dudley would have been dead as soon as word hit the street, and that's a fact."

"So Gunderson knew the cops were dirty?"

"Damned toot'n he knew. He knew of other dirty cops too but he didn't let on he knew. He played the naive stupid card, dumb as a fox as they say. Some things you just don't mess with. Better to leave well enough alone, you know, Maggie. Yeah, Gunderson was a good actor, that's for sure. He was slicker than snot on a doorknob."

"So did he ever find out it was my dad who killed them?"

"He sure did. Dudley told him."

"What! Why would Dudley tell him? I thought he was covering for my dad. Did that snake Dudley sell my dad down the river?"

"Not exactly. Gunderson found a clue, a very important clue at the crime scene. He went to Dudley, showed him what he had found and demanded an explanation."

"Was it my diary? Did he find my diary? Don't lie to me, Paul," Maggie pleaded.

Paul put his hand on Maggie's right shoulder, patted it a couple of times and said, "No, I'm sure it wasn't your diary, Maggie. That's probably long gone by now. You most likely dropped that on the way home from the church that night. It almost certainly fell down the sewer drain or got run over by a car or something." There was no need to tell Maggie the truth about this part. She would never find out about the diary, and Paul didn't want her to live the rest of her days convinced she was the one who put the finger on her dad for the murders. It was bad enough she knew about her picture at the church picnic. Paul knew if she found out the truth about the diary, that much guilt would have set Maggie back a good ways.

"What was it then? What was the clue he found?" she asked almost frantic by now.

"Don't know. That's one thing I never found out, but it was big. I can tell you that because it was enough to make Dudley sing like a canary."

"That crooked son-of-a-bitch Dudley."

"You say that now but you don't know the whole story, Maggie. Plus, right or wrong, your dad killed those cops. Remember that little piece of information?"

"Whose side are you on anyway? I know what I know and that is that Dudley ratted out my dad."

"True, but it went a little further than that."

"What do you mean? How much further does it get than selling out a loyal friend and employee?" she asked. Maggie's stress was beginning to show because with each little bit of information she discovered, her foot pressed harder and harder down on the gas pedal. Pulling over into the far left lane she yelled, "Fuck 'em. Fuck 'em all!"

"Easy, easy Spider. How's about you slow down a bit okay? I'd like to get there in one piece." Paul continued, "As far as the murders were concerned, I can vouch for your dad who would almost certainly have said, 'what a tangled web we weave.' Fact is the whole situation was a little more complicated than just selling someone out. When Gunderson approached Dudley and told him about all the clues he found, Dudley had no choice. He brought Gunderson back into the shed in his back yard. Your Dad was working at the church at the time. He saw the both of them head back to the shed, the one where he knew Dudley kept the evidence from the murders. This evidence included Eddy's bloody uniform and the hunting knife he used to kill those cops. Right then and there your dad knew he was screwed. Dudley showed Gunderson the picture of you at the picnic, which was splattered with fresh bloodstains. Then he told him the whole story about your father and why he murdered those cops. He didn't want to tell Gunderson, no indeed. It was just that Gunderson was smart. He figured out there were too many loopholes in the stories Dudley and your dad were telling him. The stories didn't match up with the clues he found."

"So what did Gunderson do?"

"He listened for a long while to what Dudley had to say."

"And what did Dudley have to say?"

Dudley was smart too. In some ways Gunderson and Dudley were two peas in a pod. They both had a lot to lose with this case. If Gunderson spilled the beans on Dudley and Eddy, the whole church and, for that matter, the whole community would tar and feather the poor bastards, run 'em out of town on a rail. But I doubt the Mafia would let it get that far. Like I said before, they would have killed them right off the bat and never think twice about it again. Plus, Dudley didn't want to stop his dirty dealings. He got accustomed to the extra income and he didn't want anything or anyone to put the kibosh on that corrupt money.

And then there was Gunderson. If word got out on the street about what those cops were doing down there in the basement, there'd be hell to pay. That's for sure. Most likely Gunderson and his family would be in jeopardy too. So the two of them put their heads together. Dudley came up with a plan. They talked about it, and tweaked it, deciphering it six different ways from Sunday.

"So, what was the plan?" Maggie asked, just about ready to jump out of her skin.

"I'm going to have to tell you that just a little later, when we get into North Conway."

"You're killing me, Paul. Killing me!"

"I'm sorry. But I'm afraid I don't want you behind the wheel of a car when I tell you that story, Maggie, or else we'll both be in trouble."

September 1, 2007

Chapter Twenty

They drove a long ways, maybe about fifty miles or so, neither one of them saying a word to each other except for Paul giving Maggie an occasional directional change or two. Paul had decided to take them on the Kancamagus Highway, opting for the beautiful view of the White Mountains as opposed to the typical boring, flat highway roadways. The destination would be the same, North Conway, but it'd be a much prettier ride.

Maggie had never seen the New Hampshire interior and she was sufficiently impressed with the twenty-eight-mile stretch of road Paul had directed her to take. The scenic byway careened through the heart of the White Mountains. The breathtaking shades of browns, reds and yellows from fall foliage coupled with the grand and glorious mountain backdrop were the perfect visual marriage. Maggie could look at that scenery for a long, long time and be very contented. She wished she had the ability to capture it in her brain and recall it anytime she wanted, especially in times of stress.

She saw plenty of places to pull over along the side of the road. There were little alcoves specially designed to view picturesque mountain vistas but she was apprehensive about stopping because she was just a tad bit afraid of heights.

Her ears muffled and then popped as the Ford climbed the nearly 3,000-foot elevation, the highest point on the highway. The road had many a twist and turn. It was truly a motorcycle rider's dream thoroughfare. She saw plenty pass her, winding around corner after corner at speeds exceeding the numbers that were clearly marked on the designated signs. Some of the motorcycles would lean so far over Maggie could swear she saw an elbow or a knee scrape over the tar.

The New Hampshire Chamber of Commerce was sponsoring a road race today. They called it the largest and longest relay race in the nation. There were banners hung from light posts and signs tacked to trees advertising the event. All proceeds were to be donated to the New Hampshire Parks and Recreation Department for the continued beautification of the Kancamagus. Runners from all over the world were taking part in the race, passing off batons to the next runner at specially marked stations along the sides of the road. Paul and Maggie would witness this race along the entire Kancamagus, right to the very end where they would get off in North Conway. Some of the runners didn't even look like they could run ten feet, but they sure gave it the old college try, most of them slower than molasses in January. Others appeared to be seasoned marathoners, all lean and agile. They made running up those hills look as easy as shooting fish in a barrel.

"Gosh this is a pretty drive isn't it, Maggie?" Paul whispered, looking out at the scenery.

"Yeah. I guess so." Maggie did think the drive was beautiful, but at that particular moment she was much more interested in looking at all the runners. Her daughter, Abbie, had been a runner in high school, competing on the four-person relay team. Her team was good and won many a first prize trophy, but she had to admit there was no event in Abbie's repertoire that necessitated the kind of endurance it took to run this kind of distance, especially on all these uphill roads. Maggie always went to watch her daughter compete. But, being in the midst of all those fit and trim runner's bodies, she had to admit she always felt like a big fat blob sitting there with her rear end hanging over the back edge of those skinny metal benches.

"Are you mad?" Paul asked, turning his head to look at her. He sensed an acute abruptness in her voice.

"No, I'm just looking at the runners," she answered. After thinking about his question a little more, and reevaluating her sharp response, she decided, yes, she was a little mad.

"I guess I'm not so much mad as I am frustrated. You know, Paul, this isn't easy for me. It seems like it's just been a little over twenty-four hours that I started this trip and my whole world's been turned upside down. Nothing from my past was true, was it?"

"Your dad's love was true."

"Duh... I know that. Sorry, I didn't mean for it to come out that way," Maggie replied apologetically.

"No problem. I completely understand. I told you—there's a lot to absorb and it won't be easy. Hey, pull over, Maggie. Let's stop over there where those runners are wading in the stream. It's just so beautiful here, isn't it?"

"You're right about that. It's gorgeous." Her spirits seemed to lift when she witnessed the spectacular mountain stream.

They pulled off the side of the road into a little parking lot where a score of runners were bending over stretching, tying their shoelaces, and sucking down some new fangled sports juice drinks. The runners held up the tiny colorful foil sports juice pouches way above their heads and squeezed them, making the blue or red contents—which Paul imagined were just loaded with la-de-dah electrolytes—flow in one continuous slimy trickle. It appeared to Paul as if those runners were eating silly string, the kind you squirt out at people as a joke. "Whatever happened to good old fashioned water?" he thought.

Peering over the edge of the two-foot high steel guardrail, Paul noticed a few of the runners had taken their shoes off and were wading in what he imagined was numbingly cold mountain water. "Let's go down there," he suggested, turning slightly to make sure Maggie was listening and then pointing to the edge of the rock lined water. For a brief moment he had déjà vu. He loved New Hamsphire. He missed the natural beauty of its land and the crystal clear waters that flowed through the hills and valleys there. Paul felt at peace here, at one with nature so to speak.

"You sure you can make it down there?" Maggie asked, concerned for his safety. She could picture the old man falling head-long into a rolling tumble and ending up with his melon stuck far into the mud at the banks of the river, like an ostrich with its head in the sand. She'd have to call on the paramedics to get the jaws-of-life to pull him out. "Wouldn't want you to break a hip," she said. "We're way out in the middle of nowhere." She did notice an ambulance strategically placed at the end of the parking lot, which she assumed was for the runners. An immense sense of relief squashed her fear of Paul plunging down the small incline.

"I can make it, don't you worry. I'm a little more spry than I look."

"Okay then, your choice. First I have to take a potty break though," Maggie said pointing to the little makeshift porta-potties placed exclusively for the runner's use. She waited in a short line to use the facility. Gathering stares from sleek, muscular men and women, she exclaimed without even being asked, "No I'm not running in the race today, okay? Happy? So, is it a crime to take a pee or don't you think I can fit through the bathroom door?" She knew what they were thinking as they checked her out. If she hadn't pissed them off enough already, she decided to light up a cigarette. Then she coughed a deep smoker's cough and hacked up some repulsive bodily fluid, which she promptly spit out on the ground. The runners stared at her, obviously disgusted, turning their heads away from her and her smoke. "These damned runners are working my last good nerve," she uttered under her breath, all the while dangling the freshly lit cigarette loosely from her lips.

When Maggie went back to the car, Paul had already started his trek down the little hill that led to the stream. She caught up to him and gently held onto his elbow, guiding him to the water's edge. He sat on the smooth rim of a large rock and started removing his shoes and socks. "What are you doing?" Maggie asked, her half-smoked cigarette still dangling from her mouth.

Paul stared at her, "Put that damned thing out, will ya?"

"All right, all right. Don't get your panties all in a wad," she answered, removing the cigarette from her lips. She placed the end of the lit cigarette into the stream, just enough for the tip to be extinguished. Then she put the butt in her shirt pocket. "When you get done dipping your toes, I'll throw this away in the trash can over there," she said, patting her shirt pocket and turning her head toward Paul. Then, when she made sure he was watching her, she pointed to the receptacle not more than twenty feet away.

"Thank you," he replied gratefully. "I'm glad to see you're becoming more responsible."

"Whatever. Hey, is it cold? That was a dumb question, wasn't it?"

"Freezing," Paul answered as he gently guided his feet into the frigid water. "That's the thing about New Hampshire. All the water is delightfully clean. Heck, any lake or stream you go in, no matter how deep it is, you can see your toes on the bottom. Only problem is, your toes are usually blue."

Maggie laughed. "True. True. Hey Paul, mind if I ask you a question?"

"Be my guest, ask away."

"Why do you shake so much?"

"You noticed, did ya? Is it that obvious?" he asked chuckling. Paul had become accustomed to his physical maladies. Like many older people, he had had many years to become accustomed to them. It still wasn't easy to see his body fade away and become frail and unresponsive to the demands of his still youthful mind. "Funny thing, you know Maggie, just when you get things right up here (he said this as he pointed his finger to his head), the rest of you goes south. Did you ever read Mark Twain? One of my favorite lines of his goes something like this: 'Age is an issue of mind over matter. If you don't mind, it doesn't matter.' I've got Parkinson's disease, if you must know. Sometimes it acts up worse than others, especially when emotional things start to bother me. But I take medicine for it and that seems to control my shaking pretty well."

"I'm sorry. I just thought it was something else. I thought it was from your nerves. I thought there might be something else wrong, but I wasn't sure. I just hope you aren't mad at me because I never offered you anything to drink like I did Scottie's other patients. I was just lazy and didn't want to clean the floor if you spilled your drink. Plus, I thought your shaking was more a mental condition than a physical one. But your Parkinson's disease gets worse when you get nervous?"

"No need to be sorry. At my age I figure I gotta have something and it might as well be this. Better than cancer, I reckon. Yes, the shaking gets worse when I'm nervous and when my medicine starts to wear off. I always took my medicine about a half hour before I went to see Scottie, so it didn't start to take full effect right away. I take it at that time every day. So you saw me before the medicine got into my system. Then, when I left after my appointment with Scottie, I didn't shake as much. The medicine started working by that time. It's just that simple. No real big mental problems to cause me to shake that much. I'd be in trouble if that were the case, wouldn't I? Especially with Parkinson's disease already working its demons on me."

"Well, I'm sorry anyways. And you're right, better Parkinson's than cancer, I guess." This answered a question that had plagued her for a while. Maggie thought it was Dr. Leonard's skilled psychiatrist's techniques that lessened Paul's trembling and twitching. But, much to her surprise, the lessening of Paul's symptoms was just the result of his medicine taking effect.

"Any other questions I can answer?"

"Well, you won't answer any of the big questions I ask you."

"Like I said, Maggie, give those a little bit of time, okay?"

"Okay then, if you say so. In that case, I'll just ask you another question. I know you were married to Pavoti, but you never talk about children. Do you have any kids?"

Paul's face immediately changed. His eyes squinted as if he was searching for something in the distance. She saw the tears start to swell up and pool in his lower lid until the old worn out lid could no longer hold back the liquid and the salty stream ran down both sides of his nose and fell away into the crevices of his mouth. "I had a daughter once," he answered, his voice breaking up.

"Once?" Then, after becoming acutely aware of his tear-laden face and saddened demeanor, she replied softly, kindly, "I'm sorry, Paul. What happened?"

"She was very young," he started to say but had to stop to compose himself a bit before he went on.

"Take your time. We're in no rush," Maggie said taking her shoes off and sitting next to him on the rock, not because she wanted to stick her feet in the water; mostly she just wanted to get close enough to put her arm around him. "Wasn't it just like life to give every last person on this green earth a hard time?" she thought.

"She was fifteen. Committed suicide. Pavoti and I couldn't figure out why she did it. Pavoti was the one who found her, hanging from a rope in her bedroom. Pavoti was just returning home from working at the hospital all day and she called my daughter's name but there was no answer. She searched the house and found her hanging by a piece of old clothesline she had taken from outside on the back porch. My daughter had draped it over an exposed pipe in her ceiling. I'd been meaning to fix that damned ceiling but I took too long doing it, I guess." Paul removed a large red handkerchief from his pants pocket and blew his nose. He continued, "So in some ways it's my fault for not fixing that stupid pipe in time. She left a suicide note apologizing, but there was no explanation as to why she did such a horrible and tragic thing."

"I'm so sorry, Paul, so very sorry. You shouldn't blame yourself. If she didn't hang herself from that pipe, it would've been from something else. It sounds as if she was determined to do this thing." Maggie held her arm around shaky Paul and squeezed as hard as she thought was reasonable, given his frail bone structure and all.

"Thank you, Maggie. As you can imagine, neither one of us were the same after that. When you lose a child it just does something to you that I can't explain. All your senses become duller. Life itself becomes muted as if you're somewhere between conscious and unconscious but you don't know exactly where. Things don't taste the same. Things don't look the same. Nothing feels the same because it isn't the same and never will be again."

"I can imagine," she said empathizing with him while gently wiping the tears from his cheek with her shirtsleeve.

"So you never had any other children?"

"No. Pavoti had enough trouble just having the one. So when our daughter was gone, it was just the two of us again. We joined a support group. We tried to mentor troubled youth in our neighborhood and around various troubled schools in Connecticut, trying to get back that feeling of parenting a little, but it wasn't the same. There were too many memories in Connecticut for us to lead even a semi-normal life again."

"I can't imagine your lives would be the same again."

"We stayed in Connecticut for about a year after it happened but, because the memories were so painful, we decided to get out of the state and move up to New Hampshire where Pavoti's brother lived at the time. He had plenty of land with some run-down shacks on it. He said we were welcome to have whichever shack we wanted, said we could fix any one of them up until they looked just like new again. So we took him up on the offer. We moved up here to New Hampshire where the state motto is "Live Free or Die." As Paul said this last part he turned his head, staring straight into Maggie's concerned face, raised his eyebrows and bent his head down, peering out over the rim of his glasses as if to make a point.

"That's right, it is the state motto, isn't it? 'Live Free or Die.' It's on the New Hampshire license plates, isn't it? Maggie's thoughts turned to the Ford Escape they were traveling in right now.

"Yes, it is," Paul answered, wiping the remaining moisture from his face with his handkerchief.

"But you didn't stay here in New Hampshire. You live in Virginia now."

"We stayed in New Hampshire for a number of years and then decided to come to Virginia where some of Pavoti's ancestors had settled. Since she was Native American, the government allowed us to live on the reservation close to the eastern shore."

They both waded in the water for a while until neither one of them could feel their feet anymore. Maggie stared at the birch trees that lined the edge of the gurgling stream. That was her favorite tree, birch. She loved how the trees were usually grouped in three or more so they wouldn't have to be alone growing up. She loved to peel the tree's black and white bark that curled away from the trunk, collect it in a pile, and put it away for future use in some craft project that would ultimately never get finished. The bark was rough on one side and soft and furry on the other, kind of like a piece of suede. The peeling bark reminded her of the remnants of bubbled scaly skin after it had been sunburned. She remembered the times when her father had mowed their lawn without a shirt on and he would get sunburned like that. A couple of days later his shoulders and upper back would blister just a little. Maggie would beg him to let her pick at it, peeling away at the layers of reddish brown-blistered skin.

Paul started to speak again, but this time his mood seemed to have lightened up a smidgen. "Pavoti and I didn't stay alone forever in New Hampshire or Virginia. We had a lot of friends in both places. We got involved with teaching illiterate children up in New Hampshire and then with the tribal children down in Virginia. We had a full life. Not as happy as it would've been if our daughter had lived, but it was full nonetheless. Pavoti was always trying to get me to work with the children or young adults. She said I had a gift of sorts—to lead people to the next level of their journey. I never saw that in me, but she obviously did or she wouldn't have pleaded with me to help her die." Paul looked away and Maggie thought he was going to cry again, but he didn't.

"Pavoti nicknamed me Alo, which is a Hopi Indian name that means spiritual guide. Of course when she got mad at me she had plenty of other nicknames. You know what I mean, Maggie?" Paul laughed a good hearty laugh, slapped Maggie on the thigh and said, "How's about we ditch this joint? Whata you say?" Maggie could tell he'd had enough serious talk, and so had she. She laughed right along with him and said, "Now you've got it Paul, yeah—let's ditch this joint!"

"Oh and Maggie—don't forget to throw that cigarette in your pocket away."

Maggie looked down at the front of her shirt. The wet-tipped cigarette had started to leak brownish liquid through the V at the bottom of her right front pocket. She reached in to grab the butt and it started to fall apart in her hand. Her pocket stunk and the smell reminded her of when she left her ashtray filled with cigarette butts outside on her back deck in the rain. Maggie wished she had brought more clothes now. She feared she would never get the tobacco stain out of her perfectly good blouse and this made her just a wee bit sad or mad, she couldn't decide which. "Hey Paul?" she asked cocking her head a little. The muscles on her face tensed. They were seized with a most inquisitive expression.

"Yes, Maggie," he replied, taking his feet out of the water and lifting them onto the rock to dry off. She followed suit, taking her feet out of the water and raising her knees up above the edge of the rock so that her heels ever so slightly rested on the corner of the large piece of granite, exposing the majority of her feet to the open air.

"You said Pavoti worked at a hospital. Which hospital?"

Paul thought for a moment, wondering if he should reveal any more information just now. With a slight hesitation in his voice, he answered her question, "She worked at the Veterans Hospital. She was a nurse. We both worked there actually. I was a Lab Tech, but that was many, many moons ago as they say."

"Oh," she answered surprised. "That's where my father was when he died. Is that how you got to know him? But my father wasn't there for very long."

"You could say I got to know him there. Yes, you could say that I guess," Paul responded carefully. "Hey, are your feet dry yet? He reached for his shoes, trying to put them on as fast as he could. He thought back on the first time he laid eyes on Eddy Payne, in Eddy's hospital room in Connecticut in March of 1965. But, even before he met this man, he knew he owed him a great big debt of gratitude.

Eddy had saved Paul's brother's life. Paul and his brother joined the Army at the same time, went through basic training together. But when the time came for them to be assigned to a specific battalion, Paul went one way and his brother went another. His brother was assigned to the 50th Infantry, 10th Infantry Division, the same regiment that Eddy Payne was in charge of. So at that infamous battle in Tunisia when Eddy saved the lives of all those soldiers, Paul's brother was lucky enough to be one of those survivors. Paul must have heard his brother tell the story a million times. He knew Eddy's name by heart.

"They're dry," Maggie answered back half in a fog. She felt as if her brain were trying to process all the little pieces of information that had been handed to her but she still couldn't envision the entire picture yet. If she didn't know better, she would have thought she had a little Rubik's cube lodged inside her noggin' with Paul twisting and turning the little colored pieces, lining some up and leaving others alone for a while until just the right moment. Then at just that right moment another set of colors would be aligned and on and on it would go until, hopefully soon, every single one of the colors would miraculously fall into place and all would be right with the world again.

September 1, 2007

Chapter Twenty-One

They had arrived, finally. Parking their Ford Escape in the small area designated for guest check-in, they noticed their car fit right in with the remainder of other cars parked in the lot, what with their New Hampshire plates and all. They may as well have been North Conway townies, for all the townspeople knew.

Maggie and Paul made their way into the hotel via a large veranda dotted with big white rocking chairs that appeared so small they almost looked as if they'd been made for a child rather than an adult. She suspected this optical illusion came about because of the sheer size of the porch. The thing was huge. To the right of the chairs were floor to ceiling windows. The panes of glass were big and the mullions that separated each glass panel had chipped white paint on them with bits of wood showing through. Maggie imagined this was done on purpose to give the facade of that aged effect. But she didn't know this for certain. It may have been that the hotel was simply in need of some maintenance but didn't have the funds to keep the joint up.

She didn't know what the tourist situation was like lately in New Hampshire. She assumed it was good in the summer and probably also in the fall. But, the severe shortage of snow in winter and the consequent dwindling of skiers most likely put quite a stranglehold on income during winter months. Maggie briefly peered in one of the windows and observed the full-length, silk-lined brown velvet curtains hanging on the inside. Even from the outside of the window she could see the dust that had gathered around the thick gold and red braiding which held each curtain back.

On the left side of the porch were a series of massive white tapered columns spaced far enough apart so as not to deny the rocking chair dwellers their view of the grand and glorious backdrop of the White Mountains.

You could just as easily have transported this hotel back to the old south, such that its architecture matched that of the plantation home in the movie *Gone with the Wind*. Maggie envisioned Scarlet O'Hara gracefully walking along this porch, smug and rebellious in the face of a great Civil War. As Maggie walked hand in hand with shaky Paul, she imagined herself in a long hoop skirt with a tight corseted lacy blouse. In her vision, the one hand that wasn't holding onto Paul was carrying a lacy parasol, which she used much like a cane, clicking the bottom on the wood of the porch with each step she took.

In the lobby, Maggie gazed around at the tall pillars of solid wood that held up the somewhat sinking ornately carved ceiling. The thick masts of wood columns stood atop of a very lavish red and black tapestry carpeted floor that appeared as though patrons from the nineteenth century had trampled on it.

"This is beautiful, Paul," Maggie exclaimed, placing her hands next to the bowl of apples on the counter.

The lady behind the counter was as friendly as she could be, given the fact that she was born and bred in New England. "Sign here," she commanded, pointing to the line at the bottom of the receipt. Maggie had a faint recollection of the frizzy haired train attendant who had asked her to sign her train ticket on the way up to Connecticut.

"Do you need my credit card?" Maggie asked the stone-faced woman.

Paul interjected, "Everything's covered, Maggie, courtesy of your father, remember?"

"Okay, okay, I forgot."

So there they stood, Paul and Maggie at the counter waiting for their room key, the large mirror behind the stern faced check-in lady boasting her and Paul's reflection. Starring at his reflection, Maggie envied Paul and this puzzled her. Why would she envy a man who had had such a hard life? It wasn't that he had a hard life as much as it was the fact that he was so accepting of that life. He knew what he did to his wife by ending her life and was willing to pay the price for it. And anyone could tell that Paul didn't want to go see Dr. Leonard just by looking at him in the waiting room every week. But he did go, even though talking about his wife made him so sad. He faced his weekly visits with Scottie with bravery and acceptance. You also knew where you stood with Paul. He told you the truth. You knew when he was happy and when he was not because he told you this too. You knew when he was cold or hot or tired or just plain contented. Yes, indeed Paul was a man in touch with his feelings. He was not only a man to admire, he was a man to emulate.

This is what Maggie envied about him, his honesty. She had never known these traits in a man. The only two men she had known intimately, her father and ex-husband, had abandoned her after only a short time, so what they claimed to be true was not. Her father had not lived to be a hundred and her husband did not honor his own wedding vows. As a result of these two facts, Maggie had learned not to place too much credence in what men had to say.

Paul placed the room key in one hand and held onto Maggie with the other, gently guiding her toward the elevator. "Hey Paul, do you miss seeing Dr. Leonard?" Maggie asked while they waited in the lobby.

"I won't be going back to see him, Maggie. Didn't I tell you?"

"No, you didn't," Maggie answered loudly. In fact she was so loud, other people in the lobby started to turn and stare at them. "Why?"

"I guess the law figured I had done my time with good ole Dr. Leonard. Plus Dr. Leonard agreed. He went to bat for me, saying I was cured or at least rehabilitated, which is kind of a joke, right? What's an old man like me going to do anyways? Kill someone? I couldn't even hold a weapon still long enough to kill anyone at this point in my life. I think it was just a formality going to see Dr. Leonard, like doing prison time, you know? I'm glad Maggie. I hated going to talk about my wife over and over every week. I loved her more than you could imagine. I just hated talking about the last thing I did to her. It wasn't going to bring her back, right? Plus talking about it just made me feel like a rotten son-of-a-bitch guy who killed his wife, which wasn't the case at all."

"I'll miss seeing you in the waiting room, especially now that I've gotten to know you so well."

"You'll see me, Maggie. Believe me, you'll see me."

Along with the room key, Paul carried a small plastic grocery bag which now seemed to be embedded in the crook of his elbow on his right arm, the weight of which was beginning to take its toll. Letting go of Maggie's hand, he shifted the plastic bag from one arm to the other while they were on the elevator.

"Do you want me to take that, Paul?" Maggie asked, pointing to the plastic bag hanging from Paul's hand. Maggie and Paul had stopped at the food market before they got to the hotel. They wanted to get some things to cook for dinner, since they were both pretty tired from traveling all day. They were much too tired to go in search of a decent restaurant. They wanted merely to veg out tonight, cook something simple and just sit and relax in their suite.

After they got settled in their hotel room, Maggie told Paul to sit and relax while she went straight to work in the kitchen. He didn't put up an argument that was for sure. He sat opposite her on the tall counter stools sipping his Jack Daniels. "Oh just go ahead and use the tongs God gave you, Maggie," he exclaimed watching her try to mix up the beautiful salad with two bent forks. "I know your paws are clean. I watched you wash them. I worked at a restaurant a long time ago, Maggie, and believe me, you ain't seen nothin' till you work at a restaurant. So at least I know what I'm getting when I watch you prepare a meal." The tiny kitchenette provided little more than a few sets of eating utensils, certainly nothing elaborate enough to do any gourmet cooking, that was for sure. "That looks great, Maggie. I sure could use some greens. A little plugged up down south, if you know what I mean."

She knew what Paul was going through because internally things didn't work as well for Maggie either. She could barely sneeze lest she leak a little down there, and she tired much quicker than she used to. This had been a more recent occurrence in Maggie's life.

Still, the thought of an old wrinkly plugged up butt made Maggie's stomach turn for just a second. Then she really looked at him. Not as the wrinkled husk of a man he once was, but instead as merely a friend who had cared enough to take her on this journey in search of her long lost father. Paul was a man who was finally telling her the truth. Maggie found herself looking at Paul at lot on this trip. Plus, soon enough she knew she would feel the scourges of old age ravage her own body. This was a fact she was well aware of because even now, in her late fifties, the once taut skin that clung tightly to muscle and bone sagged more than she would have liked. This didn't bother her too much, mostly because she rarely looked at her reflection in the mirror. She knew they were there though, her wrinkles. She came to acknowledge and expect the crow's feet around her eyes. The little lines around her mouth that sucked up her extra lipstick, fanning it out much further than it should have, didn't trouble her too much either, except that the lipstick enhanced her constant puckered mouth appearance.

What vexed her more than those two nuances in her appearance was the addition of that little flap of saggy skin under her chin. This body part took on a life of its own, flapping around when she chewed her food or talked. As the years went on, she noticed the flap of skin sagged more and more, growing as a separate entity from the rest of her body, until it eventually cascaded down her neck and onto her chest. The extra skin ultimately ending up in a pile that rested on the top of her bosom, the sheer size of it becoming enhanced by her hefty push-up bra. "Push one thing up and it shows off some other telltale sign of old age," she thought. This made her chuckle. "I can't win for losing,"

Half the time this little bit of saggy neck and chest skin became her talisman, a trinket that boasted the fact she had actually made it well into middle age. But, at the times when it did bother her, she found herself hunting through her jewelry box for the four-strand set of Barbara Bush pearls she had purchased to conceal her saggy neck skin. Mostly though, like with everything else in her life, except of course for the feelings she had for Abbie, she really didn't care about her turkey neck.

There was no doubt in her mind this trip with Paul was changing Maggie. She could feel herself letting go of more and more of the things that ruled her previous world. She didn't count nearly as much as she used to, finding it quite unnecessary, indeed, even ludicrous for things to be even. She wasn't smoking cigarettes as much either, at least not in two's. She was more than glad about the cigarettes because they were much more expensive up north than they were in the tobacco capital of the world, the place where she lived, Virginia. Most importantly, thanks to Paul, she was becoming acutely aware of her own thoughts and feelings. It felt good.

"We should get some rest, Maggie," Paul said, revealing a big open-mouthed yawn. "We've got a big day ahead of us tomorrow."

"What are we doing tomorrow, Paul? Where are we going?"

"Another train trip, Maggie. But this will be a short one. There's a tour leaving at 8:30 a.m. going from here to Bretton Woods," as he said this, he pointed out of the big picture window to the antique train station across the street. "There's a tour guide on the train that explains everything you ever wanted to know about this area. Some folks call it a tourist trap but I think it's well worth the $49.00 investment."

"God, Paul, another train trip? When will we be done traveling? This whole trip has been on wheels. I'm tired. Why can't you just tell me why we're up here in New Hampshire? Why the big secret?"

"Trust me, Maggie. You will enjoy the train ride. You'll learn more than you ever thought you could learn. It's interesting, you'll see. Now go to bed so you can be nice and rested for tomorrow," Paul grumbled, sounding a little annoyed.

"Okay, okay, don't be so cantankerous, you old goat," she joked. "Hey, Paul?"

"Yeah."

"Thanks."

"You're welcome, Maggie," Paul answered, knowing full well the train trip would be quite an enjoyable event but afterwards would not. He didn't look forward to that part, after the tour ended. But, after all, that part was the reason they came on the trip in the first place. That part was as necessary as the day was long for Maggie or at least as necessary as her father wished it would be so many years ago.

September 2, 2007

Chapter Twenty-Two

"Rise and shine," Maggie yelled, pressing her face into Paul's half open bedroom door. "Come on, Paul, or we'll be late."

"I'm coming," he moaned, gingerly edging his way out of bed. Maggie could hear his groaning. "My achy back. You gotta love old age, Maggie. You gotta love it!"

She was relieved to hear his voice because he was usually up before her and when she didn't see him in the kitchen, it made her worry that he had died in his sleep. She knew this could happen to old people or even young ones for that matter. By the sound of his voice, he didn't seem to be in a good mood at all. It was rough and then, when she saw him emerge from his room half dressed and in his stocking feet, she knew why. He just looked awful. Just so dog-gone worn out. Maggie searched in her purse for some aspirin or any other kind of anodyne, just something to ease his morning pain and stiffness.

"Are you okay, Paul?" she asked, concerned.

"I'm alright, just a little tired and sore from traveling so much. Hey, where's that coffee I been smelling?"

"Here you go," she said as she placed the mug in front of him. And, if Maggie had ever been bothered by her turkey neck and wrinkled chest, her little physical foibles could not compare to Paul's upper body. As he sat on the stool of the kitchen counter with his shirt off, she stared at the front of him from his neck to his belt buckle. It looked as if someone had sucked the meat from the inside of a chicken breast and then gently draped the skin over the bones. After seeing this, Maggie would never complain about her turkey neck again.

"What's the matter, Maggie, never seen an old man's chest before?" Paul asked, part kidding and part sarcastic.

She thought for a moment. "No, I guess I never have come to think of it," she replied truthfully.

There was no spoiling Maggie's mood. Neither Paul nor anyone else she encountered during this beautiful September day would mess it up. She felt lighter today for some reason, more resilient to what the world would or could throw at her, more confident, if you will. She had gotten up early, taken her shower and then put on some makeup, feeling quite rested and refreshed after these past few days of grueling travel. Going to bed early made all the difference. From the limited selection of clothes in her small suitcase, she opted for the black mock turtleneck sweater, or what she referred to as her "turkey neck" sweater. But, looking back at her choice of clothing for the day, after observing Paul's chicken breast, she decided never again to refer to any poultry when speaking of the human upper frontal view.

After breakfast she revisited the mirror in her room to see if her makeup had gotten smudged or her lips were "running." "Hmm, wonder if I need more makeup," she remarked, peering closely at her reflection. "Naw, that'd be like guilding the lily," she said openly in the confines of her small room. Then she laughed a big jovial laugh. Indeed, she was in a good mood today, full of piss and vinegar. She was even looking forward to the train tour.

"What are you laughing about in there, young lady?"

"Nothing, Paul. I like the young part."

"Well, you are young, at least compared to me."

"Who's comparing?" Maggie stated matter-of-fact. "Remember what you said earlier in our trip, age is a state of mind?"

"Well, if age is a state of mind, I feel like one of the first states in the union right now."

"Funny, Paul. Very funny."

"I'm not trying to be funny. I do feel like that."

"So, shall we just walk across the street to the train station?"

"Yeah. That'd be fine with me. Shouldn't we get going?"

"I have my jacket in my hand, my shoes on my feet, and my purse on my shoulder," Maggie said, looking at Paul's bare chest.

"Okay. I get the point. I'll just be a minute." Paul rustled through his also limited selection of clothes. He picked out his flannel to wear because he knew the mountains of New Hampshire could get cold this time of year, especially in the early morning. "God, I wish I didn't have to do this today," he whispered, buttoning up his well worn, quilt-lined flannel shirt.

They made their way across the street, walking over the meticulously manicured grass still wet with morning dew, then hopped or rather hobbled over the two foot cement barrier which lined the parking lot in front of the station. The old train station had been renovated but kept its original architecture. Refurbished old-fashioned mustard colored planking was laid in an overlapping pattern on the outside of the building. A recently replaced reddish colored copper patina tin roof gave proof of the building's original style.

The station was crowded. Paul had forgotten this was Labor Day weekend, the last weekend children were off from their summer vacations. For some families, Labor Day weekend was the last hoorah before preparing for the hectic new school year when they would be busy shuffling kids off to not only school, but also various after-school activities such as soccer, track, and band practice. After waiting in line for a while, Paul bought two tickets that set him back about a hundred bucks, or rather set back Maggie's father a hundred bucks.

Maggie and Paul sat in one of the train cars where there were windows you could push up or down, not in the open-air car. Paul knew that car would be way too cold, even as the train sputtered along at a mere twenty-five miles per hour. Not a fast speed but fast enough for a cold New Hampshire morning wind to cut right through you.

The train started up and was on its way, leaving in its wake a thick black trail of smoke, remnants from the old diesel engine. The engineer sounded the traditional loud train whistle, forewarning the townspeople of the train's impending departure. Pulling out of North Conway via a small rusted iron suspension trestle, the old rusted train crossed over one of the main roads in town. As it wobbled back and forth, clucking along, the tour guide began to speak. "Welcome, welcome," he said enthusiastically. "Sit back and enjoy the ride."

"He must get so sick of saying the same thing over and over again, day after day," Paul thought as he listened to the guide.

"You are traveling on one of the first diesel electric trains ever made in this country. Today our twenty-one-mile, hour-and-forty-five-minute roundtrip excursion will take us northeast, traveling through fields and woodlands and crossing the East Branch, Saco, and Ellis rivers," the guide went on.

"Hey Paul, did you live close to here when you moved up north with Pavoti's family?"

"Yep, sure did. I'll show you where I lived. It's on the way to Bartlett and you can see it right from this train."

"Really?" Maggie asked, surprised. "I'm excited now. Ever since you told me about that place Pavoti's brother owned up here, I've been interested in it. Can you see the house where you used to live?"

"Sure can," Paul answered, closing his eyes and shaking his head up and down. "Sure can," he said again as if to resign himself to what needed to be done, the imminent telling of information about the property and its original contents and all the inhabitants of the land as well. This was all information he would need to reveal to Maggie. Paul looked down at his hands that were folded neatly in his lap. They were shaking uncontrollably. Maggie was far too preoccupied to take notice of them, thank God.

As the train moved forward slowly it came upon a little clearing. Maggie spotted a few rundown houses. The tour guide got on his microphone and said something but she couldn't hear because the diesel engine was too loud. "What did he say? What did he say?" Maggie turned and asked Paul.

"He said that's Parker's Pasture."

Maggie viewed the large expanse of land dotted with old run down houses. A small patch of railroad ties led from around the back of one of the homes, eventually leading up to the tracks they were traveling on right now. The old tracks encircling Parker's Pasture were overgrown with weeds and crabgrass. The once thick railroad ties that separated those rusted iron tracks were now splintered and rotting. "That's it isn't it, Paul? That's where you used to live."

"Yes, that's it," he answered searching the land for any remnants of life. There were none of course.

"Why do they call it Parker's Pasture?"

"Because that was my wife's family's last name, Parker. I know it doesn't sound very much like a Native American name. I was surprised when I first met my wife too. I thought authentic Native Americans should have names like Running Bull, Black Hawk, or Crazy Horse. They may have had names like that early on in history, but I guess eventually they were forced to conform to our ways and, consequently, took on the names we consider normal.

Originally, my wife Pavoti, her brother Pontiac, and their whole family were part of the Pennacook tribe. It wasn't really a tribe in and of itself but more of a confederacy of Algonquian tribes that occupied New Hampshire. My wife's family stayed true to their Native American ways as much as they could. They were part of the Tribe of Nations in the Northeast. Pavoti's mother was originally from Carson Valley, Nevada but migrated east when the women in her tribe were banned from basket making. This left her tribe little to trade, reducing it to poverty. So they consequently headed east in search of a better life. She met Pavoti's father here in New Hampshire, married him, and took on the name Parker. They lived just outside of North Conway in Parker's Pasture from then on. Her mother carried on the tradition of basket making. Maggie, you should have seen some of the baskets she made. She used to bring them into town to sell to the tourists. Some of them sold for close to 500 dollars."

"Wow. They must have been beautiful."

"They were. I wish I had one to show you now. I just have a few of them left to my name. They're in my house down in Virginia. One of them was originally bright red and orange. It was made with handmade twine interwoven between small, pliable willow branches. It was beautiful in its day, but now it's quite faded and pretty worn from years of schlepping things around in it."

"It sounds lovely. Hey, not to change the subject, but tell me, Paul, why are there railroad ties along the outer rim of the property? They look like they lead right up to the tracks we're on right now."

Paul's facial expression turned serious and grim.

"What's the matter, Paul? Did I say something wrong?" Maggie asked, concerned.

"Nothing, Maggie. I'll tell you later."

"Was there something on the tracks at one time, Paul? Was there an old train on them, or did a train go right through your property?" On closer inspection Maggie noticed the tracks did not actually meet with the ones they were traveling on right now. It looked as if someone had just plopped down the piece of track randomly in the field. "It doesn't look like they come all the way up to these tracks," she said, pointing back to where the old tracks stopped, about twenty feet away from their train.

"Good deduction, Maggie. Not a whole train but you're close. There was a caboose that sat on the tracks. It was done over so nice it hardly looked like it was once part of a train. I'll show it to you when we get back to the station."

"It's back at the train station where we started, Paul?" she inquired puzzled.

"Yes, it's back at the train station. There's a section to the side of the station, off the back parking lot that houses a whole bunch of old train cabooses. It's kind of like a caboose graveyard."

"Isn't that an oxymoron?" Maggie replied, half laughing. "A caboose graveyard? Talk about reaching the end of the line. Why was there a caboose in your front yard?"

"I'll tell you in a little while," he said abruptly. He wanted her to stop asking questions. He knew he had to tell her the truth soon enough even though he didn't really want to. He was actually scared to tell her.

A hush fell on their conversation, Paul's mystifying behavior give way to a rising suspicion that had begun to fester in Maggie's gut.

September 2, 2007

Chapter Twenty-Three

At precisely 10:15 a.m. the train pulled back into the old railroad station in the middle of town. The massive diesel engine spit and sputtered a few times before coming to a complete stop. Maggie decided she had pretty much learned all she ever wanted or needed to know about North Conway, New Hampshire. The tour guide got off the train first and pulled down three heavy metal steps. They clanked as they hit the cement platform. Paul was the first passenger off and, as the tour guide reached out to grab his hand to help him down the steps, he kindly thanked him. He could use all the help he could get these days.

"You're welcome," the tour guide answered back.

Maggie followed Paul, but instead of accepting the tour guide's outstretched hand, Maggie preferred to make her way down the steps on her own.

Paul and Maggie slowly walked to the back of the building where the Caboose Graveyard was housed. It wasn't a long walk but they did go through a crowd of people waiting in line to get tickets. The tourists stared at Paul and Maggie. "Maybe people think we're a couple," Maggie said softly. Mismatched as they were, indeed she would have to agree that would be something to stare at for sure. She would have stared too had she been standing in that line.

For some unknown reason, Maggie thought back to when her daughter was in college. One random weekend she surprised her daughter by paying a visit to her at school. After she picked her daughter up in the parking lot of her dorm building, they drove along the main thoroughfare of campus on their way to the bagel shop down the road. On their way to eat, both Maggie and her daughter watched as many students stumbled across lawns and sidewalks on their way back to their dorm rooms. Being so early in the morning, Maggie couldn't figure out why so many kids were out and about. As these students made their way across empty parking lots and grassy fields, Abbie pointed at them and said, "Walk of shame." Their appearance was not good, pretty much all of them sporting severely wrinkled clothing and no bras, making Maggie think they'd slept in their clothes. And talk about bed head. As they staggered past Maggie observed their tangled knots of hair, indicating a fitful night's sleep. But somehow she guessed the cause of their knotted hair was not the result of sleeping.

"I get it, Abbie. Walk of shame. I hope you've never taken that walk," Maggie said in her motherly voice, knowing full well that if she had, Maggie would be the last person to find out.

Maggie didn't go to college, so she wouldn't have taken that walk. Since most of her classmates didn't go to college either, she supposed the definition of a walk of shame to them would be jumping from the back seat of an old Buick into the front. Maggie knew plenty of her old high school classmates who had taken that hop. Some of the less careful couples, the ones who got pregnant, even named their children after the cars they were conceived in. Maggie wished her mother and father would have done that, back seat or no back seat. Nothing would have pleased her more than having a name like Catalina or Bonneville. Even Galaxy would have been better than Maggie. She'd probably get ribbed for those names too, but she was pretty sure she wouldn't have minded that as much. She thought of Pontiac, that lucky son-of-a-bitch.

"Ma. Stop it. This is college remember?"

"Oh I haven't forgotten, believe me." Maggie replied. It was at this point in their relationship she realized that her daughter was slipping away from her. She knew she would ultimately lose a good part of her to a career, the opposite sex, and eventually her own home and family. Maggie was not able to guide her daughter in any of these areas because she was certain, had these things been tests in school, she would never have passed any of them.

While it was true that Maggie couldn't help her daughter with many things in her life, she figured it didn't really matter because that wasn't the bond that held them together. From the very beginning, their unbreakable connection had been humor. Abbie was one of the few people who "got" Maggie's witty, satirical sense of humor, often bantering back and forth with her. It was like watching a tennis match when the two of them went at it, until eventually, as Abbie started to get a little older, it became almost impossible for Maggie to keep up with her daughter's tongue-in-cheek one-liners. Abbie had a dry sense of humor, often delivering her comedy without a single expression on her face. If anyone ever came in the room while they were bantering back and forth, they'd see Abbie with her straight face and Maggie rolling on the floor, laughing like a hyena.

Even though Maggie couldn't help her daughter with her career, she desperately wanted to guide her in the boyfriend department—that is the live-in boyfriend department. It seemed lately that every time Maggie saw her daughter, she looked more and more tired. Abbie went to graduate school part-time and waitressed two to three nights a week and most weekends, often working well into the wee hours of the night.

Although Abbie flip-flopped back and forth with her career choice, she ultimately decided business was the way to go, so she was attending an MBA program at a local college. She still wasn't positive this was the right field for her, though. One thing she was resolute about was keeping the same boyfriend around. His name was Richard, but Maggie enjoyed calling him "Dick." Dick didn't work. He apparently couldn't find the right kind of job yet. He didn't go to school either. But he did have time to go to the gym twice a day.

Maggie suggested to him once, "You know it's amazing, Dick," she commented. "How is it with that buff physique of yours, that you have so much trouble finding even a job that involves some kind of manual labor? Wouldn't it be nice to help Abbie out with the bills?" she asked bluntly. Judging by their reaction, her comments didn't go over big with Dick or Abbie. Her daughter shot her a piercing stare after her mother spoke and she said, "ML, Richard will find the right job soon, give him a break will you! He just needs a little more time." Maggie shut up after that.

They turned the corner and, lo and behold, there they were—caboose heaven. There must have been at least a dozen old cabooses all balanced quite nicely on a long stretch of old railroad track leading to nowhere. Much to Maggie's surprise, all the cabooses were in pristine condition. Some were brightly colored and had additions added to their sides or tops. Some had little platforms sticking out from the ends, akin to where a deck would be on a regular house. All had been residences at one time too she was certain of that. Now the train station had taken upon itself the chore of restoring and preserving the homes that once housed many a free spirited soul.

"Was this a trend at one time, Paul? Living in a caboose?"

"Yes, as a matter of fact it was. During the '60's and early '70's it was the hippie era and these caboose things were cheap to live in. All you needed was to revamp them a little and they became nice little homes. Plus, they'd last a lifetime what with the thickness of the metal and all. The only trouble was they rusted. So that's why most of them are painted, to keep the rust from taking over and rotting them away. I sure wish there was some kind of paint old people could spray on themselves to keep them from rotting away," Paul said, laughing nervously.

Maggie ignored him. She was much more interested in the caboose houses. "Which one was on your property?"

"Over here, Maggie. Paul led her to the third one in the lineup. See— you can see the words 'Parker's Pasture' written in small letters across the wood at the top of the side window."

"Can we go inside?"

"Sure can, my dear. This one still belongs to me. I know because I have to pay fifty bucks a month for it to sit here and have other folks come and look at it."

"Can you move it anywhere you want, Paul?"

"Sure I can, but I just don't see a need to right now. I have plenty of room in my house on the reservation." Paul hesitated for a moment, but ultimately decided not to tell her what needed to be said. Not yet. Timing was everything now.

"Oh, I see."
"Come on inside. Let me show you the joint."
"Cool."

They both stood on the small simple wooden platform which could have passed for her back deck except that the view here was much more spectacular. Paul searched through his set of keys, finally settling on a small one at the end of the ring. Holding back the screen door, he placed the key in the thick wooden door lock, and with one click to the left the deadbolt was released. He turned the handle and forced the door open. Maggie stepped in behind him. It smelled musty. "This is absolutely beautiful," she gasped, looking around at the original natural bead board on the walls.

"You know the history of the caboose, don't you, Maggie?"

"Can't say as I do, Paul," she replied, in awe of the little structure. She had never been inside a caboose before. The layout was similar to an old fashioned RV but much nicer. Immediately upon entering there was a short hallway. To the left an open coat closet housed an array of various empty hangers, beckoning visitors to come in, take off their coats and sit a spell. A single green and white checked wool shirt hung on the last hanger in the corner of the closet. When Paul wasn't looking, Maggie bent over and smelled the shirt, taking a deep pull of air through the material into her lungs. The familiar odor of the garment lingered in her nostrils. Maggie closed her eyes, and for one brief moment she couldn't tell if she actually smelled or tasted the shirt.

In that instant her two senses meshed and became one so that the odors, remnants of mechanics grease and cigarette smoke, rested briefly on the taste buds in her tongue. Maggie pulled away, almost scared to breath more of the shirt's owners essence into her snout. She was right, just one whiff of that shirt and her suspicions were confirmed. This was where her father stayed, lived even. "He lived," she thought. "I was right–he lived. But how, why?"

Turning quickly around to the other side of the caboose, directly across from the coat closet was a full bathroom, shower and all. Both of these spaces boasted natural wood bead board. Not the kind you get at a hardware store nowadays either. This was the real deal. The deep, rich natural wood that had once been soiled with a buildup of dirt, smoke and engine grime had been painstakingly sanded, stained and then shellacked. The rest of the caboose featured the same natural wood. The inside glowed with a warmth and richness that was as inviting and soothing as a cup of hot cocoa on a frigid winter's day.

A small kitchen table was folded flat against one wall in the kitchen area. Someone had put a makeshift lever on the bottom of the table, allowing it to collapse in on itself and blend flush to the wall. This gave the appearance of much more room inside the cabin area. Two chairs were pushed up against the wall too, one on each side of the table. Above the table was a window from which hung tattered white curtains with faded red roosters on them. The kitchen had all the amenities of any modern day kitchen. A small gas stove stood to the left of the table. It had a metal hood with a fan and a large metal pipe that led to the outside, a way for cooking smoke and steam to escape, Maggie supposed. To the left of that was a midsize refrigerator and then a corner sink and small countertop to the left of that. On the opposite wall was an "L" shaped built in rich cordovan leather couch. It almost looked as if it had been hand sewn. The stitches were widely spaced apart and made of thick yellow string. A small TV was mounted on the wall just above one end of the couch.

Maggie imagined her father in this space, smoking his unfiltered cigarettes and drinking his coffee. Even laughing at some of the modern day sitcoms on his small TV. *I Love Lucy* and *The Dick Van Dyke Show* had been his favorites back in the early 60's. She wondered why he hadn't contacted her? Why didn't he let her know he was alive?

Maggie could see a floor to ceiling curtain hung in the doorway just past the kitchen table. She pulled it open and found a moderate sized bedroom with a large queen sized mattress laying on a high wooden platform. The platform had six drawers underneath. She assumed these were used as a bureau for the occupant, seeing as there wasn't enough space for a real one to stand-alone in the room. The walls of the bedroom were made of the same rich bead board wood as the rest of the interior décor of the caboose. The bedroom was cozy and light.

"This is beautiful, Paul. Simply beautiful."

"I know, isn't it?"

Maggie knew why it was so light in there. When she looked up, directly above the bed was what she thought was a high, glassed in ceiling. A set of small metal stairs just to the right of the bed led up to the light, airy space.

"You know what that is, don't you?"

"No, I don't"

"That's the cupola."

"Cupola?" Maggie questioned. She had a friend once who had a cupola on the roof of her house. But it was nothing like this one. The one on her house was small and completely enclosed with a big rooster weathervane sticking out of the top of it. She never knew there could be one on a train, especially one this big and open.

"Some people call it a Belvedere or, more commonly, a 'widow's walk.' See all the glass around the outside? Those windows can be opened. They even have screens in them to keep the bugs out. At night you can look up at the stars and it feels just like you're camping out in the open air. There's even a bench around the outside too so you can sit up there. There's a small table just like the one in the kitchen. It folds down too, so you can put it out of the way when you're not using it."

"May I go up there, Paul?"

"Be my guest." Maggie walked up the stairs and sat on one of the benches. Paul was right—it was spectacular. You could see for miles from up there. Maggie felt at one with nature. An air of unobstructed freedom immediately surrounded her. Now she knew why people wanted to live in these things, especially hippies.

"You know what the caboose and this cupola were used for back in the early days, don't you, Maggie?"

"I'm afraid I don't," she shouted down to Paul, who had his head bent back and was staring up at her. "Come up here, Paul. It's beautiful." She wondered how in the hell he would make it up those stairs. There was no ambulance here to save him like there was at the road race.

Maggie's thoughts turned back to her father, "How many sunsets had her father witnessed up here? How many trains filled with excited tourists had he seen go by? How many times had he thought of her? Her sisters? Her mother?"

Paul struggled up the stairs, placing both feet firmly on each stair before tackling the next step. He did this all the way to the top. When he was almost all the way up, Maggie grabbed his arm and hoisted him to the top. Paul was quite amazed by her strength. He lifted his eyebrows and said, "I'm impressed. I didn't know you were so strong."

Maggie pushed the sleeves of her mock turtleneck up to reveal her biceps and flexed them for Paul saying all the while, "See? You see, Paul? Didn't know I had so many muscles, did you?"

"I had no idea. If I knew you were Wonder Woman, I would've had you carrying my bags all this time." They both laughed.

Paul began talking, spewing out information about the caboose and its history. He spoke as he usually did, in his instructional fatherly manner. This style suited Paul. He was a natural leader and teacher. Pavoti had been right, he was good at leading people in journeys of any kind. He gave all the necessary information needed along the trip at just the right time, making sure not to overwhelm Maggie with either too much information or the wrong kind of information.

Paul situated himself next to Maggie on the long wooden bench. "Now, like I was saying, you know what this was used for at one time, right?" He glanced over at Maggie, his head tilted to one side.

"A lookout?"

"Sort of," Paul replied. "A long time ago the caboose and the conductor inside this cupola were considered to be the 'brains' onboard the train. They could oversee all the train routes from this little space up here. From this cupola to the rear platform they could assess the safety of speed around curves and gauge obstacles that might materialize during the trip."

"That's pretty cool, Paul. Pretty darned cool."

"So you like it?"

"Like it? I love it. How is it heated and cooled?"

"This little caboose she has a complete HVAC unit. Heating and cooling at your fingertips."

"Where is it?"

"Come on, I'll show you."

They headed down the stairs and outside. Paul bent over and showed Maggie the heating and cooling system bolted underneath the caboose. "That's pretty clever," she said in amazement. She could imagine her father working on it, tinkering with it to make sure everything was perfect. She wished she had been right there beside him, helping him with all his projects. She could have learned so much from him.

"Yeah. There wasn't much space on the outside of this little filly, but there's plenty of room underneath, since the wheels are so big and it sits up so high. That makes for a perfect spot for plumbing pipes and heating and air conditioning units."

"I'm thoroughly impressed, Paul. Thoroughly impressed."

"Thought you would be. That's why I took you here. That and one other reason."

Maggie's demeanor changed. "This is where he lived isn't it Paul?" she asked, pointing to the caboose.

Paul's eyes widened and his mouth dropped, showing off his lower set of tiny yellowed teeth as his bottom lip pulled away from the gum line, the result of gravity and old skin considerably lacking in collagen and elasticity. Paul was speechless that Maggie had figured out the mystery already. "When did you find out, Maggie?"

"I'm not stupid you know, Paul. It just came to me not too long ago, though I'm still not sure of a lot of things."

"You're a smart one, Margaret Lerner. A smart one indeed."

"He decided to live free as opposed to dying. Right, Paul?"

"You're half right, Maggie," Paul answered, looking over at a nearby car with New Hampshire license plates that read "Live Free or Die."

"You're only half right."

September 2, 2007

Chapter Twenty-Four

"I'm flabbergasted, Maggie. I still want to know how you knew." Paul searched Maggie's face for a clue. She had started to cry as they walked back toward their hotel. Even though she knew the truth about her father now, it didn't make things any easier for her. "I know how you must feel, Maggie," Paul said empathetically. He tried to console her but that was not an easy task.

"I've been thinking, thinking, thinking. I've been thinking way too much on this trip and you know what?" She asked sniffling softly and wiping her eyes with her baggy shirtsleeve. "Last night I went through my notes, I just put two and two together, but I still wasn't quite sure. It wasn't hard to figure out, you know. Then, after our tour of the caboose graveyard and after I went inside the little train house, the answer became as plain as day. That old caboose cinched it for me. It was that shirt actually–the green and white checked one hanging in there? It smelled just like my father, a mixture of tobacco smoke and mechanical grease."

"That was his favorite shirt. He wore it nearly every day. Your father ended up leaving that shirt behind. He forgot about it until we were in Virginia. By that time he was so busy getting settled there, he ultimately forgot about it altogether. I didn't know you still wrote things down in a diary?"

"Yes, I do. But I don't call it my diary anymore. That word gets under my skin, makes me feel as though I'm doing something wrong, you know? I do try to write some of my thoughts and feelings in a notebook every once in a while, especially when my life gets confusing like it has been these past few weeks. Usually, when I go back over my notes, the answer becomes quite clear to me. Plus it makes me feel better to write down my thoughts and feelings at the end of the day sometimes. I wondered why you or whomever you had come into my apartment to steal the stories about my mother and father didn't take my writing notebook too. But, with where I hide it, not even Harry Houdini could find it. After I lost my diary when I was a kid, I vowed never to misplace my writing tablet ever again." She looked directly at Paul. He hung his head.

"We just copied the stories and then put them right back the next day," Paul said, feeling a little guilty for barging into her private space. He had to though. He had no choice. Eddy wanted to see how she lived, check out some things that belonged to her. When they came upon the stories they knew Eddy would want a copy of them.

"Here, Maggie, let's sit here on the bench," Paul beckoned–pointing to the old wooden structure with the thick cement legs that sat at the edge of the lush green grass.

After thinking about it for a minute, Maggie said, "Don't worry Paul, I'm not upset you took my stories."

"Good," he answered, relieved.

"So anyways, to get back to my journal thing, last night I lay awake trying to piece all the parts of this trip together. I went back to the first part where it all started, the e-mail. Remember?"

Paul verified her statement. "Yes. I remember."

"By the way Paul, who the hell is Chickahominy Grits? Is there really a Native American by that name? If there is–I really feel sorry for that poor schlep."

"No, no one by that name that I know of at least. Pontiac made up the name, said you might get a kick out of it. Said you might even be easier to convince about this journey thing if you had something funny to hang onto."

"Oh I've hung onto it alright Paul, and I'd like to fling it right back at this Pontiac character. I'd like to put my foot up his ass. That whole e-mail, including the Chickahominy part, really scared the crap out of me. This Pontiac dude, he likes to scare people doesn't he?"

"No, not at all actually. He just likes to be funny, but sometimes I guess his idea of funny isn't always funny."

Maggie didn't respond to Paul's comments about Pontiac. She continued talking about her journal, "Anyways, where were we? Yeah, so when I reread my journal and everything just fit together like a glove. I bet you thought I'd be more upset, right?"

"I thought you would be much more upset. Really I thought you'd lose it completely."

"Well, I kept thinking about that part and I guess I would have been more upset if my dad had been missing for just a few years and I found all this out. But, truthfully, it's been more than three quarters of my life that he's been gone. And then I thought, "Why didn't he try to tell me all of this sooner? But it wouldn't have mattered. I think he felt the same way I do right now. He had been dead to me for so many years, coming back into my life wouldn't have done any good at all. It was too late wasn't it?"

"Your father wanted to tell you he was alive. He desperately wanted to be a part of your life, but Eddy feared reconnecting with you. He was afraid of the mob finding out and of any repercussions that might endanger you or your family. That's why this trip was so important for him. This trip was the most important thing in his life. He couldn't wait for you to take it."

"Why, Paul, why?" Maggie tried to understand her father's reasoning, but she just couldn't let go of the fact that her father was alive all these years and didn't reach out to her and her family. She had mixed emotions, vacillating between understanding and anger. "Don't you think after so many years the mob would have forgotten about all that?" she said.

"I tried to tell him that but he wouldn't listen. He had risked too much. There was no way in hell he was going to jeopardize anything happening to you or your sisters, even if it took a lifetime of separation from you all. And it did. He figured the pain would lessen over the years for you and then, after you took this trip, you'd completely understand why he did what he did. He actually dreaded the first part of this excursion for you because he knew it would hurt you so much. But he predicted you'd find out before I had a chance to tell you. And you did," Paul exclaimed, still in shock. "He needed you to go on this trip because he wanted you to feel the way he did when he left so many years ago. He needed you to take his same journey. But mostly he wanted you to experience the second part of the trip, the fun part."

"Well, I'll have to see about that part when I get to it, right Paul? So far this hasn't been the most fun trip I've ever been on, you know. I still have a lot of questions for you."

"Fire away."

"You serious?"

"Yeah, I'm serious."

"You know I was almost disappointed when I found out about my dad because I thought for a little while you were my long lost father. But, when you had your shirt off this morning I knew better. My father had a big scar on his back from shrapnel when he was in the war and you didn't have any scars on your back at all."

"You know, Maggie–I'd like for you to think of me as your dad if you can. In fact I'd like nothing more than that. I think you're just wonderful. I've thought that from the very beginning when I first started coming in to see Dr. Leonard and saw you sitting behind your computer at your desk."

"Is that why you came to see Dr. Leonard? Did my father ask you to do that?"

"No, he had no part in any of it. I told the truth before. The courts made me see a psychiatrist and Scottie just happened to be the one I picked. The rest is just coincidental. Your father wanted me to find you after he was dead because of this trip thing he planned for you. But remember that day I came to check in and you had a picture of your mother and father on your desk? It was their wedding picture remember? You also had a picture of Abbie next to it, remember?"

"I do recall that day, come to think of it."

"I asked you who that was in the picture."

"Yes, and I said it was my mother and father," Maggie replied, her mouth gaping open a little in amazement.

"Well, there you go. Life is strange, Maggie. Life is so very strange."

"You ain't kidding, Paul."

"I'll tell you what—I'll tell you the whole story and then you won't have any questions left at all, unless there's something you want to ask along the way. I'll tell you anything you want to know."

"So it all started with the plan Dudley and Gunderson came up with, remember when I told you about that?"

"Yes, I remember, Paul," she answered intrigued.

"Gunderson was fed up with everything, everyone, the dirty cops, the mob, Dudley. He wanted to just blow the lid on the whole lot of them, bash the whole mess and everyone who was involved in it to smithereens. He wanted to tell all and then just let the chips fall where they may. He figured he'd be the hero too, the one that put Durham back on the straight and narrow path. He told Dudley he'd be safe because he would have cooperated with the police. But Dudley would have no part of it. Dudley said openly to Gunderson, "You love your family?" "Your wife, kids?"

"Of course I do. What do you think, Dudley?"

"Well if you love them, you'll do as I say." Dudley informed Gunderson in no uncertain terms that he wouldn't give his friend Eddy up to the police or the mob. He didn't want to risk him or his family being killed. He also told Gunderson that if the Chief did blow the whistle on everyone, Gunderson and his family would eventually pay the price. He told Gunderson, maybe not today or tomorrow, but one day he'd be riding down Federal Hill and his brakes would give out, or he'd be painting his house and the top rung of the ladder would give way. "Anything could happen. Anytime." he assured Gunderson.

"Yeah right," thought Gunderson. "This Dudley character just wants to save his own skin. There was no way he would rat this Eddy out because he's just too selfish to give up the extra loot he makes dealing with these dirty bastard cops." But, then again, maybe Dudley was right. Gunderson didn't want to risk any harm that might come to him or his family. So, ultimately he gave in, went along with Dudley's plan.

Dudley started by reaching out to a couple of friends from his old Army days. One friend in particular, a doctor friend by the name of John Sellick who was in his platoon during the war, seemed interested in the plan, especially after Dudley told him Eddy's name. Sellick worked at the Memorial Veterans Hospital. Dudley called his doctor friend to ask him his advice. Sellick said he'd think about what to do and call him back. Dr. Sellick had an "Aha!" moment after he heard Eddy Payne's name mentioned. The name Eddy Payne kept circling around in Sellick's brain. He was so sure he had heard that name before. "Paul!" Sellick thought. "That's where I've heard that name before, from Paul."

"Sellick and I worked together for many years." Paul informed Maggie. "We had a lot in common, both being old Army guys and all. We used to meet up at lunch sometimes, reminisce about our old Army days, you know? Well, my brother John was one of the guys in your dad's platoon. They were stationed in Tunisia together. John was one of the soldiers who benefited from your father's bravery. Remember the story I told you before about your dad saving his platoon? Your father saved my brother's life. I know I must have told Sellick that story about Eddy Payne at least a couple of times." Paul admitted.

"So this doctor, Dr. Sellick, he remembered my dad's name?" Maggie asked.

"Yes, he remembered your dad's name. How could he forget? The story I told him about Eddy was one of the most heroic stories he'd ever heard about the war. So when Sellick asked if we would all help your father out by going along with a plan, Pavoti and I were happy to oblige. We both felt like we owed your father a big debt of gratitude for what he had done in the war, for saving my brother's life and all. Plus Pavoti felt so bad for him. Having lost our daughter, we knew what it would have been like had these cops done something bad to you. And, like I told you before, Maggie, Pavoti and I were more than ready to leave Connecticut."

"Well, I did put all of you together somehow, but I didn't know the whole story. It just seemed so weird you knew so much about my father. After all, he was only in the hospital for about three weeks."

"Well, your father had no choice at all. He had to go along with the plan or someone would have killed him anyways, either the rest of the dirty cops on the force or the Mafia."

"So, what was the plan? It had something to do with escaping to New Hampshire, that I know. Duh...because of the Ford Escape with the license plates 'Live Free or Die.' Because of the caboose he lived in and your land at Parker's Pasture."

"Yeah. Your father thought that would be a clever way to send you a sign, buying a Ford Escape."

"My dad—yeah he was a real prankster all right," Maggie said with just a hint of anger and sarcasm.

"Yes, he was."

"Sellick didn't mind fixing the medical records, but he wouldn't make your father ill. Well, I mean fake ill. That was up to Pavoti."

"So he wasn't really sick with that strange disease, was he? Or whatever way the coroners said he died. I still don't know what really happened to him."

"No, he wasn't really sick. I take that back. He was sick, very sick but it wasn't a sickness that would kill him. Not if Pavoti watched him carefully."

Maggie interrupted. She was puzzled. "The Honda Element— EPHEDRA—that's what made him sick, wasn't it? I tried to look that up online and the whole list of symptoms matched my dad's symptoms—penny for penny and pound for pound."

"You're right, Maggie. Boy you're a smart one that's for sure. Pavoti knew about the drug. In her tribe they nicknamed it 'squaw tea.' It's been called many things throughout history such as Ma Huang and also Mormon Tea.

The ephedra plant has a pine-like odor and is sometimes known as 'joint pine.' It's a perennial evergreen that reaches a height of about four feet or so. Some of the flowers are poisonous and resemble fleshy red cones that look like berries. Only the young stems and branches are used for medicinal purposes. Pavoti's mother used to give it to her in very small doses because she had asthma as a child and that's one of the ailments ephedra helps correct. But if you give too much of it to someone it increases blood pressure and heart rate and causes insomnia and anxiety."

"Those are all the symptoms my father had, right?"

"Right. Squaw tea also messes up lab tests. That part was easy for Dr. Sellick and myself to pull off. After your dad took ephedra for a while his lab work was much the same as a person with pheochromocytoma."

"Yes," Maggie shouted, "that's what Sellick thought he had. That's what he told my mother when dad first got sick. I couldn't remember for the longest time and now you've jarred my memory. But I'd never seen my father's death certificate though."

"It appeared he had that condition, and that's what Sellick wanted people to think, but he really didn't. That was just the ephedra working. Anyways, towards the end of his hospital stay Dr. Sellick ruled that out as his final diagnosis. Instead he decided to play around with the x-rays a bit and blame your dad's death on the shrapnel in his back. He figured that was such a bizarre way to die, no one would suspect or question his demise if Sellick put that on the death certificate. Sellick thought with the other diagnosis, the pheochromocytoma diagnosis, all the other doctors would be fishing around for an autopsy, since it's so rare and all."

"What? What do you mean the shrapnel in his back? What does that have to do with the price of oranges?"

"Everything. Sellick manipulated the x-rays to show that the shrapnel moved and was leaning on your father's adrenal glands. He blamed it for causing all of Eddy's symptoms. But ultimately, he openly blamed Pavoti for your father's death. The night before he 'died,' Pavoti gave your father a backrub before he went to bed. Dr. Sellick claimed Pavoti's backrub made the shrapnel in your father's back move around, ultimately puncturing a main artery. So Sellick claimed your father bled to death internally in his sleep. But it was all a set up, a ruse. The plan, the one Dudley, Sellick, Pavoti, and I concocted, called for Eddy's death, or rather his fake death. Pavoti was glad to help out. She didn't mind placing her job in jeopardy. She wanted to move away. She wanted to get out of the nursing field once and for all. So it all worked out nicely. Pavoti claimed to be distraught at supposedly killing a patient. And as far as everyone knew, your father was, for all intents and purposes, dead. So we all carried out the plan and then Pavoti and I moved to New Hampshire."

"So how was my father after that? He must have been pretty upset right?"

"He was sick, very sick for a long time. That ephedra really did a number on his system, brought him to death's door. Your father actually wanted to die, so Pavoti and I kept a watch on him for many, many months so he wouldn't kill himself. He was beyond sadness and depression. He would mope around all day moaning and groaning. Pavoti and I had to practically force-feed him to keep him alive. Remember Maggie–you lost your father, but he lost his whole family."

Maggie started to cry again. "I know. My dad was very brave wasn't he? Why didn't he just kill himself right off the bat after Gunderson suspected him?"

"He wanted you, your mom and your sisters to get the insurance money. Suicide claims don't pay out a blessed cent, remember?"

"Oh yeah."

"After we all moved up to New Hampshire, your father's health steadily improved year after year. He kept tabs on you through Dudley, so he knew all the things that were happening in you and your sisters' lives. As the years went on he became more content with his situation. He didn't like not seeing you but he was grateful to be able to communicate with Dudley about you all. Not to mention, he was just grateful you were all alive and safe. He lived in the basement of the house Pavoti and I did over in New Hampshire. Then one year he just announced to my wife and I that he was buying this caboose to renovate. We looked at him like he was crazy. But it came out beautiful, didn't it?"

"It sure did, Paul. My father was always good with his hands. He could fix anything, anything but this mess he was in, I guess."

"He wants you to have it. He wants you to bring it back to Virginia with you."

"Me? What am I going to do with a caboose?"

"That's the beginning of the fun part of your journey."

"Sure, Paul, that sounds like fun. We can just put a big magnet on the back of that Ford Escape of yours and tow it back to Virginia. Then I can live the rest of my life in a little metal caboose," Maggie announced sarcastically. "Seriously, Paul, how the hell would I get it back home? Where would I put it? On my back deck?"

"We'll talk about that over the next couple of days."

"Alright then, if you say so, Paul," Maggie replied, still unsure she wanted the thing and then there were all those "minor" details of how they would transport this metal monstrosity back home.

"Hey?"

"Yes."

"When did my father actually die? I'm assuming it was recently or else you would have come to me before this, right?"

"Right. He died about a month ago. He was ninety-three years old."

"He almost made it to a hundred, didn't he Paul?"

"Almost Maggie, almost."

September 6, 2007

Chapter Twenty-Five

It was hard for Maggie to believe all that had happened to her in just seven short days. Seven days that seemed like seventy years to Maggie. She felt as if she'd been propelled forward in time like a rock held taut on a slingshot. Paul had taken her back to where it all began and then, slowly and steadily he had let go, hurling her into the future, her future now. And, after adjusting to all this newly found information from the mouth of Paul Paterson, she had to admit most of it felt pretty damned good. Well, not exactly all of it mind you, just the part about knowing more about her father and her past. At least she knew more about him now, and that in and of itself was a huge relief. No more questions about the past and no more guessing or wondering. Then of course there was the cool caboose he lived in and all. Plus that cool hunk of metal sitting in the caboose graveyard was hers now, lock, stock, and barrel. What she would do with it or how she would get it home, well that was another story.

Paul filled Maggie in on some more details from her father's life. Details she had missed during the nearly forty-year vacant span. He couldn't fill her in on everything of course, just the highlights. She wondered why it took so long for a life to progress and so short a time to talk about it. In approximately four or five hours Maggie became aware of how Eddy lived after he secretly escaped from the Veterans hospital way back in 1965.

Eddy's life had not been a complicated one. Indeed it had become so very uncomplicated after he left Connecticut, mainly because that's how he wanted it to be, just plain and simple, no frills and no fanfare. Eddy had taken to fixing cars while he lived up in New Hampshire. Pavoti's brother, Pontiac, had a similar interest in automobiles, so they worked together underneath the radar of the government, avoiding taxes and all the stupid rules that went along with owning a business. Plus, with this little side business Eddy could almost assuredly keep his anonymity. They ended up being mechanics the entire time they lived up in New Hampshire, working mainly on vehicles that belonged to the locals. They got so good at it and were so reasonably priced no one in or around North Conway would ever snitch on them for not reporting their business to the tax department. Oh, every once in a while a vacationer happened by with a flat tire or busted fan belt, but not often enough for anyone to suspect anything out of the ordinary. These vacationers were usually friends or relatives of some of the locals in New Hampshire, come up to spend a little time with them in the great outdoors.

Pontiac learned a great deal from Eddy's knowledge of cars, apprenticing long enough to where he could diagnose an engine malfunction as soon as he heard the car pull into their little makeshift garage right off Pontiac's house in Parker's Pasture. When they all moved down to Virginia, Eddy gradually handed over the car fixing business to Pontiac, skilled as he was by that time. Eddy was just getting too old to spend countless hours bending and twisting to tighten a lug nut or the heavy lifting it took to haul a radiator out. And, since they were all living on the reservation by that time, it was a no brainer that Pontiac had to go legal with his car-fixing craft, what with the government looking over his shoulder so closely. All three of them, Pontiac, Pavoti, and Paul had a hard enough time keeping Eddy under the radar of the government, let alone having him be involved in a mechanic's workshop.

Eddy lasted a good while in Virginia. He kept up with the goings on of the reservation and took up a new hobby, carving. By the time he passed, he could carve almost any creature the good Lord put on this earth. He whittled away at all the spent little branches of pine and oak. Or he'd take his little carving knife to some of the great big tree stumps on our plot of land and painstakingly carve the most beautiful scenes on them, mostly nature scenes with animals and rivers and vast meadows and fields. There wasn't anything he couldn't carve including snakes, squirrels, chipmunks, geese, and any kind of bug you can name including cockroaches. When his time came for dying, Eddy didn't fear the end. He was more or less relieved to have it all over and done with. In fact, that was one of the aspects of his life he truly looked forward to, as it would ultimately rescue him from his abominable emotional suffering at the loss of his family.

Paul also informed Maggie that her father wished for his end to indeed be a beginning for her. That's why he planned the trip and all the events that went along with it. He wished that his death would bring forth all the things he wanted to tell her during his absence, and so, consequently, he plotted out her journey right down to the very last detail.

Paul and Maggie spent a couple of days in North Conway, exploring. Paul brought her back to Parker's Pasture to give her a close up of the property, the house he lived in there and where the caboose was situated. The old track of railroad it sat on was adjacent to Pavoti and Paul's home. Pavoti's brother lived in one of the other homes on the property about a half an acre away. Eddy's mechanic's garage was right next to his caboose. For Eddy, all he had to do was step out his door and he was at work. For Pontiac it was just a hop, skip and jump to get to the garage. Indeed all four of them worked closely together and lived closely together much like a real family would live, each one watching out for the other. They ate dinner together every night, and did pretty much all the other things families do together.

"Strange as it may sound, Paul, I'm tempted to live in that little caboose. I love it, really. I'd also like to get away from apartment living, especially that nosy couple in front of me. But where would I live? Where would I put this huge hunk of metal house? I can't just park it out in some parking lot somewhere can I? Even Wal-Mart with their open door RV policy would frown on that."

"Not to worry. I have a small field next to my house on the reservation. Your father and I had talked it over with Pontiac and all the other tribal elders. They loved your father, Maggie. They'd want nothing more than for you to live with them on the reservation. Then you could be right next door to me and still have your own place just as your father did up here."

After Maggie thought about the proposition more she responded, "Sounds like you've got the whole rest of my life planned out for me, Paul. How do you know I'll go along with your plan to live there? I haven't even seen the reservation yet. I'll have to think about all this before I agree to it. How far is this reservation from my work, Paul?"

"It's about an hour or so by car," Paul answered. He didn't blame Maggie for wanting to think about it. He would have done the same thing.

"Well of course it's by car, Paul. How else would I get there, by horse and buggy?" Maggie asked sarcastically. Maggie was a little peeved at Paul for assuming she'd just go along with all these arrangements he'd made. She was also a little mad at her dad, but there was nothing she could do about that. He wasn't there for her to express her feelings to.

"Ahh Maggie–not so fresh," Paul answered. "Remember one thing my dear, I'm just the messenger."

"I know, I know. Sorry Paul. But things are still kind of hard for me to take in."

"I know that Maggie. I know. Think of it this way, if you live in that caboose you'll never have to worry about those nosy neighbors of yours back at the apartment."

"How do I know you won't be a nosy neighbor?" she teased.

"You'll have to just trust me on that one, Maggie. You'll have your own space. I promise. Plus you don't have to hide like your father did. You can come and go as you please."

"So, how big is this patch of land you'll put the caboose on?" she asked inquisitively.

"It's about an eighth of an acre or so. Plenty of land for that caboose and for your privacy." Paul hoped she was asking questions because she was interested in living there. Eddy wanted nothing more than for his daughter to live next to Paul. He knew she'd be happy there. Besides, Maggie didn't even know the rest of Eddy's plan yet. Paul was sure she'd agree to living there after she knew what was in store for her down in Virginia. "I think she might do it," thought Paul.

"I'll have to think about it some more, Paul." Maggie had to admit it did all sound alluring. She loved the caboose because it was cute, but mostly because it had belonged to her father. And an eighth of an acre was plenty of land for her to live on and have her privacy. But what would Abbie say? She'd probably shit a brick. Then she'd probably admit her mother to the state mental hospital.

"Fair enough," Paul agreed. "But I'll be bringing it back to Virginia anyways. That was your father's request, whether you decide to live there or not. Pontiac and I were planning on getting some old tracks just like up here and lay them down in that field next to my house. Then we'll set up the caboose. We'll fix the plumbing . . ."

"Whoa, Nellie. How the heck are you going to get that caboose down to Virginia? Can you tell me that, Paul? How do you figure you can transport twenty-one tons of wood and steel?"

"First of all, young lady, as I've said before, your father thought of everything. He already rented a crane to lift the thing and a semi to load it on and take it down to Virginia. We're to follow in the Ford Escape. And, also for your information, the Ford Escape is yours now too, if you decide to keep it, another gift from you father. As a matter of fact this is just the beginning of many, many gifts from your father. See how much fun we're going to have in the next week or so?"

"Wow, I'm impressed. That's one thing I'll definitely take, the car. My old car is on its last leg. So when's the semi coming?"

"It'll be here tomorrow morning bright and early. Should take him about two hours to load it up and then we can leave New Hampshire. Of course it will be slow going for all of us. I'd be amazed if we travel any faster than fifty miles an hour with that heavy thing on the back of the truck."

"Cool," Maggie said in her excited high-pitched voice. "I've never traveled in back of a wide load truck before."

"Can't say as I have either, Maggie. It is kind of exciting isn't it?"

"Hey, Paul."

"Yeah?"

"Thanks. It's funny you know. I never thought this trip would turn out like this. I never thought it would have such an impact on me when I started. But learning all this stuff about my Dad's past makes me feel better. There's just something so satisfying about knowing all the things you've told me about him. I feel so much more complete now, like pieces of a puzzle that have been missing for years have suddenly been found. I'm sorry I didn't get to know him personally. "And don't get me wrong, I do love that little caboose, Paul. I loved it the minute I set foot inside of it. I'm just not sure yet about moving into it permanently. Not to mention, there's the living next to you part," she teased again.

"Funny, Maggie. Go ahead and dish out the insults, I can take them. I'm thick-skinned," he said.

"Oh I don't think you're that thick-skinned," she replied, thinking back to when she saw the old wrinkled skin on his chest. "But I do think you're a pretty good sport and funnier than I would have thought when we started this trip together."

"Thanks. I've had fun."

"You're welcome. I've had fun too."

"You know your father loved that caboose. He worked on it for damned near ten years, so it should be nice. It was such a mess when he had it delivered to Parker's Pasture. Lots of elbow grease went into that thing."

"That's my dad for you. Didn't I tell you he could fix anything?"

"You didn't have to tell me that about your father, I learned that out quick enough after we started living with him up here. I believe we would have frozen to death the first winter had it not been for Eddy's skilled knowledge of heating systems. I can guarantee, no matter how long that caboose has sat in that graveyard, that heating and cooling system are still in tip-top shape. Yes indeed, old JEMEL is a pristine hunk of metal and it was just the right size for your father's needs. It's perfect for one person," Paul hinted.

"JEMEL? What's JEMEL?" Maggie asked.

"That's the name of the caboose. Didn't you see it on that plaque above the back door when we went in?"

"I must have missed that. What kind of a name is JEMEL, or is it short for something else?"

"It stands for..." Paul hesitated a moment to gain his composure. He could feel tears well up in his tired droopy eyes. "It's an acronym. Stands for Jill, Emily, Maggie, Eddy and Linda."

Maggie bit her bottom lip as it quivered with emotion. There they stood–those two Magoos, Maggie and Paul–holding onto one another, crying their hearts out. Crying for all the pain and joy Eddy brought into this world, and all the incredible needless sadness brought about by one freakish night way back so many years ago.

September 9, 2007

Chapter Twenty-Six

Paul wasn't kidding. The crane and the semi were waiting in the caboose graveyard across the street from their hotel at precisely 7:00 a.m. Maggie had to haul ass to get ready, having overslept about an hour too long. She was up half the night trying to decide what to do about Paul's proposition, living in that caboose next to his house on the reservation. Then, after listing all the pros and cons down in her journal, she made her decision.

Even after her decision was made, she was still unable to sleep. She felt as if she could just jump right out of her skin she was so excited about witnessing with her own eyes how they would get that caboose hoisted on the semi. Plus, she'd be living in her very own home, well sort of a home, on her very own patch of land.

She told Paul first thing in the morning, even before they shared their first cup of coffee together. "Yes. I'll do it," she exclaimed as soon as he walked out of his bedroom door. "I must be nuts," she mumbled to herself. She thought of Abbie again and how she would deliver this news to her daughter.

"Great!" Paul shouted. "Your father would be so pleased right now." Somehow Paul knew she'd agree. He couldn't stop talking about her decision, going on and on about how she would love her new home.

But all the while he was rambling on, Maggie's thoughts trailed off as she imagined her new life on the reservation, a life with Paul living right next door to her. After all these years, she at long last would have a place to call her very own. She wondered what Scottie would think of all this, wondered if he would question her decision making processes. All these decisions she had been making the past week or so were so out of character for Maggie. Never in a million years would she have done this kind of thing on a whim. But here she was in the middle of a small New Hampshire town waiting for a low bed semi tractor-trailer to deliver her new home to a reservation in Virginia where she would live next to Paul, her new best friend of two weeks.

Paul and Maggie gathered their things together and threw them in the back of the Ford Escape. They locked the car up and slowly walked across the street to get a good look at the semi and the crane. The sheer size of it floored them both. They decided to wait until the crane loaded the caboose onto the semi and then they'd walk back across the street, start up their car and follow along after the huge load got situated on the main road. It would definitely be slow going indeed. "Hey Paul?" Maggie asked, looking both ways before she crossed the street.

"Yeah?" Paul answered, half listening to her. Even from across the street he was truly engrossed by the size of both the crane and the semi.

"What da you think old Scottie would say if he knew what I was doing right now?"

"He'd probably ask you to visit with him once a week until you came to your senses," Paul answered chuckling a bit but still very much enthralled by what was happening in the caboose graveyard.

"He's such a good doctor, isn't he?"

"Yes, he is good," Paul answered. "He's been good to me over the years. He's been good to you too, hasn't he?"

"Yeah, he has. He's been so good to me. I've enjoyed working with him too, even though he has some oddities."

"I know. I used to go into his office and his whole damned desk was full of magazines. If he was sitting at his desk, I could hardly see the top of his head. And he was tall."

"Well, I hope you didn't touch those magazines of his. He used to have a conniption fit when I did."

Paul laughed. "You think he misses you?"

"Yeah, probably," she replied, thinking about his question briefly. But truthfully, after watching the arm of the crane moving now, Maggie became more enthralled with what was happening with the caboose-hoisting than she was in talking about Dr. Leonard right now.

Paul kept probing. "You like working in that office, Maggie?"

"It's okay I guess. Kind of depressing sometimes though," she answered, standing on her tip-toes to get a better look at what was going on in the caboose graveyard. Maggie's attention turned back to Paul's question again. "Dr. Leonard was smart, Paul. He knew his patients and he knew what they needed. He was good at what he did. But, I have to admit good ole Dr. Leonard was lacking some in the common sense department. In fact, I don't think he had the common sense he was born with. The smart ones do the stupidest things, don't they?"

"Like what?" Paul asked.

"Like he used to water his plants with a watering can that had a hole in the bottom of it. He could never figure out why the floor was wet when he got through. You'd think he would figure out that the can was leaking, right? Especially because he had to go down the hall to fill it and by the time he got back to his office, the damned thing was half empty. Plus I kept telling him about what a fire hazard those stacks of magazines on his desk were. We were in a very old building and those piles of papers could have gone up like kindling at any minute. But he wouldn't listen to me about those stupid papers on his desk."

"Why didn't you just tell him about the watering can thing too?"
"Hey Paul?"
"Yeah?"
"Not to change the subject, but do you think we can get back to watching this crane thing? It's not that I don't like talking about Scottie. It's just that I'd like to pay attention to this caboose-lifting project we got going on here. You're ruining my buzz, Paul!"
"Okay. I'll stop talking about Scottie."
"Thanks."

Paul reached into his pocket for his pillbox. He hadn't kept up on his Parkinson's medication nearly as well as he should have during this trip. In fact, due to his shaking, he would've dropped the tablets on the ground had it not been for Maggie's steady hand helping him place the pills in his mouth. Paul took a long swig of Pepsi, again aided by Maggie's caring touch, washing all the pills down his throat in one long swallow.

Maggie watched as Paul went through this familiar ritual. She knew living beside him would not be easy, especially because of his ailments and frailty. She was up for the challenge though. In fact, nothing would ruffle her feathers with regard to her moving adventure. She had waited a lifetime to be close to her father, even if it meant just living with his ghost in a weathered old caboose.

Maggie had to admit that Paul did get her thinking about her work. Like she told him, she liked Dr. Leonard but that office, it was depressing. Most days Maggie would want to cry on her way home from work. She dreaded going back to her job. She tried to get the image of Scottie and that office out of her head.

"Hey, would you look at that crane lifting the caboose? Amazing isn't it? Looks almost like the cable's gonna bust right in half doesn't it?" Maggie said, excited.

"Wow. You're damned right. That thing is probably heavier than it looks, right Paul?"

"Twenty-one tons of heavy, that's what it is, Maggie. And it'll cost a pretty penny to send down to Virginia too."

"How much you figure it'll cost, Paul?"

"Well, the crane itself costs about $3,500 to hoist the caboose on the semi and then take it off when we get down to Virginia. The semi costs a little more, especially with the price of gas like it is now. So your father figured it'd be about thirty-five dollars a mile. Multiply that times about 600 miles to Virginia and it comes out to $21,000. But, just in about one month's time the gas has gone up so much I figure it'll be closer to about $25,000. Add that to the crane costs and you're looking at close to $30,000."

"Where did my father get that kind of money?"

"He worked a long time, remember. No taxes, nothing really to spend his money on except sending some home to you through Dudley. Add that all up and you've got yourself a windfall so to speak. He was a great mechanic, Maggie. Folks came from all parts of New Hampshire to have him work on their cars. He made a killing here in North Conway. He shared with all of us too. He paid for food, heating, and lights. Plus, when he moved down to Virginia after he got out of the mechanic business, he took to selling some of his carvings in our crafts store on the reservation. Clear profit it was for him. There you have it–he saved nearly $500,000 in total. After you take away the money for the caboose shipping, the crane, the Ford Escape, and the Honda Element, it leaves about $400,000 for you to do with what you like, Maggie."

"You're kidding, right, Paul?"

"No, I'm not kidding at all. It's yours, every last cent."

"Where is it then, Paul? It can't be in a bank account or the government would trace it back right?"

"No banks, Maggie. Your father didn't believe in them. I'll show you where he hid it when we get back home. Your new home, remember?"

"Yes, I remember. How could I possibly forget?" Maggie turned her attention back to the crane. She felt as high as a kite right now. Maggie reached in her pocket for a cigarette and suddenly realized that she hadn't smoked in nearly two days. Even now she just reached for the cancer sticks out of habit. Looking at the half empty box of cigarettes, she decided to throw them away in the nearest trash barrel. As she made her way to the barrel she realized something else, she wasn't counting anything. Nothing. Not even the number of steps it took her to get to the trashcan. In fact, she hadn't counted anything for a while now, at least in the last six or seven days. No counting toothbrush strokes. No counting as she chewed her food. "Maybe getting away from that office and my ratty apartment and my routine did me more good than I thought," Maggie contemplated.

She stared at Paul with his head crooked back, his mouth was opened wide in pure amazement as he watched the strength of machine lifting machine and the placement of a twenty-one ton caboose onto the monstrous flat-bed semi. The effects of Paul's Parkinson's medication hadn't manifested itself yet. She knew this because as he looked up at the crane, Paul's head wobbled back and forth and up and down. It reminded her of one of those little plastic dogs people used to put in the back window of cars, the ones with the bobbing heads that turned when the car turned or bounced when the vehicle ran over a bump in the road. As Paul stood still on that beautiful crisp bright morning with the spectacular backdrop of the snow-crested mountains of New Hampshire, Maggie knew that he couldn't help his bobbing head. The movements his head made were completely out of his control, his old wrinkled orb moving up and down purely of its own volition. An onlooker would have no choice but to follow along with each and every movement, most likely finding the rhythmic motions of his bobbing head hypnotic, and guided by a force much greater than could be explained in earthly terms. The closest word in the English language Maggie could come up with for Paul's uncontrollable movements would most likely be—destiny.

September 9, 2007

Chapter Twenty-Seven

"What kind of power you got hidin' under the hood of that semi?" Maggie asked the driver. The cab on the damned truck was massive and looked more like a two-story condominium than something you could drive on the interstate. The flat bed semi was big too and that was no exaggeration. Forty-eight feet long, to be precise. The drop deck three axle flat bed and attached cab weighed in at a whopping 32,000 pounds and that was without any added weight. Add that to the twenty-one ton caboose and you'd be pretty darned close to the semi's weight limit of 80,000 pounds. All the cars, trucks, virtually everything in the parking lot next to the caboose graveyard had been cleared out to accommodate the sheer size of both the crane and the semi.

Yellow crime scene tape boasting big black lettered words DO NOT ENTER in repeating three to four inches intervals hung taught from the corner of the train station depot all the way across to the other side of the parking lot. The place looked like a murder scene investigation with all that yellow tape spread all over the place.

The truck driver proudly smiled a wide toothy grin, affectionately patting the immense wheel well of his semi as if it were a baby's bottom and replied, "This here little (he emphasized the word little) gem she's got a Mack six-cylinder inline engine."

"No way a six-cylinder engine could haul over 42,000 pounds of wood and steel. I don't believe it," Maggie emphatically exclaimed to the truck driver.

"M'am this 6 cylinder ain't the kind you're used to. It's not like what you got in your standard Honda Accord car. These cylinder's is big, every one of 'em. Plus, most of the power comes from T & A," he shouted back, laughing so that his great big belly shook like he was Santa Claus.

This sounded as if it might have a sexual connotation to it but Maggie suspected T & A probably had a double meaning of some kind. She looked at him puzzled all the while sizing him up from top to bottom, all six feet three inches of him. She figured him to be about 350 pounds, most of which had settled in his midsection. She figured the shirt he was wearing, an old ragged cotton button down, used to fit him about a 150 McDonald's super-sized meals ago, but it sure didn't fit him now. Maggie pushed her sunglasses up closer to the top of her nose. She was glad she'd put them on this morning because if one of those buttons on his shirt let go, she'd sure as shit have been blinded by it. She smiled, thinking about what those buttons would've said had they been able to speak, probably panicked words something along the lines of, "HELP ME..." Maggie eventually landed her gaze on a great big scar that traveled across the entire expanse of the truck drivers deeply lined forehead. "Zipper face," she mumbled. She probably wouldn't have even noticed the scar had he worn his bangs longer, but because of a receding hairline, this was not possible.

"T & A," the driver repeated, "Torque and Attitude. The semi has the torque and I have the attitude. It's a team effort. Oh and this little scar you been staring at," the truck driver said sarcastically, casually pointing to his forehead, "that's from a long haul I made last winter. I ended up slipping on some black ice in North Dakota. Flipped old Bessie here more than three times. We're no worse for the wear though. See, she's got a scar too." He pointed to the hood of the cab. Of course Maggie's short stature prohibited her from seeing the scar on the hood of the cab so she just had to take his word for it. She thought it was odd that he referred to his truck as if she were his female counterpart. Being on the road for so many hours at a clip probably necessitated some form of companionship, Maggie surmised, even if his travel companion was made of steel.

Maggie had to admit she didn't feel too confident about the driver's accident last winter, but allayed her fears by attributing his mishap to the wrath of Mother Nature. And, after viewing the truck driver's wide girth, the grease spots on his old shirt, and the large bag of candy on his dashboard, Maggie's fear switched from black ice to a massive heart attack. This would not be good, especially while he was hauling her new home back to Virginia. She mentally switched gears, trying to focus on a more pleasant subject. She took out a little pad of paper from her purse and wrote down–torque, flat bed semi. This word torque and its meaning sparked an interest in her. She would definitely have to do more research on it when she returned home. Feeling a pair of eyes fixed on her, she slowly turned around only to find Paul staring directly at her, sporting a great big grin. "What are you smiling at, Paul?" she questioned.

"You. Pretty interested in that engine aren't you, Maggie?"

"Yeah, so what?"

"Like I said before, you and your dad were cut from the same mold. You both love cars and I guess, from what I'm hearing today, trucks too."

"Come to think of it, I guess you're right," she answered. Her mind was going a mile a minute now, contemplating the truck's ability to move all that weight, what kind of diesel mileage it got, the use of the computerized system with regard to emissions, and of course, the never-ending mystery of torque."

The caboose was finally in place, all tied up and secure enough for the long journey ahead. Maggie and Paul made their way back to the Ford Escape, started up the engine and situated themselves close to the back taillights of the semi as it left the train depot parking lot and was ready to roll on the main road. It would take a lot of patience from both Paul and Maggie to follow behind the semi and its newly acquired load, especially for over six hundred miles. The trip back to Virginia would be a long one, that's for sure, probably taking them a good two or three days. This would bring their two-week trip almost to its end. Maggie was sad about this fact, but she knew that a new life awaited her back home, one that was different from anything she had ever known before. Plus, as Paul mentioned earlier, more surprises were waiting for her back on the reservation.

Finally, after three grueling days of driving, stopping and then driving again, they crossed the Virginia border. It was early morning, September 12th. After spending the night in a Best Western, Paul and Maggie waited in the lobby for the truck driver to appear. It was 8:00 a.m. on the dot. The truck driver was late. He was supposed to meet them at 7:45 a.m. Again Maggie worried about the heart attack thing. It was 8:05 and then 8:10, and Maggie began to freak out a bit. Finally at 8:15 a.m., a half hour late, the truck driver appeared. They made their way over to the restaurant across the street, Bob Evans, all you could eat. Maggie thought as she looked over at the mammoth truck driver, "I bet they hate to see this guy come through the door."

By 9:30 a.m. they were on the road again. With only a little over a hundred miles to go, they should make the reservation by mid afternoon, if traffic cooperated with them of course. Maggie began to get more and more excited with each mile that passed. Paul drove the last bit of the way because she had a really hard time concentrating on the road. "Do you know what torque means with regard to semi's, Paul?" she asked, bouncing in her seat like a little kid as she asked the question.

"I have an idea but I'm not real sure," he replied honestly. "I know who will know though."

"Who's that? Don't tell me, let me guess–Pontiac, right?"

"Yep, Pontiac. Remember he used to work on cars with your father? He'd know for sure."

"Does he still work on cars? I mean does he still have that garage down in Virginia? On the reservation?"

"As a matter of fact, he does," Paul answered slyly.

"Did they get along good? I mean Pontiac and my dad?"

"They got along famously. Your father was the great teacher of auto mechanics and Pontiac was like a sponge, soaking up all the information on cars your dad dished out. Plus, you'll see, they both had the same sense of humor. Neither one of them were politically correct either. They slung insults back and forth to one another all day long. Pavoti used to call it 'banter.' I used to call it just plain rude and crude fun."

"What kinds of insults?" Maggie asked innocently.

"Well, for one thing, although they were both mechanics, they each had other hobbies. You couldn't help it what with all the extra time they both had up in New Hampshire and even down in Virginia. Once their work on cars was done, there wasn't much else going on. And you know, your Dad couldn't very well step out in the open too often. He kept a low profile for sure. So, remember what I told you before, your Dad took to carving old pieces of wood in his spare time. Pontiac took up cooking. So, you can imagine what kinds of things they teased each other about."

"Like what?"

"Pontiac used to refer to your father as "Paddy wanker, the resident whittler." And your father used to say that Pontiac wanted to be a "Sioux chef". He would spell out the word SIOUX, as if Pontiac didn't understand." Of course both would laugh hysterically after they said their comments. That was just one example. They went at it all day long, bantering just like Pavoti said. You'll like Pontiac, Maggie. I know you will."

"How old is he?"

"Let's see now," Paul answered, trying to remember. "Pavoti was the oldest in their family, Pontiac was the youngest with a nearly seventeen year span between the two of them. There were a couple other brothers and sisters in between. We used to keep in touch with them but, as time went by, we lost track. Some moved way out to the northwest and one moved to southern California. I think, as far as I can remember, Pontiac is in his early sixties now. Yeah, I would put him at about sixty-three or so. Hard to believe, because I knew him when he was just a kid."

"He ever marry?" Maggie asked Paul.

"Never. He used to say, "Who would want to marry a car?" But Pavoti and I agreed, he didn't get married because he couldn't find a female version of your father, someone with a great sense of humor and a love of cars."

"Too bad," Maggie replied sadly. "I think some people do get married to their cars though. Look at potbelly up ahead of us. He calls that big rig "Bessie" and he acts like she's his soul mate."

September 12, 2:00 PM

Chapter Twenty-Eight

The semi pulled onto the reservation at precisely 2:00 p.m. Following close behind were Maggie and Paul in the Ford Escape. The big rig pulled around the curve of the large winding dirt road and on into a small cul-de-sac overlooking the Mattaponi River. On the cul-de-sac were two average sized houses, one was Paul's and the other one belonged to Pontiac. Paul pointed out to Maggie which one was his, but she had figured that part out already. She saw the Honda Element parked in the driveway of Pontiac's house, the same car she saw on the highway, the one with the word EPHEDRA on the license plate. In the middle of the two houses was a good size chunk of land with quite a long stretch of railroad ties plopped in the center of it. Pontiac stood beside the ties with a great big grin on his face.

Paul and Maggie got out of the car and walked up to Pavoti's brother. "Happy to see us, Pontiac?" Paul asked, extending his hand out for the elderly red-skinned man to shake. Pontiac ignored Paul's outstretched arm and instead, with the force of a wild mare at the head of a stampede, he grabbed Paul and lifted him off the ground, shaking him like a rattle. "Whoa Nellie," Paul screamed. "Put me down. I'm old and frail remember?"

"Old and frail, my ass," Pontiac shouted back. "And who is this you got with you?" he asked, already knowing what the answer would be.

"This here is the infamous Maggie," Paul answered proudly.

Pontiac took hold of Maggie's hand. He held it up in a royal gesture, bowing as he did this, cocking his head slightly and lowering it just enough to kiss the topside of her right hand. "Pleased to meet you m'lady," he said, as if she were the Queen of England.

"Pleased to meet you too. You're the same guy I saw in this Ford," she said glaring at him. She turned around slightly, pointing her finger toward the Escape. "And also in that Honda," she said, pointing to Pontiac's driveway."

"Indeed I am," he royally replied in his best English accent.

"Good to meet you, Injun Joe," Maggie said, snickering.

Pontiac's face changed, unsure of what to make of her comment. After about thirty seconds, he grinned, went along with it and replied, "Good to meet you too, Lucy Leprechaun."

They both laughed. So did Paul, probably more than the two of them put together. He knew this would be a good meeting and that they would become the best of friends just as Maggie's father and Pontiac were the best of pals.

Maggie looked back in Pontiac's driveway. She had noticed another vehicle in his gravel driveway. This one was covered by a large tarp. Wondering what was hiding under that tarp, she walked over to it, lifted the cover and peeked underneath. "Wow," she exclaimed excitedly. "This car is beautiful. This yours, Pontiac?"

"Sure is m'lady. It's a beauty isn't it?"

"You're not kidding. Nice looking hotrod. You like Pontiac's Pontiac?" she asked smiling.

"You know your father had a great sense of humor, and apparently you take after him," he remarked, smiling back at her. "Your father picked this old 1964 Pontiac convertible up for my birthday one year. Really it started out as a joke you know? But we ended up working on it off and on for years, refurbishing the whole car from top to bottom. Now look at this beauty, will ya? I might let you drive it sometime," Pontiac added. "If you're lucky!"

"Gee thanks, Pontiac. You know I'll definitely take you up on that offer."

Meanwhile the three of them stood in front of the railroad ties catching up on the trip until a large noise boomed right behind them. Maggie jumped. They all turned around and looked up. The crane was slowly making its way down the dirt road that led to Maggie's new property. Smoke billowed out from two rusted exhaust pipes on either side of the large windows on the cab. The man behind the humungous steering wheel appeared no bigger than a tiny ant as he sat in the driver's seat. The crane was monstrously big, just like the one in New Hampshire had been, it's long horizontal jib looming over them as it got closer and closer to the semi with its attached caboose cargo that lay on the adjoining flat bed.

Maggie thought back to those vending machines in the grocery stores or at amusement parks, the ones with moveable cranes that would go backward and forward. Every time Abbie saw one of those damned things with all the cheap little stuffed animals mounded inside them, she'd ask her mother for money to see if she could win something. Trouble was, after you put the coins in, you only had one chance to go backward and one chance to go forward. So, consequently you needed to pick out exactly what you wanted and then strategically make your two moves with the crane arm even before you pressed any buttons. The one time Maggie tried it she got a hold of some cheap trinket that she ultimately deposited in the trash just outside the sliding glass doors of the grocery store.

Paul, Maggie, and Pontiac hauled ass to get out of the crane's way. "If that arm ever fell on anyone, they'd be dead in a second," Paul announced, as if that thought hadn't crossed Maggie and Pontiac's minds already.

The driver of the crane and the driver of the semi worked together, hooking the caboose to the crane in six strategic locations, three on each side of the caboose. This was not a job for one person. The crane operator went back inside his cab and moved the appropriate levers, then the hoisting began. The noise was deafening but in about five minutes the Caboose was lowered onto the railroad tracks on the vacant piece of land, Maggie's land. From the edge of the semi circular cul-de-sac Maggie proudly gawked at all three homes together. She smiled, thinking to herself, "This is my new house now, my father's home."

It would also live on in perpetuity if she kept it up as her father had, commemorating his hard work, selflessness, and love for his daughter. And, if Abbie had the inclination to live in it as well, there was always that option too. But she highly doubted Abbie would reside in a caboose.

Speaking of Abbie, Maggie had to call her daughter to inform her of her new address. After thinking about it more, she decided to write Abbie another letter rather than call her. This would enable Maggie to deliver the information to her daughter in a more subtle way than a phone call and would also give her more time to get settled in her new caboose home. She also had to cancel her apartment. She had so much to do. Suddenly she became overwhelmed.

Paul noticed Maggie's reddened face. "Is everything okay?" he asked.

"Fine, Paul. Just feeling a little overwhelmed. So much to do now, I guess."

"You've got plenty of time, my dear. You're home now. Why don't you relax for a while. How do you feel?"

"I feel great, Paul. Just great."

"I feel great too," Pontiac agreed.

"Who's asking for your two cents, Pontiac?" Paul kidded.

"Two red cents," Pontiac replied, laughing.

"Go inside and see what it's like after the move, Maggie. It's pretty sturdy but some things may have shifted during the long haul."

She nodded in agreement, "Right. Some things may have shifted. I better check it out." Maggie stayed in the caboose for a long time. She sat on the edge of the small bed with the patchwork quilt on top of it. She rested her head on the pillow, the same pillow her father had used. After just a few minutes she dozed off. Paul had come in to check on her and covered her up with another blanket. He let her rest. He was pretty tired himself after the long trip, but there were things to do now, more surprises in store for Maggie so he'd have to forego resting for a while.

Maggie was awakened by loud voices just whooping and hollering away. She was startled at first, having to get her bearings as to where she was. She felt more at ease after she remembered where she was then rose slowly, stretching her arms out and yawning a great big satisfying yawn. She looked at her watch. It was 5:30 p.m. Peering out of the little window over her new kitchen sink she saw a whole bunch of people gathered in a large circle outside. They were all wearing the most colorful clothing she'd ever seen. Resting on some of their heads were long brightly colored beaded headdresses with a variety of bird and turkey feathers sticking out of them. "Oh boy, a pow-wow," she thought. She opened up the little door with the sign that read JEMEL hanging over top of it. Stepping out onto her little makeshift porch with the red lacquered iron railings, there were people everywhere, all yelling and screaming her name. She was overcome with emotion. Holding her hand over her quivering mouth she stood in amazement. They all motioned for her to come down and join them. She did so willingly.

They seemed to be standing around something. It was something old. As they parted their circle and beckoned for her to come into the center of it, Maggie noticed an old beat up rusted out car. She wondered why on earth they were all dancing around a stupid old jalopy like that. They must have carried that hunk of junk onto the grassy patch of land in front of the cul-de-sac while she was sleeping. As she approached the center of the circle where the car was, everyone around her began to dance. Someone started beating on a set of drums. She looked around. It was Pontiac. He grinned at her. In fact, he couldn't stop grinning at her. People began to move. Maggie stood by the old car while her new neighbors danced up to her, twisting and turning, bending and hopping, each one of them laying down something in front of her. Mechanic's tools. They were laying down mechanic's tools as she stood there in pure amazement.

One laid down a couple of gear wrenches, another a set of floor jacks, and still another an air compressor. Each person that set down a tool named what it was and what it was used for, as if each person had been scripted beforehand. There were screwdrivers and pliers, universal joint sets, and heavy-duty impact wrenches. One person wheeled over a 36" creeper made especially for sliding under cars to fix their exhaust systems. Pontiac stopped playing the drums. He picked two things up and came over to her. One was an incandescent work light. "This is a necessity!" he exclaimed, laying it at her feet.

Maggie stood in awe. She couldn't believe what was happening to her. All these gifts were just for her. She loved every single one of them. Secretly, Maggie had wanted every single one of these tools ever since she could remember because, secretly, she had wanted to tinker and fix car engines ever since she was a little girl. She was certain her father had known that little fact about his daughter too.

Pontiac took her hand and led her around to the backside of the old jalopy. He walked with her, still holding her hand until they came to the old garage. Above the garage was a sign that read:

Maggie the M_____.

The letters after the second *M* were covered with a piece of cloth with a string attached to it. Maggie looked in back of her. The whole reservation was there. Pontiac stared at Maggie and excitedly asked, "Are you ready?" Paul stood by silently at the edge of the garage.

"Ready for what?" Maggie asked in between sobs.

"Ready for your future, Maggie." He proudly announced. Everyone started yelling again. They all knew what the sign said, everyone but Maggie that was.

"I guess so," she replied softly, still crying.

Pontiac pulled the little piece of cloth hiding the other seven letters. MAGGIE THE MECHANIC the sign read. Pontiac stood looking at the sign and then gazed back at Maggie. "Don't worry, he said empathetically. I'll teach you everything there is to know about fixin' cars. I'll teach you everything your father taught me. I'll even teach you about my culture, my way of life, but only if you want to learn it, that is."

Maggie felt as though she would pass out, she was so overcome with happiness. She dropped to her knees. Pontiac tried to get her to stand up again. She kindly waved him away. Kneeling, she peered up at the crowd, which had now circled Maggie once again. They were making the familiar funny hand gesture, the one Pontiac used the first time she saw him in the Ford Escape. "What does that hand gesture mean, Pontiac?" she asked almost afraid to hear what the answer would be.

"Do you remember a long time ago when your father used to stir his coffee in the morning? Do you remember how much you liked looking at him doing that?"

"Don't tell me, Pontiac. That's the coffee stirring hand gesture? It isn't, is it Pontiac? Tell me it isn't," she said. She couldn't help but burst out laughing. Wasn't it like her father to invent this hand gesture and use it with all these people. They probably got a big kick out of her dad with his constant teasing and practical jokes.

"It is. After your father read your stories, he started using that hand gesture whenever he ran into anyone. He used it to say good morning and good afternoon, and he used it to thank people. He used it for any kind of greeting. Well, you get the point. It caught on quickly. Now everyone here uses it. You can too now, Maggie, see." Pontiac held his hand up and made the sign slowly so that she was easily able to emulate it.

"My dad, the trendsetter," Maggie said still laughing.

Paul stepped over to Maggie and held out his hand for her to stand up. She lifted one foot and then the other, standing next to him trembling uncontrollably. He wrapped his arms tightly around her stocky frame. "Look," he said, pointing his open hand around to all the colorful people who had gathered around the garage. "These are your people now. All your pain and suffering is over now, Maggie. You can rest. You are safe and welcome here. Come and live with us. Be a part of our lives as your father had been."

Without a moment's hesitation, Maggie blurted out, "Yes." She said it softly at first and then louder and louder, repeating it over and over until the whole group was saying it too. "Yes, yes, yes, yes," they all shouted.

Paul began to speak. The crowd grew silent to listen to the wise old man. He looked directly at Maggie the whole time he was talking. "There are many things I can tell you today but nothing will be as powerful as the trip we just took together and the lessons you've learned along the way. As we took that trip together and I saw you change, I couldn't help but think that we must all be willing to get rid of the life we've planned, so as to have the life that is waiting for us. It's true Maggie that your father committed that crime way back in 1964, but, believe me, he paid the ultimate price for it. Now you have traveled his journey and felt his pain. You know what he saw and how he felt back in 1965. My grandmother used to say, "When your horse is stuck in the mud, sometimes you have to move him backwards before he can go forward." Your gift from your father was that passage back in time and that passage has led you here, to this spot, to discover your true talents."

Maggie interrupted Paul, tears in her eyes, "Thank you, Paul. Now don't you think you've done enough talking on this trip? Don't you think it's my turn now?" Maggie joked, afraid that anymore of his sentimental speech would send her into a fit of uncontrollable crying.

"Well, excuse me!" Paul kidded back.

"I just want to say one thing to everyone here, especially you Paul. THANK YOU!" she yelled. "I know I'll enjoy living here with every one of you, except maybe Pontiac that is." She turned around to wink at Pontiac who was standing right in back of her. "But I guess I have to get along with him, seeing that he's going to teach me about fixin' cars and all. Right?"

"Don't you forget it," Pontiac answered back, shaking his head and winking back at Maggie.

Maggie stepped back and stared at Paul lovingly. She mouthed the words, "Thank you." Looking out over the crowd she did the same, mouthing the words "Thank you" to each and every member of her new clan. Then, peering up into the heavens to a world she did not know yet, the world where both her father and mother now called their home, and, furrowing her brow, she sensed an overwhelming spirit of forgiveness descend upon her. Raising her arms up into the air and pointing them toward the heavens, she made the infamous coffee stirring hand gesture and declared with profound humility and gratefulness, "Thank you, mom and dad. You gave up everything for me. Everything."

September 13, 2007

My Dearest Daughter, Abigail M. Lerner:

It seems I've come full circle, my dear. I'm back safe and sound. And, as luck would have it, I've acquired a bit of property along my journey and now have a new address. Oh not to worry, I'll still be living here in Virginia, just not in my old apartment (thank God!). I am also going to be totally immersed in heavy metal, but not the head banging kind, unless of course I hit my noggin on the doorway. I know this all sounds peculiar to you, Abbie, but I can assure you, after we have a nice long conversation over a hot cup of coffee, all will become crystal clear. My new address is on the upper part of this envelope. Give me a call when you receive this and we'll set up a date for you to come and visit. You'll love it. I know you will!

I do have so much to tell you, my darling. Remember when I mentioned that my traveling partner, Paul, knew your grandfather? Well, it turns out he knew my dad much better than anyone could have imagined. It also seems your grandfather was a bit of a magician, and his specialty was a most ingenious disappearing act!

More surprises, my beloved Abbie—I'm in the midst of learning a new trade!! Yes, darling, I'm in the middle of gearing up to make a career change. After many years of working for Dr. Leonard, I'll be giving my two-week notice to dear old Scottie as of tomorrow morning. I'm not looking forward to telling him of my new line of work since he's really been a gem to work for. But, truth be told, I'm dreading going back to that stuffy psychiatrist's office even to work my last couple of weeks. Oddly enough, it was quite by accident that I've fallen into my new craft. I hadn't even thought of switching careers, but something came along and put a wrench in the works, and now I'll be doing what I love. The transition was so smooth I never had to think twice about it. In fact the decision was almost mechanical.

There are so many changes, Abbie. We'll be talking for hours when you come and visit. Remember my love of cars? Well, it seems I've got my sights set on a certain Pontiac. And what a beautiful specimen of a machine he is.

As a sidebar, along my route home I stopped by my old stomping ground in Durham, CT, picked up a newspaper there and came upon your Aunt Elsie's name in the obituary column. I didn't know the old gal was sick. You remember her, don't you, Abbie? She was your father's youngest sister. She used to come visit us at Christmas until she got that awful Bell's Palsy. Then she never left the house because it looked as *though someone stuck a fishhook through her jaw and was reeling the whole right side of her face in. Your father used to say she had the spirit of Christmas but the face of Halloween! It was an awful joke really. I always liked Aunt Elsie, although I never thought she was the sharpest crayon in the box. I always referred to her as the "slow" Lerner.*

Anyhoo.....I hope you're happy Abbie. Are you happy? It's just so important to be happy. I am now, after living in a fog for so many years. I'm finally quite content. Please tell me you'll try to find your true calling and not wait so many years as I've done. Life's a journey, Abbie. Enjoy the ride!!

Love to you always and hope to see you very soon.

Your mother,

*Margaret Lerner
A.K.A. The Journeywoman*